ANY DAY NOW

A Novel

Gordon J. Brown

RED DOG
UK

Published by RED DOG PRESS 2022

First Edition

Hardback ISBN 978-1-915433-07-7
Paperback ISBN 978-1-915433-05-3
Ebook ISBN 978-1-915433-06-0

www.reddogpress.co.uk

To
Angela

Enjoy
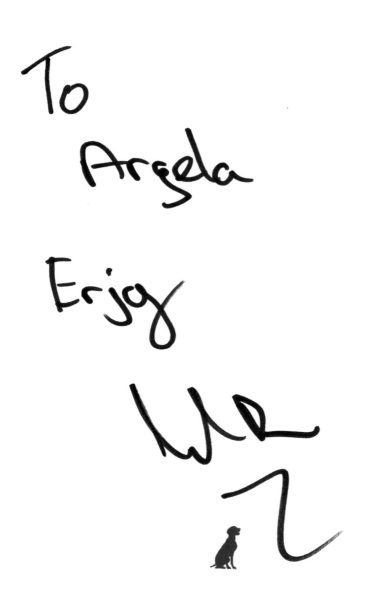

1

Monday, June 21st, 1982

THE RESULTS WAIT...

Why am I always waiting?

Take this morning. I'm sitting against the hall wall, rubbing at the anaglypta that coats the inside of most of our house; bursting bubbles with my finger nails. An action that'll bring the wrath of Mum down upon me when she spots the damage. And spot it she will. Mum has the eyesight of a bird of prey.

My action is not a conscious one and Mum will assign a seven on the internationally recognised *'Angry at Catherine'* scale for this. Seven brings a statutory three-night grounding, no TV, prove you've done your homework tariff. Severe, but doable only because it's a Tuesday morning. Had it been a Friday, the grounding would have spanned the weekend and, for an over-active sixteen-year-old, that is *not* doable.

I burst a few more bubbles and stare at the letterbox, willing the faded gold flap to open and a formally addressed, A4 envelope emblazoned with my name to drop to the worn carpet.

The postman is either late or has no mail for us. The former is unacceptable, the latter even more so. I check the hall clock and sigh. I'm on the cusp of being late for my summer job. Even at a fair run it's a fifteen-minute journey to the hair salon. Work starts at nine. It's now eight forty-three.

I rise, tiptoe to the front door and press my face against the frosted glass panel. This provides little additional insight. Our front door lies at the top of ten steps. At best, without opening the door, you can see someone coming when they reach step three. There's no shadow and the clock ticks over to eight forty-four.

'*Why am I waiting?*'

It's been a week since they were supposed to arrive. Five days since Jenny Meadows got hers, and four days since Karen Shields called to say hers had also arrived.

The exam results.

Karen and Jenny, my two best friends, were keen to share and to bathe in their success—which didn't help on two fronts. Firstly, I'm certain that my exam results, when they arrive, will not warrant the attachment of the word success to them. Secondly, the late delivery has convinced Mum that my results have already arrived and that I've squirrelled them away. I have some history on this front that means repeated denial has been less effective as each day passes. So much so that, despite me forcing my mother to phone the school, coupled with—of her own volition—two calls to the council, she hasn't bought any of the three steps of the waiting excuses she was offered:

The Stock Response from the school: 'The Results Are In The Post.'

Nor, when she called the council, *Vagueness*: 'We Know These Things Happen'

And certainly not on the third call, *The Lie*: 'Sorry About This, But We Will Contact You In Due Course To Check Your Daughter Has Received Them.'

Mum now has me in deep in her crosshairs; my bedroom has been searched five times.

The three-step excuse process irritates Mum as it is used too often for her liking. Take the following exchange in the bank last week as Mum, in discussion with the bank clerk, me in tow, a queue like an executioner's behind us, tried to close her bank account.

The Stock Response:
Mum: *'Look I want my money. And I want it right now.'*

Bank Clerk: *'We are working on that. Closing an account is a complicated business. Someone will be in touch.'*

Vagueness:
Mum: *'You said that last week. No one, and I mean no one, has been in touch.'*

Bank Clerk: *'Have they not? That is odd. Are you sure?'*

The Lie:
Mum: *'Of course I'm bloody sure. Why else would I be here?'*

Bank Clerk: *'Hang on I'll check my records… Ah, it seems someone did call but no one answered your phone.'*

As far as my mother is concerned, I am past steps one and two and firmly at three.

A liar.

I'm now running late for my work just to prove to Mum that the delay in the results reaching her hands is not down to my devious ways. There is a fatal flaw in this plan. Even if the results do turn up today, she'll assert, unless she sees them drop through the letterbox herself, that they arrived days ago and only now, under severe pressure, am I giving them up. The lowly *scores on the doors* that I am expecting will add massive weight to her theory. The best bet would be for me to leave for work, and to let the postman deliver, if he delivers, unsupervised. And that will end thus:

'Catherine your results arrived this morning.'

'Can I see them?'

'I opened them.'

'Why?'

'Because I'm your Mum.'

'But…'

'Do you know what you got for English?'

'How could I? I haven't seen my results.'

'Guess?'

'Guess what?'

'Guess your mark?'

'Mum, just give me my results.'

'Well if you don't want to guess your English result, maybe you can explain why you did so badly in Maths. I thought you liked Maths. Did you really want such a low mark?'

'I don't know what my mark is.'

'And Geography. Do you know I was top of the class in Geography in school?'

'Yes.'

'What mark did you expect to get in Geography?'

'I…'

'Did you try hard enough?'

'Please just give me my results.'

'And wait until Mr Jonty next door hears about your History mark. He has spent an age telling you all about World War II.'

'We didn't do World War II in History, Mum.'

'Well, you should have. Maybe your mark would have been better. And French? Did you even go to the class…?'

Where in the hell is the postie when you need him? There's no point in trying to track him down. He won't upset his routine by digging into his pre-prepared piles of letters for me. I'd asked him, last Valentine's Day, to check his bag, because I'd expected,

4

but didn't receive, a card from Tommy Creadie. The resultant ten-minute diatribe on the intricacies and nuances of the sorting and delivery of mail left me in no doubt that all post goes through the appropriate letterboxes in a strict order that cannot be violated.

I could open the front door and look out. Our bungalow lies on a quiet tree-lined street, and I'd be able to spot the postie if he was en route. Better still, if I stand on the pavement, I can see twenty houses down.

That isn't an option.

Mum is sleeping. Last night she had 'the girls' around for her Wednesday Club; a long-standing event that moves from house to house each Wednesday, as 'the girls' take it in turn to host the evening. There are six of them in the gang. Mum has known them all since her schooldays, and the Wednesday Club is a wine and gossip fest that maxes out on both. Given the thumping ABBA singalong I had to endure at two this morning, Mum is lined up for a killer hangover.

'I'm not hungover, just tired.'

Mum's tired a lot lately. Seven days a week tired. Unemployment does not sit well with her. Opening the front or the back door will rouse her, and that would raise the question of why I've not left for work.

Where the hell is the postie?

I hear the bed creak in mum's bedroom. Mum is rousing. *Sugar and junk.* Okay, don't panic yet Catherine—is she toilet bound or is she kitchen bound? Is she heading to throw up in the loo at the rear of the house or is she heading for a gallon of her favourite post booze drink, IRN-BRU? The latter would mean she is kitchen bound. Bog bound, and I might escape unnoticed if I hide behind the hall table. Kitchen, and I'm screwed. The kitchen door is right next to me. I jump up and place my hand on the front door handle, ready to run.

'Are you still here?' she shouts.

The croaking voice echoes down the hall from inside the bedroom

'Catherine Day, I'm talking to you.'

The use of my full name means Mum's hangover is a doozy.

'Just leaving Mum.'

'You're late.'

The bedroom door stays closed.

'I know Mum. I'll be alright. The rush at the salon won't start 'til ten.'

My job, now school has broken up for the summer, is as the assistant's assistant at a local hair salon. It pays less than picking coins out of the stank, but it still pays. I have three responsibilities; wash hair, clean the floor and do anything else that my co-workers deem necessary. And that can be any shitty job going. They hit a new low last week when I was designated the task of unblocking the loo. The resultant battle with the salon's waste plumbing rendered my jeans, T-shirt and trainers in need of nuking. That night I'd scrubbed myself raw in the bath for over two hours, only to emerge still feeling like I'd just had a swim in a sewage treatment plant.

'Well, get going, Catherine. I'm too tired for any of your games.'

'Just need to pee first.'

'Go at the hairdressers, I need to use ours.'

The bedroom door cracks open and the smell of stale booze flows along the hall as Mum emerges in a swirling oversized T-shirt. Her rabbit slippers are on the wrong feet and her hair is courtesy of the South of Scotland Electricity Board. She glances in my direction and I have enough nous to open the front door.

'So, get,' she says.

'Okay Mum, I'm off.'

I leave and shut the door, scanning to the left, the direction the postie will come from. He's not on the immediate horizon. I count to one hundred, slowly, and decide I'm pushing my luck in an altogether bad direction. Mum might glance out of the living room window and what is a seven for the anaglypta mutilation will rise to an eight—four days grounded, no TV for a week, and dishwashing duty for a fortnight. It's Jenny Meadows' birthday party on Friday night. There's no way on this good green planet that I can miss that. I'll take the seven on the chin and pray I don't transgress again before Friday.

I start to run.

2
CHAIRWOMEN

THE USUALLY PERMANENT fug of hairspray and vapour that permeates the hairdressers is still only light when I enter. In an hour from now the plate glass window that looks upon the main road will be a grey curtain of moisture, and the atmosphere will be so thick you could cut it with a pair of shears.

'It's nice of you to join us, Catherine,' says Maggie.

Maggie Hamilton, the owner of 'Hair It Is', is a pocket battleship of a woman. At four feet ten, she's never out of high heels and sports a hairstyle that adds three inches of neon red to her height at all times, regardless of current trends in the coiffure world. The salon is her life. Her passion. Seven days a week she conducts affairs from an oversized till that sits at the rear. Emerging from behind it for special customers only. The size of that till gives evidence to the real passion in Maggie's life. Money. With an apartment in Greece and a taste for the more expensive restaurants and clubs in Glasgow, she milks the salon for all its worth—and then some. Take today, Pensioner's Day. On average, the expected discount for such individuals, in most other establishments, is of the order of a third or more. Maggie gives ten percent off, and that only applies to a cut'n'blow-dry and above. When you consider that her prices are twenty percent higher than the competition in the first place, the discount isn't anything of the sort. Yet that doesn't reduce the demand for her services. Maggie could fill every day of the week in her January-bought diary. Supported by three senior stylists, a couple of juniors, an assistant and me—she's the queen of maximising hirsute cash flow.

The salon is a throwback to the early seventies. Maggie is not one given to replacing *perfectly good* equipment unless it's pronounced dead by her equally tight-fisted husband, Richard. Two sinks, both chipped, squat next to the till. Mirrors adorn both sides of the salon, running the full length of the walls. Two nineteen sixties bought chairs facing each one. Three dryers are lined up to my left, and a pair of battered wooden chairs lie near the door for those that arrive early. Between the chairs is a microscopic coffee table that was reclaimed from a skip. It's buried under a pile of magazines, some of which were published before I started secondary school. The ceiling lights are a single row of flickering fluorescent tubes that spark and fizz their way through the day. The linoleum floor, once a mottled sea scape of vibrant green, has a dirt grey track down the centre and is worn thin from decades of foot traffic. Look hard and the darkest corners reveal the original colour. Unlike other salons there are no glossy pictures of models with outrageous haircuts to be found. The only item that decorates the walls, save the slabs of mirrors, is the price list. The point size of the type more suited to the bottom row of an eye chart.

Behind the till lies the back shop, hidden by a peeling, sliding door. If the front is trying to fight wear and decay, the rear lost the battle many moons ago. A battered wooden table attended by two even more distressed chairs sits in one corner. A row of coat hooks—*customer only* coat hooks—hang above the table. An electric hob, manufactured before World War II, hunkers down next to the table and, on top of it, an industrial grade kettle waits. On the table sits a tray filled with an assortment of teacups, saucers and a single tea pot, none of which match. The teapot, a three-pint metal affair was *rescued* from the local church. For *rescued* read *stolen*. A two-pound bag of sugar and a carton of milk fight for space along with a half-filled packet of digestives. If Maggie had her way she would do without the tea for the customers. But she can't. It's part of the *experience*. Still, she tries to put people off by purchasing the cheapest tea and utilising UHT milk. It hasn't worked. All haircuts come with a cup of tea. It's the golden rule of hairdressing.

I should really describe the small toilet that lies beyond the back shop, but I won't. I've never quite found the right words to do the space justice. Let's say I'd nipped to the cafe two doors down before I came in, rather than use the salon bog.

'The floor needs swept,' says Maggie and points to the tired broom that's standing next to the sinks.

I nip into the back room, drop my coat on the pile on the floor and grab the last of the lurid yellow aprons that we have to wear. Once back in the salon, I start on the task of sweeping up, interspersed with calls to fetch tea, fetch brushes, fetch rollers, fetch, fetch and fetch. The real rush kicks in as expected at ten. Every single slot today is booked, as usual, and today, as usual, all are booked by regulars. For as far ahead as Maggie's diary will allow, the regulars have a Tuesday appointment. Lose that slot and you'll never get it back. It's rumoured that a few patrons have put theirs in their wills. As a result of the Tuesday ritual, everyone knows everyone at any given time of the day. Like an endless cheese and wine party, the flow of gossip never dies. Gossip is the life blood of existence in here. The fresher and juicier the better. If I ran the Daily Record, I'd have a journalist on tap full time. If it's going on then it's being talked about in this salon but, be wary, there are unwritten rules that have to be adhered to on chat:

Rule Number 1: The customers sitting in the four main chairs have the floor. With the 'two-to-two' 'back-to-back' set up, shouting is the norm. Customers talk to the mirrors, not to each other. Sitting here designates you as a **Chairwoman**.

Rule number 2: When you're at the sink having your hair washed, you can only join in if one of the **Chairwoman** asks you to. Otherwise, you lie back and listen.

Rule number 3: The waiting chairs are silent chairs. Only in extreme circumstances are the occupants allowed to speak.

Rule number 4: Staff can only ask the mundane questions of life: 'How are you today, Mrs Lundie? Will it be the usual, Mrs McLang? Isn't the weather terrible/good? How does that look, Mrs Jackson?' Any other views are mute unless asked for.

For my part, as the lowest of the low, I could sew up my lips save for the odd 'Is the water too hot, Mrs Craig?' For this I'm grateful, because just listening to the flow of chat in 'Hair It Is' has been the best educational experience of my life.

By ten thirty, a four way yack-fest is in full flow and the Chairwoman are:

Chair 1: Mrs Lidia Todd

Biog: Claims to be in her mid-fifties (but is probably mid-sixties), likes people to think she has much more money than she has. Her husband, Gerald, lost his job (admin clerk in the Post Office) eight months ago and has two years to go before his pension kicks in. Lidia has never worked a day in her life and despite pressure from Gerald would be mortified if she had to.

Chair 2: Miss Wilma Hunter

Biog: Sixty-three and single. Never married but has had a string of toy-boys in the last fifteen years. Was the Managing Director of a clothing firm and sold it for a mint. Unlike Lidia, Wilma has cash to burn. Could easily afford the more upmarket salons in town but loves the vibe in 'Hair It Is'.

Chair 3: Mrs Rowena Laidlaw

Biog: Forty-nine, married three times and is in the process of divorcing hubby number three. Smokes like the proverbial stack and works in Cachet and Wratt Medical Supplies as the buyer. She is frequently abroad on 'buying trips' and bores the salon rigid with stories that start with the phrase '*When I was in…*'

Chair 4: Mrs Vera Lynn

Biog: Seventy-four and tells everyone she was born before the *other* Vera Lynn and that means the *other* Vera Lynn should change her name. Has a son who is something very big in the city down in London (although she is vague on exactly what big means). Vera is the de-facto queen bee of the salon and likes a little gin in her tea.

'I'm telling you,' says Lidia Todd. 'The best-looking film star of all time was Alan Ladd.'

'Alan Ladd was a midget,' replies Wilma Hunter. 'You do know that they used to make his co-stars stand in a hole to make him look taller.'

'That's a pile of crap, Wilma Hunter,' Lidia shoots back as her hair is tugged at by the stylist.

'I heard the same story,' says Vera Lynn. 'Five feet six inches he was, that's why he made so many movies with Veronica Lake—she was only four feet eleven.'

'Who the hell is Alan Ladd?' says Rowena Laidlaw. 'If we are talking good-looking film stars then I give you Mr Tom Selleck.'

'He doesn't count,' says Lidia. 'He's on TV, not the pictures.'

'He was in Coma,' spits back Rowena.

'What's that?'

'A film.'

'Never heard of it. Was it a dirty movie?'

'No it *was* not.'

'I like Tom Selleck,' adds Wilma. 'But if you are talking real looks, then you need to go with Rock Hudson.'

'I hear he prefers men to women,' says Rowena

'Where did you hear that?'

'When I was in Los Angeles…'

Lidia cuts her off, 'So what if he does, each to their own and I agree with Wilma; he's gorgeous. Him and Stewart Granger.'

'Lidia, what do you know? You think your Gerald is gorgeous,' says Wilma. 'And, in my book, that's a brand-new meaning for the word gorgeous that I've never come across before.'

'My Gerald was a stunner on our wedding day.'

Vera laughs as the stylist asks her to tip her head back. 'Stunner, Lidia. Are you referring to his breath?'

That gets a laugh from everyone but Lidia.

'Gerald suffers from Sjögren's Syndrome,' she says. 'He can't help the smell.'

'More like 'Garlic Syndrome',' says Wilma.

'Or 'Forgot to Brush My Teeth Again Syndrome,' adds Rowena.

'Or maybe it's just 'Lidia's Cooking Syndrome',' suggests Vera.

'You three,' Lidia says. 'Are a pair of swines.'

That gets a bigger laugh.

'Let's ask young Catherine who the hotties are in the film world,' says Vera turning to me.

I'm washing Mrs Connor's hair.

'Eh,' I say, wondering if Maggie will shoot me down for speaking.

'Well, Catherine?' Vera asks.

'Eh,' I repeat, conscious that any answer I give could lead to a verbal doing. 'Eh.'

'Well come on girl,' says Vera. 'It's not a bloody inquest.'

'Mel Gibson,' I say.

'Oooh,' sighs Wilma. 'Good call. A little bit of Australia booty.'

'Now that's one didgeridoo I'd like to get my hands on,' says Lidia.

'You do know that you *blow* a didgeridoo?' says Vera.

'Oh yes, I *so* do,' replies Lidia.

More laughter.

'Now that's a story that would make the newspaper,' says Lidia. 'And talking about newspapers, Catherine...'

The laughter stops.

'Lidia,' snaps Vera, before glancing at Maggie. Lidia opens her mouth to talk again. Maggie raises a finger to her mouth and silently shushes her. All four of the chairwomen are looking at me in a decidedly awkward silence.

What is this about?

'Okay, what about Tony Curtis?' says Wilma breaking the spell, and they are off again.

And so it rolls through to lunchtime when I'm allowed twenty minutes to grab some air and a hot pie from the City Bakeries next door. I cross to the railway station and drop onto one of the platform benches to devour the grease bomb in my hand. I skipped breakfast this morning after studying myself in the bathroom mirror. I'm certain my stomach is expanding faster than it should. I'm a slave to a packet of crisps and a Fry's Chocolate Cream when I have the spare cash. I'm also big on cheese and toast, and last night I did in four plain bread slices of the stuff. Skipping breakfast is my way of fighting the flab. Only that just makes me hungrier by midday. As I was paying for the pie I'd added a Yum-Yum to my order and a can of Coke. That will just about wipe out my wages for today.

When I get back to the salon the cast in the four chairs has changed and we are in for a new round of gossip. This time the conversation revolves around Hathaway Cottage and a long-held suspicion that it's a house of ill repute. The latest piece of evidence being supplied is from Walter Sullivan, son of chair number 3's occupant, Sonia Sullivan. Walter is a painter and decorator who was recently asked to quote for a makeover at Hathaway Cottage, an out of place stone-built oddity that sits between the shops opposite the salon. Walter was afforded a brief tour of the cottage to estimate the job and was surprised to discover that of the six rooms in the cottage, five were bedrooms, each furnished with a double bed. The owner, Roslyn Black, is a widower in her early eighties and lives alone. All the bedrooms were unoccupied at the time of Walter's visit, but Sonia Williams managed to repeat the phrase 'Five bedrooms—all *doubles*,' over a dozen times before she was relegated to the sinks.

When the last customer is shown the door at five o'clock, we prep for tomorrow. I'm forced, as usual, to ask for my pay which is made up of coins from the tip tray. I have to point out that one of them is a US quarter and Maggie feigns surprise. She taps me on the shoulder as the others exit and holds me back.

'Catherine how are things at home?'

I look a little bewildered. Maggie's not given to pleasantries. 'Fine, Mrs Hamilton. Why do you ask?'

'Hard for your mum bringing up a girl on her own and you being at such a sensitive age.'

'Sensitive age?'

'Yes, the sexual exploration age.'

That phrase causes me to step back a little.

'If you ever want to talk about such things, please let me know,' she adds.

15

I'm now in a new world of confusion. Maggie Hamilton's total conversation with me in the two weeks I've been here has been an unflinching blend of instruction and berating. This enquiring and downright awkward offer is as out of place as a dry Glasgow weekend in August. I'm at a loss as to what to say. So, I say nothing.

'I know that your mother is, shall we say, *struggling*. She's always been a bit of mystery to me.'

By mystery she means that Mum has never darkened Maggie's doorstep for a haircut. She uses a far cheaper alternative down the road. As a result, Mum has never been the victim of the patented 'Hair It Is' Chairwoman interrogation. In that instant, I suspect an ulterior motive to my employment. If you can't get the low down on the woman because she won't come to the party, why not see if the daughter's tongue is loose. As the thought forms I zip my lip.

Maggie notes my reticence.

'Please don't be fooled by this gruff exterior, Catherine. My door is always open.'

I nod in weak appreciation of the offer and make for the exit.

'And Catherine,' she says. 'Just because it's in the news, don't worry. Remember it'll all be tomorrow's fish 'n' chip paper.'

I want to ask what's in the newspaper, but at the same time I just want the hell out of here. This whole nicey-nicey Maggie routine has me creeped out. I mumble some thanks and push through the door into a chilly summer's eve.

Just because it's in the news, don't worry.'

Don't worry about what?

For a few seconds I stand still, processing what Maggie has just said. Clearly there's something in the newspaper that relates to my mum. Was this Maggie stepping up to be some pseudo nosey-parker auntie that offers up her shoulder and wisdom to lean on, in return for a little inside info?

I begin to walk towards the pelican crossing, mind spinning.

'And talking about newspapers, Catherine.'

Lidia Todd had said that, plunging the salon into an uneasy moment of silence driven by Maggie's shushing finger. Lidia admonished for some transgression.

'And talking about newspapers, Catherine.'

I press the button to cross the road and stare at the John Menzies opposite. What newspaper? What newspaper was Maggie or Lidia talking about. One in the past or maybe one that is sitting on the rack right now. Todays' news.

'I know that your mother is, shall we say, struggling.'

The little man flips to green and I cross. I walk straight into John Menzies and head for the newspaper's shelves. I scan them, half-expecting to see a picture of my mother on one of the front covers, but today you can't move for coverage of the birth of Prince William to Charles and Diana. There isn't a front page that doesn't feature the news. If there's a story about my Mum in one of the papers, it will be hard to find. I remember a commentator last night on Scotland Today saying that tomorrow would be a good day to release bad news as it would get lost in the blizzard of William-mania.

Is Mum buried under that blizzard?

I pull out the handful of coins that Maggie had handed me and try and calculate how many newspapers I could buy. Certainly not them all. I pick up the Daily Express and flick through it. The paper is thick with royalty and nothing obvious jumps out. I put it back and lift the Evening Times. More princely stuff. I try the Daily Record. The same.

'Are you buying one of those, or do you think we've become the new local library?'

I turn around to find the shop's manager, a gruff man called Leadingham or Meadowland or some sort, at my back. He's a Rottweiler to the local kids. Convinced anyone of school age has only one reason to be in his store. Shoplifting. I put the paper back down and shrug.

'Well?' he says.

I shrug again and slide past him, his eyes following me out of the door. Outside I almost bump into a woman pushing a pram, and spring away to avoid sending the baby into the road.

'Catherine, mind where you are going.'

'Sorry, Mrs Johnston.'

'Don't worry, dear.'

Mrs Johnston is a solid lump wrapped in a brown tweed coat. She lives four doors down from us. The kid in the pram is her daughter's, but the gossip in the salon is that she takes the kid out a lot because she thinks that people think the baby is hers. Another 'Hair It Is' customer fighting the age monster.

She stares at me and then says, 'I'm so sorry to hear about your Mum.'

'Mum? What about Mum?'

'Oh, eh, I, eh, thought you knew? Oh I'm so sorry. I didn't mean to…'

'What about Mum, Mrs Johnston?'

She shakes her head, tightens the belt on her coat and wheels the pram away without another word. I now have alarm bells ringing so loud in my head that I'm sure others will be able to hear them.

I shout after her, 'What about Mum? Has something happened to her?'

She keeps going and my mind goes into over drive. Mum? What about Mum? What? What was in the papers? Was it bad? *How bad?*

'Hi Catherine,' says Mr Roach, the fishmonger, who is closing up his shop. 'It's a terrible thing, but you'll get through it.'

'Sorry?'

He throws a padlock and also walks away.

'What, Mr Roach,' I shout. 'What's a terrible thing?'

He ignores me.

What is going on.

Is Mum in trouble?

Is she injured? An accident?

Is she…?

Is she…?

…dead?

3
SALON GOSSIP

I RUN HOME, so fast that I burn out before I reach the corner of our drive. I slow to a jog then to a walk, still pushing on as hard as I can. Our street of 1930s-built bungalows that come in any colour, as long as it's white, are each set back from the road. Each is fronted by pristine gardens, all shining bright with summer colours, lawns mowed to bowling green perfection, flower beds weedless, the foliage trimmed with porcelain nail scissors. All of this passes in a blur as I drag myself towards our house. Thoughts of exam results and gossip about movie stars are banished.

Is Mum dead?

I ram my key into the front door lock with such force that it snaps clean in two. I drop the stump on the doorstep and stare at the lock, expecting it open under sheer force of will. I kick at the broken piece of key on the ground and can feel tears beginning to rise. I close my fist and batter the door frame. I push at the doorbell and repeat. Such actions will have consequences. I have a key for a reason. Quiet entry the expected norm because of hangovers. I keep up the attack on the door but no shadow appears in our hallway.

Is Mum lying in the bedroom? Lifeless?

I change tack, sprint around to the rear, vaulting the gate that guards the back of our house. I pound on the back door with force but still no one comes. I pummel the kitchen window. I'm in full panic mode. Mum could be in there. Dead. Or dying... I slam my fist on the door's glass panel and it explodes. Glass showering inwards, scattering across the kitchen linoleum. I leap back, clipping my hip on the small wall that surrounds the dirt brown square that we call a lawn. I fall to the ground, my arm scraping down the roughcast of the wall. The assault on my body savages whatever sane thought processes I have left. Instinct takes over and I scream, a throat bursting noise that I didn't know I had in me.

'What the hell?'

Mum is standing at the door, staring through the broken pane at me.

'Mum,' is the only word that tumbles from my mouth.

'Catherine, what the...?'

I burst out crying and she opens the door.

'Catherine,' she says bending down.

I collapse into her arms.

She lets me cry a little before gently helping me to my feet. She smells of lavender and rose oil, taking me back to my earliest memories. To flickering recollections of love and care. To skinned knees, broken bones and falling out with friends. To overfilled baths and Mum's bed and snuggling on the sofa. To kind words, wise words and no words. She helps me up, guides me into the house and through to the living room where I fall into a chair. She vanishes and reappears a few minutes later with a tray in hand. Two mugs of sweet tea and a packet of bourbon biscuits lie on it. She lays my mug on the chair's armrest, dropping two biscuits beside it. Taking up the chair opposite, she sips at her own tea and waits. Mum is good at waiting. She excels at. A black belt, tenth dan with knobs on. Patience a virtue that pervades her soul. But only when she's had a drink. Sober she has the patience of a hurricane. Her silence suggests that drink has already been taken.

My sobbing stops as the sugar and caffeine from the hot liquid and biscuits flood my system—the chemical reaction working its magic.

And still she waits. Her brown eyes gazing at me, hands crossed on her lap, her upper half swaying slightly. She'll speak first. A gentle probing question to unlock whatever demon it is that I'm suffering under. It's *our* way.

On the mantelpiece, a brown lump of Bakelite dulls the ticking of the mechanism inside it. The ancient clock unwinding its eight-day movement a tad slowly. Losing a few minutes every day. If not reset regularly it can be a quarter of an hour slow by the weekend. Enough to ensure I miss the train to town or the bus to the park or some sort. It's my job to wind it up and keep time straight. It used to live on my gran's sideboard. Mum's mum. She won it in a church raffle back in the dark ages and was convinced it was an antique of note. She would often tell me that one day it would be mine. That one day I could sell it and buy the *bestest* house in the whole world. When I was fourteen, Mum, short on cash, took it to the pawn broker who offered her ten quid for it. She thought she was being ripped off and went to another. He offered seven quid. By the time she had visited two more, eight quid and another tenner, she took the clock home and found the money somewhere else.

The clock chimes the half hour.

'Okay Catherine, take it slowly and tell me what is going on.'

I gather my thoughts and relay what happened. As I speak my deductions come out muddled, and the rationale for my actions as insane.

'Okay,' she says once I'm finished. 'Let me get this straight. Maggie Hamilton at the salon mentioned something about me

ANY DAY NOW

and the newspapers. But she didn't say what. Then you bumped into Ira Johnston and Les Roach, and they both told you I was dead?'

'Not dead, Mum. Mrs Johnston said she was sorry to hear about you and Mr Roach said it was a terrible thing.'

'And you took that to mean I was dead?'

I nod.

'And you ran straight here, and trying to get in, you broke your key? Then you tried to break in through the back door because you thought I might be lying lifeless in the bedroom?'

I nod again.

'And if I was dead in the bedroom,' she adds. 'How would Ira or Les have known about it?'

I say nothing.

'And you thought that was the news in the papers? That I was dead.' She pauses. 'I think you might have heard I'd passed on before the papers got the story. Don't you, darling?'

I blink a lot as I process that.

'And, Catherine, if I was dead, would someone not have come to the salon to tell you.'

I feel stupid.

'I wasn't thinking straight, Mum. I just... panicked.'

'And now we have to find the cash for replacement glass in the back door and a new front lock. Where will that come from?'

From the money you spend on booze.' I open my mouth to utter the words and manage to stop myself.

I realise that I'm angry at myself and the booze chat isn't for now. It isn't for ever. I've been down that line before and, no matter how I approach it, I always come off feeling like I'm trying to deny Mum a little bit of pleasure in an otherwise crap world.

'A wee drink now and again is the only thing I have, Catherine.'

GORDON J. BROWN

'I'll save up from the salon money and pay for both,' I offer.

I know that won't work. If I did do that, I may as well bury myself in my bedroom until school goes back in the Autumn. I don't have an expensive lifestyle, but bus fares and sweets eat most of what I earn. Mum stands up and walks to the window to stare out on the road. She swigs from her mug and speaks to the window.

'It wasn't supposed to be like this, Catherine.'

I wait, knowing there is more.

'After all I've done, it wasn't supposed to be this way.'

She drinks some more tea, and her head moves slowly as the sound of a passing car enters the room.

'I thought things would be better by now, Catherine. You know, not scratching around for pennies all the time. I'd sell this house if I could. Take the cash and buy us a small flat somewhere, and then we'd have a little bit of spare money.'

I shuffle on my seat, my head still wrapped in my act of stupidity, the words of Ira Johnston, Les Roach and Maggie Hamilton muffling what Mum is saying.

'But I can't even do that, can I?' she says. 'Not with our mortgage. There would be nothing left.'

The mists part a little as I realise what she is suggesting. I don't want to move away from here. I don't want any conversation that has that as an option. This is my home. *Our* home.

She says, 'Maybe I *can* make it work. Maybe I'm just not looking at it in the right way.'

I find myself wondering if I should ask questions that might lead to questions that don't need answers.

'Would you like to move, Catherine?'

I find my voice on that one, 'No.'

'It might be better, darling. Less stress. A new start.'

Is this to do with the shattered glass? The bust lock? The newspaper? My stupidity? Moving has never been mentioned before.

'We could move somewhere far away,' she continues. 'I've always fancied the Outer Hebrides, the Isle of Harris. It's beautiful. When you stand on the beaches you could be in the Caribbean except you can still nip to Spar for a bottle of Grants and a Tunnock's Teacake. A small cottage by the sea. Just you and me, Catherine. A log fire for the winter and deck chairs on the sand for the summer. We could buy a giant freezer, fill it and, come October, we'd hunker down 'til Spring. No visitors. No TV or radio to bring us bad news. Just an endless pile of books and a panoramic window to watch the storms batter the coast, while we're safe and snug inside. How is that not heaven?'

Heaven? Really? No friends. No TV. Sitting in a house twenty-four hours a day? She can't be serious. That's not heaven. That's hell.

'Mum, I have school.'

'They have schools on the islands and it would be a chance for you to make new friends.'

'I don't want new friends. I like the ones I have.'

She ignores that. 'Think about it. Fresh sea air, fresh sea food, a fresh start. When I was your age, I would have loved the chance to start all over.'

'I'm sixteen, Mum, not sixty. I've hardly started the first time around, never mind a second.'

'You're never too young to try something new?'

'You're never too old, Mum. The phrase is you're never too *old.*'

She turns to look at me. I can see tiredness in her eyes and it's not just from the booze. She has bags where none existed not long ago, or at least none that I noticed. And is it me, or is she standing with a slight stoop? Mum's not young. Not as young as some of the other mums.

'I had you late in life, Catherine. But that meant I had more time to be with you.'

A well-used phrase.

I'm not sure I saw any more of her than my friends saw of their mums. Mum was forty-one when she had me. And she looks every day of her fifty-seven years now. I never think of her as old. You don't. Mums are mums. And all mums are the best mums. True she didn't hang out too much with the other mothers. She has always had her own set of friends: the Wednesday Club. I know that being a single mum did raise issues for her, and me. As did the lack of a dad. I've got in more than a few fights over my status as a bastard and mum's as a harlot. And if you think those descriptions are harsh, there's been far worse said in the past.

'So what are we going to do with you?' she says.

Mum is road-watching again. I'm reckoning that my punishment is an easy nine on the scale. And that is hard, hard time. As she gazes out the window, I have questions. *What is in the newspaper? Why would Ira Johnston be sorry about Mum? What did Mr Loach think was a terrible thing?*

I sip at my tea and wonder if this is one of those moments in life—the ones that you look back on. A junction on the path you are walking. But, at this point, Catherine, you can only turn left. You have no choice. The other path is now closed. The one that would have led to a more recognisable future.

Or am I overthinking it all.

A new path.

4
BACK TO SCHOOL

Wednesday, 3rd November, 1982

CHANNEL 4 STARTED today. I sat in front of the telly at three thirty in the afternoon and stared at the blank screen until four o'clock when the new Channel 4 logo emerged from a black screen and a new quiz programme called Countdown came on. I just wanted to say I'd seen the birth of a new TV channel, and waiting in front of the telly was more exciting than I'd thought it would be. A good wait. But as I sat there, stationary, I knew that to counter this, there are the bad waits in life. Waiting outside the headmaster's room to get the belt for throwing mud at Mark Brost. Or waiting on the youth club leader to call Mum because *'Catherine decided it was a good idea to set fire to a bunch of church newsletters is the nearby woods.'* Or being spotted with Mark Brost in said woods, after setting fire to the newsletters and knowing someone would tell on us. Those are bad waits. Ones designed to muck with your head. To allow your brain cells to paint endless pictures of doom and gloom about what will come next. Of what will be, could be, might be.

Catastrophe thinking in action.

Will I get four of the belt or six for the mudslinging—or is there a new number for transgressors like me. Eight, ten. Will my hands bleed? Will I be able to write after? Ever? Will the headmasters hand slip and slice my wrist open with the leather?

Will I bleed out on the floor? What about me kissing Mark Brost in the woods, the smell of burnt paper in the air. Him trying to touch me where I know he shouldn't and failing. Me touching him where I know I shouldn't and succeeding. Will I be barred from the club for that? From school? From life.

Catastrophe thinking.

Then there are the exciting waits that involve no thinking, no guessing at the future, the ones that you don't even know you are participating in. The invisible waits. King of those is waiting for the summer holidays to finish. No one thinks of the invisible waits as waiting. You don't wait on a good thing to end. You don't wait on a movie to finish or Top of the Pops to be over. You don't wait on a slice of cake to vanish or your birthday party to conclude. Yet they are waits. You just don't notice them because they are waits that you enjoy.

This year the summer holiday wait raced past far too quickly. And now I'm in the world of waiting for each school day to finish.

Looking back over the summer wait there are four things of note that *didn't* happen.

I didn't get a nine for smashing the back-door window. I didn't even get a one. I was punished by not being punished. A wait in itself. Waiting for Mum to realise the error of her parenting ways. When the glazier turned up, she didn't realise her error. When the locksmith arrived, she didn't realise her error. She simply let it all slide. I went unpunished.

The second non-happening of note was the lack of a smoking gun in the shape of a newspaper article with Mum's name in it. That took a little bit of thievery to dispel. Our local newsagent bundles the unsold papers for collection by the delivery van each morning. Tying them up in string and dropping them at the shop's back door first thing. Scissors in hand, I had sneaked out of the house at five forty-five the day after the day that Mum didn't die. I'd slid from my bedroom window to avoid the front door and, convinced I would be caught at any moment, snipped the string on the bundle of yesterday's newspapers and took a copy of every paper. The Express, Sun, Record, Herald, Evening Times, Scotsman—even the Times and the Guardian—plus the local rag. I spirited them into my bedroom and scanned each from front to back.

Nothing. I found nothing about Mum. I even checked the obituary columns—just in case.

Over the next week, I haunted a few libraries asking for back copies of the newspapers from the days before the incident. I think I read most of them for up to a week prior, but still found zip.

The third in a series of summer nothings occurred when I met Ira Johnston and her baby two weeks after she first threw me into a tailspin. Jenny and I were hanging out near the salon. We'd blown through almost all of our spare cash and were sharing a packet of Polo Mints.

'Catherine, we really know how to live it up.'

I was showing Jenny that I could push a fair slug of my tongue through the hole of the mint I was eating, when Ira rolled into view. Her daughter's baby, Sean, was ensconced in the same Silver Cross pram that Ira had occupied some twenty-five years earlier. To Jenny and me, it looked like the same pram that Ira's great granny had probably occupied. Ira is all hustle and bustle. She's nicknamed the White Rabbit. Always late for something, but never able to tell you exactly what. On the spur of the moment, I'd decided to intercept her.

'Mrs Johnston?'

'Catherine, I don't have time to chat. I'm late.'

'It's just a wee question.'

'I'm really too busy, Catherine.'

'Please?'

'Be quick then.'

'I bumped into you a few weeks ago, outside John Menzies. Do you remember?'

'Not especially.'

'Well, I did, and you said something to me.'

'I did?'

'Yes. You said you were sorry to hear about my mum.'

'Really?'

'Really.'

'And?'

'What did you mean?'

'I've no idea. Now excuse me, I need to go.'

With that she pushed off. A non-event. Although it wasn't quite a genuine non-happening. For a moment, just after I told her what she had said to me outside John Menzies, there was a small flicker in her eyes, and she'd glanced away. A little tell that could be something or nothing. An indication of a lie or a twitch brought on by years of being late? I'd asked Jenny if she had seen it, but she'd just told me I'm being paranoid. And I probably am... maybe.

Non-happening number four centred around my exam results. Let's say they were better than I had anticipated but worse than Mum expected. I managed to scrape together a fifth year at school consisting of English (I'm halfway decent at writing stories), History (Mr Jonty, him of next door and World War II knowledge fame, may actually be very useful this year), Home Economics (Mum says I really need to learn to cook), Biology (I hate Chemistry and Physics but you need to take one of the three) and Maths (because you have to). Mum briefly mentioned the possibility of me going to university next year, in between her increasing flights of fancy.

'Catherine how do you fancy moving to France?'

Or…

'I know someone that lives in New York, at least I did a long while back. How good would that be as a place to live?'

Or…

'I hear they need farm workers in Australia and provide accommodation.'

Or…

'Do you think working in a canteen on a northern Canadian coal mine would be a good job?'

Or…

'I read once that there is good money in alpaca farming in the Andes.'

Or…Or…Or…

Thankfully we are still in our house, although Mum's drinking is now running out of control. She's still unemployed. A short stint in a local estate agency didn't end well when she was found asleep, in the bed of one of the houses she was supposed to be selling, half a bottle of vodka next to her. It's a rare day when I get in from school and she's not already three sheets to the wind. She's out for the count by seven most nights. My minor worry over developing a paunch has faded. As Mum's spend on booze has increased, the quantity of food on the table has fallen. Breakfast is a slice of toast at best. Dinnertime is optional. If I have the money, I grab a pie or a bridie from the City Bakeries, otherwise zip. Going home at midday for food isn't advisable. Mum rises about twelve and her mood is three steps down from foul. Teatime is a hit or miss affair. Too much vodka in Mum's system and I make my own food, if there's any in the house.

I work at the hair salon on Thursday evenings and all-day Saturday. What money Mum used to give me has dried up. I've no idea how she is paying any of the bills. The postie drops copious volumes of final demands and ominous buff-coloured envelopes through our letterbox. I gather them up each morning and leave them on the hall table for Mum to read. They are still there when I come back in the evening. Most find the bin at some point.

I picked up a warning letter from the assistant head at school last Monday about the state of my clothes. The school insists on a shirt, tie, dark skirt and sensible shoes—frowning on fashion items. I have one shirt that I grew out of last year. It was white when it was bought but has now established its own unique colour—that sits somewhere between grey and grime. My tie is shredded at the bottom from catching it in a drawer in the Biology lab. My shoes are more scuff than shine, and my skirt, despite my enforced diet, is a little tight. Mum and I are off shopping on Wednesday after school. Drunk as she was when I came home from school with the letter, crying, she was black affronted that I had note from school about my clothes.

'Catherine Day?' says Mrs Lionel, our history teacher.

I snap back to the moment, sitting at the back of the classroom—realising that my name may have been said a few times and I'd missed it.

'Yes, Mrs Lionel?'

'Good of you to join us, Miss Day. Now can you tell me what is considered the most important historical moment of the nineteenth century?'

I love when I get the easy questions.

'Sorry Mrs Lionel, can you repeat that?' I say, playing for time. Not that it'll make any difference. How can you answer a question like that? Where do you even start?

'Can you tell me what is considered the most important historical moment of the nineteenth century?'

I give that a few seconds and then offer, 'Eleven fifty-nine and fifty-nine seconds on December the 31st 1899.'

That draws a moment's silence.

'I'm sorry?' she says.

'That was the most important moment of the nineteenth century.'

'What was?'

'Eleven fifty-nine and fifty-nine seconds on December the 31st 1899.'

'Is this your attempt at being funny, Catherine?'

I've drawn the full attention of my classmates. They are now looking on, waiting on developments, happy that I'm providing a minor but welcome break from the Napoleonic Wars.

'No, Mrs Lionel.'

'Then explain yourself.'

'Well, Mrs Lionel, the most important moment has to be eleven fifty-nine and fifty-nine seconds on December the 31st 1899.'

'And, pray tell, why would that be?'

'Well, that's the time when the whole of the century is complete. Full up. No more room left. Everything that was ever going to happen has happened.'

'Interesting.'

'To be more accurate, Mrs Lionel, the most important moment is actually not in the nineteenth century at all.'

'It's not?'

'No. It's actually twelve o'clock midnight on the first of January 1900. By then the century is definitely over. At eleven fifty-nine and fifty-nine there is a still a whole second left, and a lot can happen in a second.'

'Like what?'

The fact that Mrs Lionel is giving me the time of day on this is throwing me a little.

'Eh,' I stutter. 'Someone important could die or maybe someone that would rock the next century could have been born.'

'Anything else you'd like to add?'

I should call it quits, but as is my want, I don't.

'Well,' I add. 'that moment was also very important for another reason.'

'And what is that?'

I'm praying that Mr Jonty next door didn't feed me a whopper as I draw a breath.

'That was the day that someone created a time machine.'

A few of my fellow classmates laugh.

'A time machine, Catherine?'

'Yes.'

'You are saying that in the eighteen hundreds someone invented a time machine.'

'Yes. On the very last day of the century.'

'Explain?' she says.

I scratch at my head. My hair so needs a wash.

'Well, there was this boat, Mrs Lionel. It was called the SS Warimoo, I think that's its name, anyway it was sailing from Vancouver to Brisbane. Well, the Captain of this ship, he was called Captain John Phillips by the way. Well, Captain John, on the 31st December 1899, was plotting his position in the Pacific Ocean and realised the ship was near the international date line. Do you know what that is?'

'I do,' she says, turning to the class. 'Does anyone else?'

John Last raises his hand. 'It's where Tuesday becomes Wednesday.'

'Kind of,' says Mrs Lionel. 'I'll explain later. Go on, Catherine.'

'Well, Captain John also realises that they are near the equator. So, he turns to his first mate and says something like 'look where we are' and maybe he added 'look *when* we are.' And the first mate maybe looks a little confused, but the Captain does some checking and orders his boat to change course. Now, after a bit of fiddling around, Captain John stops the ship in the middle of the ocean. Right on a very special spot. Just where the dateline meets the equator.'

'And what did that mean for him and the ship?'

I'm being given a very long run of rope here.

'Well,' I continue. 'Once the captain parked the boat, he made sure that it was positioned in such a way that the left-hand side of the boat was in the 31st of December 1899 but the right-hand side was now in the 1st of January 1900. That's what happens when you cross the dateline. But he also made sure that the back of the boat was in the northern hemisphere and the front was in the southern hemisphere. And that meant the back of the boat was in winter and the front was in summer. So, he figured, if you stood right in the middle of the boat you were standing in two different days, two different months, two different years, two different seasons and two different centuries, all at the same time.'

'And that is the time machine?'

'Well, if you jogged around a bit, you could jump back and forth from the 31st of December to the 1st January. From 1899 to 1900. Is that not time travel?'

Mrs Lionel moves back to the black board, rubbing slowly at her chin. As she retreats, she asks, 'How do you know all this?'

I'm feeling good about this.

'Our next-door neighbour is full of that type of shit.'

And the spell is broken as the class bursts out in laughter.

'What did you say Catherine?' Mrs Lionel says, turning back to me.

I cringe.

'Sorry?', I say.

'Headmaster's study, Catherine.'

'Oh, come on, Mrs Lionel. It was a mistake.'

'Move! Now!'

I rise and, with the class still laughing, I scowl at Mrs Lionel. I had been doing so well. I mean who else, other than Mr Jonty, knows that little nugget of history around here. This is so unfair.

I don't move.

'Headmaster's study,' she repeats.

'This is rubbish, Mrs Lionel. It was a slip of the tongue.'

'Go this instant.'

'Shit.'

'Now.'

I walk to the door and stop, 'Mrs Lionel, what *is* considered the most important historical moment of the nineteenth century?'

'Headmaster's study,' she says.

I stand my ground.

'Catherine Day. Don't make this any worse. Go to the headmaster's study, right now.'

'Not until you tell me what is the considered the most important historical moment of the nineteenth century?'

'You will do as you are told, Catherine.'

'So will you.'

'Pardon me?'

'You are a teacher, here to teach me, and I'm asking a perfectly legitimate question in my quest to be a good pupil.'

'You are being an insolent pupil.'

'I'm being an inquisitive pupil. Isn't that what you want?'

'I'm not listening to anymore of this. Please leave.'

I take a step towards her. 'Not until you answer the question.'

'I will do no such thing.'

'Do you know what I think, Mrs Lionel?'

'I do not care what you think. Now leave the class.'

'I think, Mrs Lionel, that you don't have an answer to the question you asked me. I don't think you have a blind clue as to the most important moment of nineteenth century history. Not one single blind clue. And do you know what else? Do you?'

'Leave now!'

'Mrs Lionel,' I add. 'I also think that you are one moody cow.'

The 'ooh' from the class is universal and I can feel me pushing that age-old self-destruct button, but I can't stop myself. *Don't want to* stop myself.

'What did you say, Catherine Day?'

'You see, Mrs Wax…'

She bristles at her nickname, derived from her habit of digging around in her ears for wax before popping what she finds into her mouth. The name pushes the confrontation towards a cliff edge… and I dive over.

'You see, *Mrs Lionel*, I knew a really good story that you didn't, but because of a slip of the tongue, you are punishing me rather than encouraging me. I said 'shit'. So the shit what? My neighbour, Mr Jonty, *is* full of shit. That's a fact. We are all full of shit. You are full of shit, Mrs Lionel. Right now. In your gut. A whole stinking pile of shit just waiting to get out. So why am I being punished? Everyone is full of shit.'

She moves towards me, and we are now two boxers in a ring. I have a good four inches on her height wise. In first year, I'd have been hauled by my ear to the headmaster's room. Not now. I'm sixteen and the dynamics here have shifted.

'Answer my question, Mrs Lionel, and I'll go.'

I'm surprised to see tears in her eyes. She skirts around me and exits the room, leaving me standing. There's a collective intake of breath from the body of the kirk as she slams the door.

5

THE PUNISHMENT WAIT…

'Catherine, you are so right in it,' says Jenny Meadows, one my best friends.

Jenny is sitting two rows back from the front of the classroom and she's spot on with capital letters on that one, along with their two brothers. I am *so* in it. I look at the class and then at the door trying to figure what to do next.

'I bet she's gone to get the heady,' says Jenny. 'Boy, will you catch it.'

'I didn't do anything,' I plead, knowing that's as far from the truth as I'll get today.

The class breaks into the cacophony that accompanies the absence of a teacher. Chatter and nonsense—me briefly at the centre—but sliding to a speculation thing that's better discussed on a one-to-one basis. Heads turn to each other as my classmates debate my fate. The thought of legging it is high on my Top 5 of things to do right now. If I stay, well if I stay, what am I waiting on? I'm not certain where Mrs Lionel has gone but I'd guess Jenny is on the money.

She's gone to get the heady.

So, do I stand or run?

I look at my classmates: heads occasionally turn to check I'm still there but attention spans are short, and my antics will soon be relegated below the chat on last night's TV or on who is wynching who. A few are already out of their chairs. A couple are perched on their desks. Deidre Smith has moved to sit on the windowsill, legs crossed showing off enough thigh to easily rival me for the attention of the boys. Callum Taylor is a prime example, with the subtlety of a brick toilet, he's resting his chin in cupped hands, staring at Deidre like a salivating dog eyeing a bone.

I spin around.

Bugger this wait.

I march out of the classroom to another collective 'ooh', turn left and head for the main staircase. Dropping to the ground floor, I pick up the pace. The headmaster's study lies near the end of this corridor. I could find it in my sleep and I'm walking so fast now I'm on the edge of running; a one-hundred-line punishment if caught. There's no one outside the headmaster's room and, without hesitation, I rap the glass door and enter.

A fierce mountain of fat, Miss Rennie, the school secretary, lifts her head from the typewriter. Her eyebrows rise at the intrusion. She defends her boss's territory with the skill and tenacity of a knight in armour, this office the moat to her king's castle, her desk positioned as the closed drawbridge to the royal chambers beyond. No one passes without her say so. I shouldn't have even entered without being called in.

'Miss Rennie,' I say, walking up to her desk, raising her eyebrows further, 'I was told to report here by Mrs Lionel.'

'Mrs Lionel is in with Mr Young right now.'

Not unexpected.

'I'd like to see them both. Right now.'

The forcefulness in my voice catches Miss Rennie a little off balance, but she recovers quickly. 'If you were told to report here, then go back out into the corridor and take a seat where you are supposed to.'

'No,' I say.

Her eyebrows reach new heights, 'I'm sorry.'

'I said no. I'm not sitting out there. It's both embarrassing and, frankly, an abuse of power.'

'What?'

'The bell will go soon, and I'll be subject to no end of insults as my fellow pupils walk by. And you well know that. It's why the chairs are out there. There's plenty of space in here for pupils to wait.'

'You'll do as you are told young lady.'

'No, I won't.'

If I had pressed the self-destruct button in the classroom, I am now pulling a grenade pin.

'Go sit outside, right this minute!'

'No.'

'Go now!'

'Or what?'

'Pardon.'

'Or what? What will you do if I don't go?'

'Don't you mouth off to me.'

'You like your little position of power don't you, *Indigestion*.'

Her face glows red as I drop in the nickname.

'How dare you?'

'Oh, I dare alright, Miss Rennie. I *so* dare. What gives you the right to order me around? Eh? You're not a teacher. You're not the headmaster or the assistant head. You're the school secretary. Where in your job description does it say that you can tell pupils what to do?'

'I'll not listen to this.'

'Then leave.'

'Me? Leave?'

'Exactly. If you don't want to listen to this, then leave! I'm not going anywhere, so if you don't want to hear what I have to say, leave!'

Her face colour flushes to sunburst red.

'You cheeky cow!' she spits.

'Language, Timothy,' I say, lifting Ronnie Corbett's phrase from the sitcom *Sorry*. 'I'll be reporting that language to Mr Young. *Cheeky cow*. Not very nice coming from the school secretary. Now I'm going to go in and see Mr Young.'

I round the desk and Miss Rennie stands up. Another face-to-face with an adult in under ten minutes. She reaches out and grabs me by the arm. I look at her hand and then her eyes.

'Remove your hand!' I say, lowering my voice, going for menace but probably coming out with nervous.

'Leave this room…' she starts.

I yank my arm free and reach out for the doorknob to the headmaster's office door.

'Don't you dare…' she says.

I open the door and walk in.

My future changes in that instant.

And much for the better.

I smile.

In front of me Mrs Lionel and Mr Young are wrapped so tight in each other's arms that it's hard to tell where one starts and the other stops. Given the intensity of the kiss I'm witnessing, I'd guess we are in full tongue exchange mode here. Mr Young's right hand has a firm grasp of Mrs Lionel's left breast. Mrs Lionel's right hand is squeezing buttock. It takes them both a second to realise that someone has walked into the room. A second too long. A whole second for me to take in what is going on and realise the implication. That this could be the story of the decade in school and it's breaking right in front of me. Mr Young and Mrs Lionel in passionate embrace, me in the front row. Me knowing there's a *Mrs* Young and *Mr* Lionel waiting at home for them both. Me knowing that I have just bagged the get-out-of-jail-free-card of the century—if I can hack a little blackmail or, maybe, I could choose to be the supernova at the centre of the school scandal universe for a few days.

The two fly apart as soon as they see me. Heading for opposite sides of the room. Magnets with the same pole. Mrs Lionel's top button on her blouse is undone and Mr Young drops his hand to his crotch to hide the bulge. Neither say anything, and behind me I can hear the sharp intake of breath that signals Miss Rennie was as in the dark over this little love tryst as the rest of school.

With Mis Rennie in the know, bang goes my blackmail opportunity, hello supernova.

'Derek,' Miss Rennie breathes.

Her voice sings of betrayal. It has been rumoured for an eon that she fancies Mr Young, and her tone has just sealed the deal. Boy this moment keeps giving. I've moved from a possible suspension, for that was the reward my behaviour in the class could have warranted, to a far less excluded world.

'Mr Young. Mrs Lionel! Whatever are you doing?' I say, with a flamboyant show of throwing my hands to my mouth.

I didn't know that I could smile quite this hard.

6
CATTLE WRANGLING

Friday, 16th September, 1983

THE QUEUE IS as slow a week in jail. It always is. The smell of human despair hangs in the air. A damp cloth weighing down on the shoulders of my fellow benefit claimants. The space around me is a dank sea of depression. It takes real skill to design such surroundings. The geniuses behind the interior seem to have had one goal—make the wait so miserable that you'd rather pull your nose hairs out through your ears than stay a second longer than necessary. Soul-sucking is as good a description as I can come up with. Faded colours are the norm, or rather faded grey is the norm. Walls, floor, plastic chairs bolted to the floor, counters, the hair of the men and women behind the counters— all grey. Only the ceiling breaks the pattern. Once white, it's now a clouded brown from an eternity of fag smoke. The cigarette fug in here is as thick as syrup, and it's not yet nine-thirty.

A couple of summers back, UB40 released a single called 'One in Ten', a reference to the near ten percent unemployment of the time. Things aren't much better today. When I'd worked in 'Hair It Is' I was exposed to endless, often harrowing, stories of men and woman who had lost their jobs. The pain and anguish that followed, as they failed to find a new job and had to rely on government hand-outs. The ability to support themselves ripped away as businesses 'downsized'—the phrase of the moment.

'Downsizing? Downsizing? Firing people, Catherine. It means they are bloody firing people.'

I was never upsized in the first place. I joined the ranks of the unwashed straight from school and the dole queue seems to get no shorter. Jobs no thicker on the ground. Today is my signing on day. I don't want to be here. No one wants to be here. No one wants this wait. A more obvious methodology to strip you of your pride would be hard to create. The people in the queue shuffle forward a few feet each time someone finishes at the desk. Most wear black. An appropriate funereal touch. A few wear grey in an attempt to blend in with the background.

I think back on that day in school when the scandal broke over Mr Young and Mrs Lionel. It never quite matched my expectations. I'd been ushered from the headmaster's room, mouth wide open, by Miss Rennie. Of course, I'd spread the word, and the gossip zipped around school on roller skates. Mrs Lionel returned to teach class a week later but she was never quite the same. When Mr Lionel appeared three days into her return, threw a set of keys at her, and announced he was leaving, she rushed after him and could be seen crying in the playground as he stormed into the distance. It transpired that her mood swings had been down to a rocky time at home. As to Mr Young, well, last I heard, he was still with Mrs Young, but had asked for, and received, a transfer to a school out Edinburgh way. Miss Rennie stayed on and is rumoured to fancy the new head. But, as with all things school wise, the flame of scandal was snuffed out by the day-to-day machinations of life, and my moment in the limelight faded.

I never did apply for Uni. I knew my results were never going to deliver that option. I managed to pass just two out of the five Highers I sat; a C in Home Economics and an A in English. With no intention of doing a sixth year, no university and no prospects, Maggie Hamilton had offered me a full-time job sweeping and cleaning. I'd lasted six weeks before I'd walked, after Wanda Craig complained that my hair-washing was not up to standard. I'd squirted half a bottle of Vosene into her hair before I'd stormed out.

I've had a couple of jobs since, but nothing that's made me want to rise in the morning singing from the high heavens. With the nights closing in on the autumn of 1983, I'm in danger of joining the long-term unemployed. I haunted the Jobcentre a few months back but that desire has passed. If it wasn't for the compulsory need to go through the motions, I'd avoid the place altogether. Sure, there are jobs on offer and I'm certainly not too high and mighty to put in a day's graft, but the jobs on offer are a Machiavellian blend of those that require specific skills I don't possess or those that require a lobotomy. The six by four cards that pepper the rows of boards promise a world of employment, but it's all a PR exercise for the ministers who like to say, '*Look at all the jobs out there*'.

I shuffle forward another few feet.

'I'm going to blow the lot the 'morra,' says the man behind me. 'Don't care. Rangers play the 'Tic and we owe them a humping. I've got tickets and we're hitting The Old Toll at eleven, be slammed by two, and at Ibrox in time for kick off. Then a Ruby Murray at the Koh and on to the casino. By Sunday, I'll either be happy and rich, happy and poor, miserable and rich, or miserable and poor. Depends on the result and the wee ball on the roulette wheel. Anyway up, I'm having a right day, the 'morra.'

He has just announced this to everyone within earshot.

The woman in front of me turns, 'And is that the responsible thing to do, Billy? Is it?'

Billy shrugs. 'Aye, it is, Isobel' he replies, 'It's my responsibility to enjoy life now and again.'

'It's your responsibility to look after Lizzie and the wanes. Can they live off a Rangers win and fresh air?'

'The whole of Glasgow can live off fresh air if the bears win.'

I'm the tennis umpire to their conversation, head flicking back and forth as they spar.

'Aye, well, don't expect me to stay quiet about your plans when I see Lizzie tonight,' Isobel says.

'Aye, like playing bingo is any better than the casino,' Billy adds.

'Billy, Lizzie spends a fiver, max, at the bingo. You blow your Bru cheque most weeks in the casino and live off her cleaning money. You're a lazy bastard!'

Billy stretches and yawns. The verbal attack isn't fazing him.

'And you're a broken record, Isobel. An *old* broken record. I've told you before, give us a decent job and I'll pack in the casino.'

Isobel laughs. 'Pack in the casino? Pack it in, Billy Caldwell. If you got ten grand in your pay packet, you'd put it all on black and blame the Pope when it came up red.'

The conversation has attracted a fair audience, happy at the diversion.

'Aye, Isobel, and if they gave you ten grand, you'd install a pipe to the Martini factory and wrap your big mouth round the open end from now to Christmas.'

'Better a bottle of Martini than a bottle of Grouse.'

'Nice whisky.'

'How would you know? It doesn't sit in your gob long enough for you to taste it. Why not just drill a hole in your stomach and feed it right in?'

'Not a bad idea, Isobel! You could do the same but you're that skinny, it'd go right through you.'

'And you're a fat slob, with greasy hair, bad breath and a nose picking habit that won't quit, but I don't hold that against you.'

'And the fact that you have the fashion sense of a dead badger, and the facial hair of a Yeti isn't an issue for me.'

This is clearly a well-worn path. Neither are rising to the other's bait.

'You know what Billy Caldwell?'

'What?'

'If I were Lizzie, I'd take one of those fancy kitchen knives you bought at the Barras and carve out your heart.'

'And if *you* were Lizzie, I'd give you a hand.'

'Have you two thought of taking this show onto the stage?' I interrupt. 'As an audience? I'd pay.'

'He needs to take his show off a cliff,' replies Isobel.

'Aye,' says Billy. 'And she needs to take hers up her scrawny backside.'

We all shuffle forward.

'I'm Catherine,' I say to Isobel.

'Nice to meet a better class of person.'

Billy jumps in, 'Isobel Caldwell, you wouldn't know a better class of person if they walked in here wearing Calvin Klein, driving a Roller and had a degree from Oxford.'

'Is that what you think makes for a better class of person, Billy Caldwell? Eh, posh gear, an overpriced car and a piece of paper that says you smoked weed and drank yourself stupid for four years?'

'You are both called Caldwell,' I interrupt.

'That's my idiot brother,' Isobel replies.

'You mean the brother of an idiot,' says Billy.

'So you've been doing this for a while,' I guess.

'What?' asks Isobel.

'This—the back-and-forth thing.'

'Since he was a wean. He's my wee brother. I've been digging him out the shit forever.'

'You? You dig me out?' Billy laughs. 'Who got you a decent lawyer only last week to stop your spending a week in Cornton Vale on remand?'

'And who gave me the bloody dodgy tellies in the first place that put me up at the Sheriff Court. I should have known better than believe they were legit.'

'I wasn't the one that tried to pap one off to the local polis.'

'You told me they were ex-rental stock.'

'They were.'

'Aye. Only in that they had been stolen from Radio Rentals two nights earlier.'

'How do you think I could knock our twenty-six-inch colour tellies at £100. They're 500 quid new.'

The queue moves and Isobel is one from the front.

'You don't fancy a telly, do you?' she asks me. 'Only we managed to plank half a dozen before the polis raided the flat. Fifty quid and its yours.'

'Sorry, I don't have fifty pence.'

'Well, no harm in asking.'

Isobel is called up to the desk.

AN HOUR LATER and I'm back in the house, reduced to watching late morning school programmes on BBC2. The school's *maths* programmes. I think I'm watching them as some form of masochistic punishment for my lack of progress on the job front. Mum is still in bed and I'm planning to be gone by the time she wakes up. But, before I go, I'll try to clean up a little.

Hoover, dishes, a bit of polishing and bung my clothes in for wash. Mum's drinking session last night will deafen her to all but a nuclear bomb this morning. It was that heavy. Before I pull on my Marigolds, I pick up the phone. I'm surprised to hear a dialling tone. We've been cut off for weeks, but Mum has somehow managed to find the cash to get us reconnected. I dial Jenny Meadows' number. She answers after a dozen rings.

'Hello,' her voice is sleepy.

'Hi Jenny.'

'Catherine, I'm on night shift. I just got my head down.'

'Sorry. But are you off tonight?'

'Yes, but I'm in for a night in front of the telly, before you ask. I'm knackered.'

Jenny volunteers at an all-night refuge in Finnieston. She's in the same position as me on employment, but during the last year at school she'd helped out at the refuge when she could and has never quit. The woman behind it is a friend of Jenny's mum. It's not something I can see myself doing, but I admire Jenny's spirit and generosity. I think things are bad in my house with Mum but Jenny sees a lot worse.

'I just need a little company, Jenny.'

'I really am tired.'

'Get some sleep now and I'll bring over my back copies of Smash Hits and a bottle of something later.'

I've known Jenny since before primary school. We love our music. We've ploughed the furrows of music fads in tandem. Early glam rockers, disco queens, punk maidens, new wave freaks, electronic robots and, of late, new romantic nuts. Her Spandau Ballet and the Kemp brothers. Me Duran Duran and Andy Taylor. I tried to get tickets for the Rio tour last year and failed. Jenny saw Spandau Ballet back in April and didn't take me. I've dug her up on that endlessly. To be fair she was invited by Doug Wallace, whose old man is Glasgow polis and knows some people at Tiffany's. She did ask Doug for a spare ticket for me, but he told her he couldn't get one. I suspect he could have, but with his eyes on Jenny, he didn't want me deflecting his little cupid's arrows. With music in our blood, one of Jenny and my favourite things to do is to surf back copies of Smash Hits and chat about concerts we never went to, singles we never bought and albums we couldn't afford.

'Catherine, I'm going to say 'no'. Is that okay?'

I inject as much disappointment in my voice as I can, and end with, 'Sure.'

I hang up the phone, and a few seconds later it rings again.

'Changed your mind,' I say after picking up.

I hear pips and then a voice says, 'Sorry.'

It's not Jenny.

'Who is this?' I ask.

'Isobel.'

'Isobel who?'

'Isobel Caldwell.'

I scrape my brain for the name.

'From the queue at the Bru,' she adds.

'Oh.'

'It was only this morning. Have you forgotten me already?'

'How did you get this number?'

'My cousin works behind the desk.'

'And they gave you my home number?'

'Yes.'

'Is that allowed?'

'Probably not, but look Katy, I have a job offer for you.'

No one calls me Katy. For reasons that escape me, my name has never been shortened. Save Jenny who sometimes pronounces Catherine as 'Can' but she's just lazy.

'A what?'

'A job. You know the sort of work where you get money in your hand at the end of the day.'

'You're offering me a job? Why? Do you work at the Job Centre or something?'

'What? And claim the Bru? Be serious. The centre are not the only ones that have jobs on offer.'

I pause. Taking a moment to steady my thinking.

'Look,' I say. 'I'll be straight with you. I don't like being called like this.'

'Like what?'

'Out of the blue.'

'This is not out of the blue. We met this morning.'

'In the Bru queue.'

'Does that matter? We met, and I have a job that you would be great for.'

'I…'

'Just hear me out and if you don't like it, then hang up and I'll not bother you again.'

'I…'

'Two minutes.'

What else am I doing?

'Two minutes, you say?'

'Max,' she replies.

'Okay.'

'Right, I'll meet you at the café next to John Menzies in ten.'

'Sorry?'

'The café next to John Menzies. It's not far from your house.'

'You know where I live?'

'Aye.'

'How?'

'My cousin.'

'They gave you my address as well?'

'Well how else was I going to find you?'

I'm not sure how to answer that.

'Just tell me what you have to say on the phone!' I say.

'No chance! Phones are not safe.'

That's enough. I hang up. The phone rings again. I leave it. It rings itself out only to kick back in again. I leave it again. It dies. Then rings. Dies. Rings.

'If you don't answer that bloody phone, I'll throw it in the bin,' mum shouts. Clearly, she's not as out for the count as I thought.

The phone rings once more and I lift it.

'Don't hang up on me!' says Isobel once she has put her money in the phone box.

'I don't want your job.'

'How do you know? You don't know what it is.'

'I'm hanging up.'

'Okay. Suit yourself. I'll just come around to your house.'

'You can't.'

'Why not?'

'You just can't.'

'Of course, I can. Put on the kettle. I'll see you in five.'

'No. Don't do that!'

I need to keep this away from here.

'I'll come to the café,' I say. 'But if I don't want the job, I want you to promise to leave me alone.'

'Aye, sure. See you in ten minutes.'

'Who was that?' shouts Mum as I hang up.

'Just Jenny,' I lie. 'She wants to meet up for a cup of tea.'

'Do me a favour, I'm out of Askit powders. Can you bring me some back from the shops?'

'Okay.'

'And Catherine?'

'Yes.'

'You know that I love you?'

Mum's not given to such outbursts when hungover.

'Sure, Mum.'

'I mean it. Always remember that. Never forget what we had!'

Had?

I grab my coat and leave, confused by the conversation but, once out on the pavement, I forget about Mum, take a deep breath, and wonder why some stranger I met in the Bru would track me down? What kind of job would they have to offer? Certainly not one that I'm going to take. Of that, I'm sure. Isobel's conversation with her brother this morning doesn't have me thinking that I'm about to be offered a role as an admin assistant with the Church of Scotland. Stolen tellies don't bode well.

The café is a steaming broth of humanity and I regret agreeing to a meet here as soon as I cross the threshold. I recognise half a dozen faces and there's at least another four people with their backs to me that look familiar. Isobel is sitting in the far corner, near the serving hatch. She waves and points at the spare chair on the other side of her table.

Sam's Café is old school—a throwback to the late fifties. Rickety wooden tables and chairs dot the space, reassigned their location in perpetuity, depending on the customer's will. The floor is a sea of cracked linoleum and the walls sport fading posters of boxing fights between fighters I've never heard of— all from the era when Sam used to pull on gloves. Sam is in his seventies and tells anyone that will listen that he's selling up soon. Maggie Hamilton thinks he first told her that in nineteen sixty-three. Sam claims that he only started the café when he picked up a bad injury to his elbow while boxing. He says he was a couple of fights short of a stab at the title. As to what title, no-one knows. And, as to the injury, sometimes it's his left elbow, sometimes his right. It doesn't impact his ability to hump bins or move furniture but makes a sudden and dramatic reappearance when he's regaling someone about his boxing lineage.

I wade through the cigarette smoke and sit down opposite Isobel. She's hugging a mug of tea, a slice of Sam's patented tablet on a plate in front of her.

'Hi Katy, what's your poison.'

'Nothing for me. I don't have much time. And it's Catherine, not Katy.'

'Katy, Catherine, same side of the same coin, but Catherine it is. What have you got to do today that you need to leave so quick?'

'Personal stuff.'

'I hate that stuff. Gets in the way of having a good time. You know? Mum stuff and all that.'

The smile on her face flashes a warning to me. Why mention Mum stuff?

'This tablet is gorgeous,' she says.

'Sam is well known for it.'

'He should sell it to other shops.'

I'm not in for chit-chat.

'What is it you want?' I ask.

'I like that,' she says, nibbling at the corner of the tablet 'Straight to the point. No messing around.'

Sam pokes his head out of the hatch and looks at me. I shake my head, indicating I don't want anything, and he vanishes.

'Look, Catherine, things ain't easy at the moment,' Isobel says. 'Jobs are hard to come by. Money's as tight as Dave Lee

Roth's trousers. I know it. You know it. And we all need a little folding to be walking around with. Don't we?'

I don't answer, leaning in a little. Isobel's voice sounds too loud to me and with the radars that pass for ears around here I could do with her toning it down a bit.

'So, this is the game, Catherine. We run a little courier business.'

'Who's we?'

'Me and my idiot brother.'

'I thought you were both unemployed?'

'What? Because we sign on at the Bru? I'd be off my head not to claim that money. Everyone else does. But it's not enough to live on. Anyway, our courier business is a little special. We're not into shifting documents for Dullsville Limited, or dropping pressies off for Granny Smith. We move items of high value for certain clients, if you get what I mean. Discreet.'

'If this about drugs, then I'm not only gone, but I'm calling the police.'

Her face hardens, 'Hey I'm doing you a favour here. It's not drugs and don't ever threaten to call the police on me again.'

'I'm leaving,' I say. 'I shouldn't have even come here.'

I start to rise, and Isobel speaks, 'Do you want Warrant Officers back at your door?'

I stop, bum off the seat, 'Warrant Officers? What are they?'

'Catherine, I really am trying to help you. I'm not here about drugs, I promise. I just think I can put a little cash your way, and we both end up happy.'

I want to ask more about the Warrant Officers but leave it. I sit back down.

'Look,' she says. 'You and I know there's no magic job out there for us. No one is going to phone and tell us that Paul

Young needs a wee friend to chat with, and pay us a hundred quid a day for holding his hand? Not going to happen.

'So,' she adds. 'All you have to do is deliver the odd parcel and you get fifty quid in your hand for each one. That easy.'

'And what's in these parcels?'

Why the hell am I even asking.

'So, you're interested?'

'No.'

And I'm not. Not really. But at the moment I have tuppence in my pocket and there's no food in the house. I've a hole in my only decent pair of shoes, and my jeans have more patches than original denim.

'Who's your friend, Catherine?' says a voice from behind me.

Maggie Hamilton appears at the side of our table as if beamed down from the Enterprise. The woman can be as stealthy as the SAS. Before I can say anything, Isobel jumps in, 'Hi, I'm Isobel, Catherine and I here are old friends.'

'Hi Mrs Hamilton, how is the salon?' I ask, trying to shut Isobel out.

'Everyone needs their hair cut, save the bald and the wild.'

Her stock answer.

I wait for her to leave, but Isobel is a little too interesting for that.

'And what do you do Isobel?' she asks.

'I wrangle cattle.'

That rips the wind from Maggie.

'You what?'

'Cattle,' Isobel repeats. 'I'm a cattle wrangler.'

Confusion reigns on Maggie's face.

'What does that mean?' she asks.

'Well, you know what cattle are?'

'You mean cows.'

'And bulls.'

'Yes.'

'Well, I wrangle them.'

'Wrangle?'

'Yip, you've got it.'

'I'm sorry, Isobel but I don't think I do. What is wrangling.'

'Have you ever watched Bonanza?'

'The telly show?'

'That's it. Well, they have a ranch with a load of cattle on it.'

'Yes?'

'And they spend all day wrangling them.'

'I'm still a little lost.'

'That happens to my cattle.'

'What does?'

'Some of them get lost. That's why I need to wrangle them. That's my job. Cattle Wrangler.'

'And is there a lot of call for that around here?'

Isobel shakes her head, 'Sadly not, but I live in hope. Anyway Mrs Hamilton, me and Catherine were chatting.'

'Well, it was nice to meet you Isobel and, if you don't mind me saying, Catherine, you could do with a haircut.'

Maggie isn't one to take a cold shoulder well, but she moves away.

I run my hand through my hair. I could do with two haircuts, but with no money that'll have to wait.

'What did you say that for?' I ask.

'What?'

'That I'm a cattle wrangler? Because it's true. At least that's what I've put down as my profession at the Job Centre. There's no chance of a job coming up as a cattle wrangler in Glasgow.'

'Not that. Why did you say we were old friends?'

'Well, we are.'

'We are not. I only met you this morning.'

'What does it matter? We'll become good friends.'

I stand up and push the chair away. 'I'm leaving for good this time. I don't like this conversation or where this is going.'

'I'll give you a bell in a day or two. It's easy money.'

'I don't want it.'

'They all say that to begin with, but there's really no risk at all. Fifty quid a delivery and as many deliveries as you can handle.'

I turn away and notice that a few too many eyes are looking in my direction. A few too many for this encounter not to be a talk of the steamie moment. Strangers are noticed around here.

7
CUT OFF

I GO FOR a walk to clear my head of all things Isobel, and arrive home after dark to find the house a cold, lightless shell. Twilight has descended but there are no lights on that I can see. I push in through the front door and flick the light switch. Nothing happens. I throw it a few more times. Zip.

'Mum?' I shout.

There's no reply.

I enter the living room and try the big light. Nothing.

'Mum?'

Still no reply.

The fuse box is in the hall cupboard. I head for the kitchen first, to dig out the old torch that lies in what mum's refers to as *the drawer of crap*. I find it under a knife sharpener we've never used and next to a ball of pink string. I try the torch, but either the batteries are dead, or the bulb has gone. We have no spares of either. I root around a little more and pull out a half-empty packet of candles. A bit more digging and I uncover a box of matches and light one of the candles. I pull out a saucer from the cupboard, drip some wax on the centre and fix the candle to it, giving it a few seconds to dry and grip. Once I'm sure the candle will stay upright, I walk back to the hall holding the saucer, and open the cupboard door.

I'm a dab hand at putting new fuse wire in. A small roll of wire and the correct sized screwdriver sit on top of the fuse box. I throw the main power switch and remove each of the grey lumps of plastic and check them. All are intact. I put them all back, throw the switch and try the hall light again. Still nothing.

'Mum,' I shout.

There's still no reply.

I cross to her bedroom and shout through the door. If she's fallen back asleep I'll catch it, but more likely she's nursing a bottle of Grants. I knock on the bedroom door. I knock three more times before I push the door open to look in. The smell of stale alcohol and Mystique, Mum's perfume of choice, is thick. The room is dark, and I push the candle ahead of me. Mum's bed is empty. I retreat to circle the house, pulling the curtains closed as I do so. I re-enter the kitchen and try to turn on the electric cooker but it is as dead as the lights. I open the fridge and no light comes on.

THE POWER WAIT...

Not again.

Two words that haunt this house. I'm thinking, with some confidence, that we've been cut off by the SSEB, short for the South of Scotland Electricity Board or, as Jenny's dad calls them, the PLEBS. I'd noticed some final demands over the last few weeks, but assumed that Mum would, as usual, stave off disconnection with an injection of cash from her mysterious source. After all, the phone was back on. Clearly the magic money-well is a little drier at the moment than she would like.

We've been here before and it's not pleasant. *No* hot water, *no* hot food. *No* nights in front of the telly, *not* making toast on the three-bar electric fire. Waking up in the dark. Going to bed in the dark. All lie before me, even if Mum comes up with the readies—reconnection is not swift.

I open the fridge to reveal the wasting food—a half a pint of milk and a scraping of margarine. There's nothing else perishable that can go off. Not that the non-perishable goods are substantive—a couple of bottles of IRN-BRU are it. The bread bin has two slices of a plain loaf on the turn, and the only fillings available in the cupboard are a quarter jar of fish paste or a half an inch of hardening jam. There are a couple of tins of beans and one of macaroni, if I fancy them cold. So, milk, and a jam sandwich it is for tea. I take my feast through to the living room to eat and contemplate my encounters with Isobel.

THE MUM WAIT…

Thoughts of Isobel vanish when I notice an envelope propped up against the clock on the mantlepiece. I pull it down. It's Mum's hand-writing. Scribbled on the outside is a single word— Catherine. I open up the envelope and pull out a sheet of perforated note paper. I read by candlelight:

'Sorry about this. I need some time to myself. I know this isn't fair. See you soon. Mum.'

I re-read the note and turn it over. The reverse is blank. I read it again. What does it mean? Where has she gone? For how long? She said nothing when I'd left earlier. Or rather, when I think on it, she had:

Never forget what we had.

That was what she'd said as I'd left to meet Isobel. Not what we *have* but what we *had.*

Past tense.

Questions pile on questions and I sit down, note on my lap, sandwich untouched at my side. After a while I rise and venture back into Mum's bedroom. The candlelight reveals a made-up bed. The usual detritus that lies around her room; shoes, underwear, tops, trousers, plates, glasses, bottles—is noticeable by its absence. That's unusual, as cleaning the room is a once in a while optional extra in her life. I flick open the collapsing ancient wardrobe. I can't tell whether there are clothes missing but the rail looks light on items. Three old cases lie at the bottom, but they have lain there for an eon. Careful not to catch the candle flame on the bed covers I peer under the bed and my heart sinks. The battered leather suitcase that once belonged to my gran is missing—a rectangle of dust free carpet betraying where it had lain. That's no overnight bag. That case did both of us for the few holidays we have taken. I check the dressing table. It's cluttered but all the essentials are missing.

I stand next to Mum's bed, looking down. When I was wee, I'd sneak through here most nights and slip between the sheets. Mum never complained. She'd just roll over and tuck me in. It was the safest I ever felt. The journeys from my room to hers became less frequent as birthdays passed. But they took a while to stop altogether. Even when I started secondary school, I had the occasional need of Mum's warmth. I touch the fading bed cover, rubbing my finger along the coarse fibre.

Where have you gone?

And for how long?

I leave the room, drink my milk, eat the sandwich, listen to the silence.

Once I've washed up, I double check the mantelpiece. With no electricity and no Mum, I'm hoping she's left some cash, but there's nothing.

I know this isn't fair.

No kidding Mum. No money. No power and no idea where you've gone. There had also been a few other bills, most in red, lying on the hall table this week. They're all missing. No doubt in the bin. I wander to the hall and pick up the phone. I call Jenny's number. It rings out. I try again. The same result. I look at the receiver. I could call Karen Shields. I *could.* Except it's been six months since I last saw her. Unlike Jenny, Karen, a once firm buddy, had found a new set of friends, and has all but cut me off since she got a job. She would still take my call. Of that I'm sure. Still offer some advice. Still ask if I wanted to come over. Maybe she'd be more dispassionate about the situation. Tell me that I needed to get a straight head on and find out where Mum is. Be logical.

Logical.

The Wednesday Club.

They would know. Mum has seen a lot less of them lately, preferring her own company, but they have known each other for ever. I could call some of them and ask if they have heard from her. I reach under the table to retrieve the torn address book. It's not there. A scribbled mess of numbers and names, many crossed out, written in a rainbow of pen and pencil colours—it has been under the table since I was a kid. I play the candle over the floor. It's definitely missing. I don't know any of Mum's friend's numbers. I squat on the floor staring at the phone realising, for the first time, just how cut off I've become. Beyond Jenny, I've no real friends. I've no idea how to get in touch with any of The Wednesday Club. I don't even have the number for Uncle Rod, Mum's younger, and only, sibling. Not that he's been a figure in our life. The occasional phone call and a card at Christmas.

Our life.

Not *my* life. But *our life*. Mum and I. A team? No, that's not quite right. Not anymore. Not a team. Not for a while. More like a vague partnership. Vodka has loosened the ties.

Self-pity lies this way. I rise, trying Jenny's number again. It rings out once more.

Back in the living room, the clock chimes seven, and I wonder just what in the hell I'm going to do.

Wait?

What else is there?

At eight, I go for a walk. Not far. A circle of the roads around us, passing homes with dancing lights and shadows behind curtains. The sounds of weekend life revving up. I pass a few neighbours on the pavement, nodding at them. Each time I wonder if I should engage. Open up a conversation. I don't. I only have one thought on my mind: Where's Mum? That won't make for good chat. Not unless I want to send a neighbourhood telegram scuttering on its way.

Anabel Day has gone missing. She's done a Jenny Agutter. Gone walkabout.

That'll do the rounds soon enough without me starting it off.

'So, are we good?'

I spin. Isobel is standing a few feet away.

'What are you doing here?' I ask.

'Friday night, where else would I be?'

I notice a black car parked along the road. I don't know much about cars, but I recognise the BMW badge. Exhaust is dribbling into the night and there's a shape in the driver's seat.

'I told you, I'm not interested,' I say.

'I know.'

She's changed clothes and is wearing a blue jump suit with a black and white striped top underneath, a denim jacket on top. Her hair is messed up Madonna style. Black Doc Martins cover her feet.

'So, I'll ask again, why are you here?', I say.

'We're off to Panama Jax and I just fancied a wee toddle around to see the area. My flat is a bit cramped and maybe I need somewhere new to live.'

'You're thinking of moving here.'

'Maybe? Can you sing?'

That throws me.

'Sorry?'

'Can you sing?'

'Why?'

'You're a good-looking girl. Need a bit of a makeover right enough. A haircut. A few wee lessons in the old slap. And some clothes that aren't from the stone age would help. But under there I see some sparkle and shine that wants to get out. I know a few guys and even a few girls that wouldn't mind wynchin' you.'

I'm taken aback. I can't remember the last time anyone complimented me on my looks.

'A wee belter like you could do the business.'

'What are you talking about.'

'Flash a bit more leg. I bet you've got great legs. High heels would do you wonders. You're a bit skinny, but there's plenty out there like that vibe. Lanky. You look like you've got nice boobs too. Pity you hide them away under that manky jumper. Bet you don't even need a bra. And if you could sing. Well?'

I can't help but look down on the seasoned old Shetland knit that I inherited from Mum's cast offs. I always thought it said something mysterious to others. A girl from the country. In town checking on her city cousins. The rough and ready look.

'I need to ask you a question.' I say ignoring her line of chat.

'What?'

'In the café today. You talked about Warrant Officers?'

'And?'

'What are they?'

'Did your mum not tell you?'

'About what?'

'Oh, that's embarrassing. Very embarrassing.'

'What is?'

'A warrant sale, that's what's embarrassing.'

I wait on more. She obliges, 'It's when you owe money, can't pay and they set up a warrant sale.'

'Who sets up a what?'

'A warrant sale. It's when warrant officers come around to your house. All legal and above board. They tot up the value of everything you have, well, really, they just make up the value. Pennies on the pound as they would say. If you don't find the cash to pay the debt, they auction it all off. Did they take your stuff?'

'What stuff would they take?'

'Furniture, telly, everything.'

'No-one took any stuff.'

'That's something, but things must be bad if your gear was going up for auction. If you still have it all, I take it your mum must have found the cash to settle the debt.'

'I never saw any Warrant Officers.'

'Maybe they came when you were out.'

'So how did you know about this?'

'How does anyone know about a warrant sale?'

'I don't know.'

'The newspapers. They have to advertise if you're subject to a warrant sale. Now I need to go. I'll see you around. Here.' She hands me a piece of paper. 'My phone number.'

As Isobel heads for the BMW, I stare at the piece of paper, before shoving it in my pocket. A few seconds later she waves at me as the car passes. I don't get a proper look at the driver. I walk back to my house, my thoughts jumping from Mum to Isobel and back. From my legs to the Shetland knit. And Warrant Officers.

'Mum,' I shout as I walk in the house, just in case.

Silence.

I slump back on the sofa.

Warrant Officers.

That has to be what Lidia Thomas was referring to when she mentioned the papers and was shushed by Maggie that day in the salon. Everyone must have seen the notice. No wonder Ira Johnston and Les Roach had said what they did. How had I missed it when I stole the papers?

Were they really going to auction off all our stuff? I look around. How much would they get for it all? And all the while Mum said nothing.

Embarrassing. Very embarrassing.

And now the electricity has been cut off. Was that the last straw. Is she leaving me here? Running out. Me picking up the pieces. She wouldn't do that. Would she?

Two hours later I've phoned Jenny so often I've lost count, but she's not in. Didn't she tell me she was in for a night in front of the telly? I think on going around to hers, but I have no money for the bus and she's miles away.

I'm being abandoned here.

I get up and wander to the kitchen. I fix up a second candle and decide to call it quits. It's too early for bed, but I need the oblivion that sleep brings. Let the morning light shine some sense on all of this. I check the doors are locked and bolted, and do the same for the windows. It's not something I ever do but, tonight, it's the right thing to do.

THE SLEEP WAIT…

Two hours, six minutes later. No sleep. No sign of sleep. The wait that gets longer the less you want it to. The wait that provides all the time your head needs to think about all the things that you don't want to think about. And most of it centres on Mum.

'I read once that there is good money in alpaca farming in the Andes.'

'I had you late in life, Catherine. But that meant I had more time to be with you.'

'A wee drink now and again is the only thing I have, Catherine.'

'Sorry about this. I need some time to myself. I know this isn't fair. See you soon.'

I slide from the covers and pull back the curtains, looking out on the back green. I glance up. No stars. There are never stars. Not here in the city. The moon is up there somewhere, but down here natural light is banned; down here streetlights, car lights and window lights rule. Orange and white. I wander to Mum's room and stare at the bed. I sit down on the edge. I pull at the cover, revealing the sheet beneath. I slide my hand to the pillow. Swing my legs up. Drop my head on the pillow. Push my feet under the blankets. Inhale the scent of Mum.

Sleep.

8
THE SMALL NASTY STUFF

'*CATHERINE?*'

'Mum? Where are you? I came home last night, and you weren't there.'

'*I know. I'm sorry. I just need some time to myself.*'

'Where are you?'

'*Safe, Catherine. Safe and there is no need for you to worry. I'll be back soon.*'

'When?'

'*I don't know.*'

'I woke up this morning and was going to call the police.'

'*That's why I phoned. I'm fine. I'll keep in touch.*'

'But what do I do, Mum? There's no electricity.'

'*I know.*'

'And I don't have any money.'

'*I know.*'

'So, what do I do.'

'*I'll be back and fix everything. I promise - just hold tight!*'

'Hold tight. I haven't even got money for food, Mum.'

'*I know.*'

'Is that all you are going to say? What can I do without money?'

'*You have your Bru money.*'

'Not 'til Thursday.'

'*Where is your last payment?*'

'You took most of it.'

'Did I?'

'Yes. From my purse.'

'Sorry.'

'Mum, you can't do this to me.'

'I know.'

'Stop saying that!'

'Catherine?'

'What?'

'You know you're special. Have I ever told you that?'

'Yes.'

'I mean really special. That's why you're called Catherine.'

'Mum, come home!'

'It's a special name for a special person. One day you'll know what I mean.'

'Come home!'

'Soon but don't forget how special you are. There are people out there that will want to find you.'

'Mum, what are you talking about?'

'Be careful. I've always told you to avoid strangers, haven't I?'

'I'm not a kid.'

'I know.'

'Mum, this isn't fair. You can't leave me here. You just can't.'

'I know. I love you, special girl.'

Click.

That conversation had taken place three days ago, the morning after she'd vanished. I've hardly left the house since, mostly scouring it for stray cash. My Bru money is gone and I've two days to go before I get any more. I've never had 'no money'. I've had 'some money', even 'not enough money' but never 'no money'. 'No money' is an evil land where life is lived at the edges. The edge of hunger, the edge of comfort, the edge of despair. I found ten pence stuffed down the back of the sofa yesterday on my fifth deep dive of the cracks and crevices. I almost cried. I think I would have, had I found a pound note.

The kitchen cupboards are down to crumbs and dust. The fridge empty. I even resorted to lining up stuff that can go to the pawn brokers. In a fit of angst, I've spent the last twenty-four hours on a cleaning marathon. As much to take my mind off the situation as anything else. I've exhausted the cleaning products in the house. With no electricity, I've hand washed every piece of linen and every slip of clothing. All are on the line or draped over tables and chairs throughout the house. I've brushed the carpet and beaten the rugs. The bathroom has been bleached so heavily that it makes my eyes water. The windows are the cleanest they've been in my lifetime.

When I had run out of stuff to clean, I set about a mend and improve run. Ancient paint from under the stairs was de-skinned to cover up ancient scrapes and scratches on wood and walls. I found a few rolls of anaglypta, but with no wall paper paste I tried glue. That didn't go well. This morning I dug what garden tools we have from the shed. I've weeded, dug over and tidied up as best I can. I started crying when I found myself on my hands and knees with a scrubbing brush and a bucket of cold water, cleaning the stone steps up to the house. It took a while to shake that moment out, all the time wondering how hard would it be to replace the broken tiles on the roof.

And now I'm sitting in the cleanest house in Glasgow. Tired, dirty and hungrier than a bear in Spring, but in a clean house. Breakfast was a wet lump of flour mixed with water. My stomach cramped up at that.

Three days since Mum left and I could eat cardboard. Shoplifting is on my mind, except I'm not brave enough. Midge raking the bins behind the shops is also on the horizon. Begging from the neighbours got me some milk and sugar yesterday. Two days back, I'd blagged a meal at Jenny's; a luxurious feast of tomato soup, grilled chicken and a pot of Ski yoghurt. Jenny's been on back-to-back night shifts since then. I called Karen only to discover that she has moved out of her parent's house and in with her boyfriend through in Edinburgh. I almost asked if I could come around anyway.

Bru day is the day after tomorrow.

Money day.

I've opened all the letters that have come through the letterbox and now know the depth of Mum's debt. I can almost smell the return of the Warrant Officers.

I root around the back of the chair I'm sitting on, digging deep. Praying that the magic money fairies invaded the house last night and secreted coins. I come up empty and take a pointless trip to the kitchen. I wonder what baking soda tastes like.

And that's enough.

Just enough.

I stamp through to the hall and pull the piece of paper that Isobel gave me from my pocket. I dial the number.

'Hello?'

'Hello, who is this?'

'Catherine.'

'Hi, Catherine.'

'Do you still need parcels delivered?'

'Always.'

'Fifty quid a go?'

'Yip.'

'Today?'

'If you want.'

'And it's not drugs.'

'It's not drugs.'

'How many parcels.?'

'One. Everyone starts with one.'

'And I get paid fifty quid?'

'Yes.'

'In cash?'

'Yip.'

'Today?'

'After delivery.'

'Where do I meet you?'

'You don't.'

'What do I do?'

'Can you get to Central Station in an hour.'

'An hour?'

'Go to the shell and wait.'

'That's it?'

'That's it.'

The shell is a fifteen-inch howitzer shell from World War I; a slug of ordnance that stands upright near the toilets in Central Station. It's as tall as I am. Mum said it used to sit in the middle of the concourse. She calls it the Dizzy Shell. A 'dizzy' is her slang for being stood up on a date.

'You'd see no end of men and women, girls and boys, hanging around the shell trying to look like the person they were waiting on was due soon.'

The ten pence I found is enough for a bus ride to town. If I'm quick, I can make it to Central Station in time. I blank the voice in my head that's screaming how bad an idea this is. I strip and cold wash myself, douse in perfume and put on the only decent clothes I own. All the time I finger the ten pence piece. Constantly checking it is there.

I arrive at the bus stop without bumping into anyone that I know. I jump on and head to the back of the bus where I drop into the rear bench seat.

'Hi Catherine.'

I turn. Lidia Todd is sitting at the other end of the seat. Cash must be tight for her to take to public transport. In the salon she used to boast about how big her taxi bill was.

'Hi, Mrs Todd.'

'Where are you going, Catherine?'

'Just into town for some window shopping.'

'And some food, I hope?'

'Pardon.'

'You're wasting away, Catherine.'

'I'm fine, Mrs Todd.'

'You don't look fine. Is your Mum not feeding you?'

'Honestly, Mrs Todd I'm fine.'

'How is she?'

'Mum's good.'

'I haven't seen her in an age.'

'She's not out much.'

'And things at home are okay?'

'Yes, Mrs Todd.'

I look out the window. It's a good forty minutes into town. I think about moving seat.

'Only I know that you're struggling to get a job, Catherine.'

I blank that one.

'I was only saying to Maggie Hamilton the other day, that young Catherine needs a job. You were a good worker in the salon. Pity about the Vosene and Wanda Craig. That took some washing out, I'll tell you. But I think Maggie might take you back if you apologise to Wanda.'

'I'm still in my fifties.'

'Fifties?' he laughs. 'The last time you were in your fifties, Lidia Todd, Marc Bolan was at number one. Catherine,' he says looking at me. 'She's sixty-seven.'

Lidia's breath explodes from her nose, some snot flying out. 'I am *not* sixty-seven.'

'Jesus, Lidia. I'm sixty-eight this month. Sorry, I got your age wrong.' He winks at me. 'You're sixty-eight.'

'Take that back.'

'Take what back, Lidia? Time? I can't do that.' Again, he looks at me. 'My name's Drew McCreadie by the way.'

'I'm Catherine Day.'

'Nice to meet you, Catherine. How old do you think Lidia is?'

There are dangerous questions and there are *dangerous* questions. I'd never heard Lidia tell anyone her actual age. Few of the women in the salon talk about how long they have been on the planet, but Lidia certainly gave the impression that she'd been born well after the First World War.

'I don't know,' I reply.

'Well, I do,' he says. 'You see I was born on the same street and same year as Lidia here. Medwyn Street in Whiteinch. 1915 was the year, and Lidia here was born two doors down.

I turn to examine Lidia, who isn't taking this conversation well at all. I mean, I thought mid-fifties was old but sixty-eight is so ancient that I'm amazed she's still alive.

'Are you sixty-eight, Mrs Todd?'

'That is absolutely none of your business Catherine, and if you say that to anyone else, I will have words with your mother.'

'About what?' I ask.

'About prying into things that have nothing to do with you.'

'Like you asking about my weight?'

'That's different. It's plain to see you are too light.'

'Aye,' says Drew. 'And it's plain to see that you're sixty-eight.'

He turns around and shouts out. 'Hey, does anyone else on this bus think Lidia here looks her age?'

There's another half a dozen people on the lower deck. All bar one, a man in a dark suit, turn around.

'How dare you!' shouts Lidia.

'Catherine,' says Drew. 'I made a mistake.'

'You did?' I answer.

'I missed a trick here. I should really have given Bruce Forsyth a call before I got on this bus.'

'Why?' I say, more than a little confused.

'Well, we could have played a game of 'Play Your Cards Right'. Only instead of guessing if the cards are higher or lower, we could have guessed Lidia's age.'

'I'm not standing for this,' spits Lidia.

'I know,' replies Drew. 'You're sitting for it.'

'I'm getting off.'

'Who's stopping you?'

'You always were a bad one, Drew McCreadie.'

'And you were always a sponger. So was your family. The Walters were famous for it. Always pretending to be better than they were. Who was it that had the money in the family? Your mum's sister. Right? Carol, wasn't it? Your aunt. She married wealthy, didn't she? I heard that your mum and her stopped talking over the amount of money your mum owed her. Thousands some said. And never paid back.'

Lidia rises and, as she passes Drew, she slaps him hard across the face. Drew takes the blow with amazing grace, rubbing his cheek and smiling. Lidia storms to the front of the bus and demands to be let off; her dramatic exit is spoilt when the driver ignores her order and makes her wait two minutes until we arrive at the next bus stop. When she gets off, she turns her back to the bus and waits for it to leave.

'Gosh,' I say to Drew as we draw away from the stop.

'Sorry about that,' Drew says. 'She's had that coming for an age. You just happened to give me a good reason to let rip.'

'Is she really sixty-eight?'

'Aye. Why, what does she tell people?'

'Well, when I worked in the hair salon, she'd give the impression of fifties.'

'I heard that her husband left her.'

'Really? I missed that.'

'A few weeks back. Got his pension from the post office and decided he'd had enough. I'm not one to talk bad about people, but Lidia Todd rubbed a lot of people up the wrong way when she was younger. All airs and graces. Told everyone that would listen that she was waiting for the right man. I doubt Gerald was what she had in mind, and he seems to have seen sense. Albeit he took a while.'

'How do you know all this?'

'My sister is a hell of a gossip. And to be fair, so am I. I moved here a few years back and was amazed to see Lidia at the shops one day. I've not seen her in decades. Never knew she was even alive. She blanked me. Recognised me but blanked me. Well that got my back up and it didn't take much to find out a little about what she had been up to. I just wish she hadn't stormed off like that just now.'

'Why?'

'I was having fun.'

I thought back to the salon and the disdain that most of the others held for Lidia. She was guilty of talking down to people and never missed a trick to tell anyone how much cash she was spending. No one really believed her.

'Maybe that was a bit much,' he says, staring out at the passing world. 'After all, I really didn't know her that well. But you know how these things build in your head. You wait for the right moment to say the right thing. Sometimes the moment arrives and sometimes it doesn't. Then you pounce and it... well, it never pans out as you thought it would. I sometimes think the waiting is more cathartic than the event itself.'

'Cathartic?'

'Liberating.'

'And you don't feel liberated?'

'Not really. But it was fun!'

'But why have a go at her?'

'I've been waiting a while.'

'For how long.'

'Oh, a long, long time.'

'And you just happened to bump into her today, on this bus?'

He leans over the back of the seat into the wash of hot air rising from the engine under my seat. 'If I'm honest I've lost count of how many times I've been sitting here in the last few weeks building up the courage to speak to her. After she blanked me, I did a bit of detective work, talked to my sister and followed Lidia. She uses this bus a lot. Goes for a walk on Glasgow Green most days, then comes home. She gets the same bus, at the same time.'

'And you've been on the bus with her each time?'

'Sad, isn't it? You'd think at my age I'd learn to let go of something that happened decades ago.'

'So, what did she do to you?'

Drew rubs at his forehead and stares past me.

'Daft, isn't it?' he says. 'The things that you hold onto in your head. The moments you play over and over, working out what you *should* have done. What you *should* have said. What you *could* have done. *Could* have said?'

I nod, not really understanding.

'So stupid but I can't let them go.'

'And?'

'I was fifteen, a pimple-loaded boy. It was just before the great depression and the roaring twenties were still roaring, just. I was too young for the clubs that had sprung up but, like every teenager, I secretly wanted to be part of the goings-on. Only there was no such thing as teenagers back then. There were children and there were adults. Nothing lay in between. I was in short trousers, and the closest I got to a night out was a walk in the park with my parents on a summer's eve.'

His eyes glaze over as he talks. The bus rumbles down Victoria Road, filling up with passengers that push both Drew and I against the windows as the seats next to us fill. The person sharing Drew's seat isn't happy at the fact Drew is turning to talk to me.

'Anyway,' he continues. 'I was a wee bit of a rebel back then. I'd saved up some money, bought a second-hand suit and had it adjusted for me. I still have it. A blue striped double-breasted beauty—nipped in at the waist, it has four pockets. My trousers bulged out around my knee and tapered in at my ankles. I even had a felt fedora and a pair of patent leather black brogues. I looked as sharp as a tack in it. But, as they would say now, I was all dressed up with nowhere to go. I'd put the whole shebang on in my bedroom and imagine myself up at the Locarno or the Albert Ballroom waiting on my chance to ask a girl for a dance. Back then, my mother and father would visit my aunt on Sundays, and leave me and my sister at home. One Sunday, with the sun splitting the sky, I couldn't resist putting on my gear and heading for the park. Sunday afternoons back then were big for promenading. Young ladies in their best get-up circling the boat pond, while young men would hang around hoping to catch the eye of a passing maiden.'

The bus is heading through the Gorbals. We'll hit town soon.

'I wasn't the only youngster there in a suit,' he continued, eyes wandering to the bus roof as he travelled back in time. 'There were always a few. Rebels like me. And there were always girls to be seen. I felt like a million quid. And along came Lidia Todd; Walters as she was then. She was wearing a flowery afternoon dress. They had dresses for every time of day back then. It was a bit on the small side for her. Her mum and dad were like us all, little spare money, so Lidia, like many, was wearing the dress to death and she was one summer past a good fit. One of the lads that I was standing near got mouthy and shouted out to Lidia that he knew a good tailor that could let her dress out. He didn't quite say it like that but you get the idea. Well, and I don't know why, I jumped to Lidia's defence and told everyone within earshot that the lad was an idiot and that Lidia looked lovely. That was a mistake. The lads rounded on me, and I got a right verbal doing. I backed away and almost knocked Lidia down. I apologised and she stared at me before saying, *'Drew McCreadie. Just because you've bought some moth-eaten suit doesn't mean you get to talk about me!'* That's what she said. *'Drew McCreadie just because you've bought some moth-eaten suit doesn't mean you get to talk about me.'*

He stops talking. The phrase is a trigger to a bad place for him. I can almost feel the sadness descend.

'Anyway,' he continues. 'She walks off, laughing. Me standing like a lemon and the lads doubling down on the abuse.'

'How long ago was this?'

'More than sixty years ago.'

'And you've been thinking about that one incident all these years?'

He nods as the bus swings into St Enoch's Square, the terminus.

'Was it that bad?' I ask.

The bus pulls to a stop.

'Catherine,' he says as he rises. 'A lesson from me to you. It's the small nasty stuff that stays with you, sticks in your head. It hangs around waiting to pop up now and again. A sniper waiting on their next shot. To pull that trigger. To chip away at you, bullet by bullet.'

'And,' I say, before he has to exit the bus, 'did today help? After all this time, did it make you feel better?'

He shakes his head, a sigh falling from his lips, 'No. Not at all. In fact, I'm already thinking about what I really should have said to her.'

With that he gets off, me behind him, and I watch as he vanishes into the crowd. I look up at the clock that sits on the subway building next to the terminus. I have ten minutes to get to Central Station. I set off along Argyle Street before swinging up Union Street, dodging the shoppers and workers, thinking on what Drew said.

The small nasty stuff.

Is that what I'm about to get involved in? The small nasty stuff?

9
THE DIZZY SHELL

I REACH THE entrance to the station and skip up the stairs into the glass-roofed cathedral that covers the concourse. The place is awash with people, and I need to push through to get to the shell.

The Dizzy Shell

I just hope *I'm* not about to be dizzied. I feel faint from the lack of food, and I'm glad I met Drew on the bus. His story distracted me from thinking about my stomach for a wee while. I rub the top of the bronze-coloured shell, realising that I have no idea who I'm meeting. A sea of humanity washes past me, most glancing up at the boards that range along the first floor of one wall, announcing the departing trains.

A little further along from me is a newsagent. I catch a man in a dark suit looking at me. I think it's the man from the bus. The one that didn't turn around when Drew shouted out. He has a distinctive beard. I caught sight of his face as I'd got off. He looks away, dropping a newspaper back on the rack, and is swallowed by the crowds.

The clock next to the departure boards tells me it's ten o'clock. A boy, trailing his father, hand in hand, skips by, a roll and something gorgeous being forced into his mouth. The smell of cooked sausage almost floors me. How hard would it be to steal the roll from him and run? For a fleeting moment, I consider leaving the shell and following the boy. Another lad zips by. He has a mouthful of jam sandwich. You would think that people would have the common decency to find somewhere less public to consume their food. Don't they realise there are hungry people nearby? It's no different to lighting a cigarette next to a smoker who has quit. Inconsiderate. Selfish. Cruel. There should be a law against it that carries an instant penalty.

Guilty. Now hand over the sarnie to Catherine Day. That or a week in jail.

Catherine's Law.

Or maybe that should be a month in jail and treat Catherine to a full slap up at Rogano's with all the trimmings. Or maybe a sausage supper, washed down with a bottle of Tizer. What about a full Scottish breakfast, a mug of tea and enough toast to build a raft?

'Isobel says be on the next train to Mount Florida.'

I only catch a fleeting glimpse of the man that says this to me. A blur that's wearing a docker's jacket. I jump up on the shell's plinth and try to spot him but he's lost to the masses already. I look up at the board. The next Circle train that passes through Mount Florida is in five minutes. I've not got enough cash for a ticket. Had Isobel told me that I was going to Mount Florida I could have walked from my house, it's that close. Famous for housing Hampden Park, it's a tenement heavy area, only a few miles from my home. On football match days, it's a place to be avoided. Hampden hosts international games and cup semis and finals. It holds all sorts of records for attendance. I think of Drew McCreadie. If he had taken a wander down to Hampden Park back in 1937 he'd have been one of near on a hundred and fifty thousand souls going to the Scotland v England game. A world record. I only know this fact because Maggie Hamilton's cousin's boy, who fancies me, thought I'd drop my knickers, being so in awe of his knowledge of all things football.

I aim for the appropriate platform. With fifteen to choose from, and trains leaving every few minutes, I double check the platform number and the time. With no ticket, getting on board will require sleight of hand. The guards at the entrance to the platform would be easy meat during rush hour. You could flash more or less anything at them, pretending it was a ticket, and get by. At this time of day, it could be trickier.

With three minutes to go before departure, I reach the platform. I'm in luck. There's only one guard on and he's talking to a woman with a large suitcase at her feet. I nip behind his back and make it onto the platform with a sigh of relief. A bright orange, six-carriage train awaits. On the Cathcart circle line, a loop that takes in ten stations in Glasgow's south side before returning to Central Station, Mount Florida is the fourth stop. A ten-minute trip, max. I jump on the front carriage, hoping the on-board guard starts checking tickets from the other end of the train. I choose a chair next to the doors. If the guard reaches me before Mount Florida I'm planning to jump off at one of the in between stations and wait for the next train.

With a blast of his whistle the guard on the platform sends us on our way.

'Tickets.'

I jump at the sound. Damn! The on-board guard was sitting on one of the front seats all the time. How in the hell did I miss her? She's looking down on a young couple two seats from me. There is one other person between me and them. I get up and walk down the train. Thankfully the carriages are connected in such a way that I can pass through all six. As I reach the first connecting door, I realise that there are nowhere near enough people on the train to make four stations without the guard reaching me. Even if I sit right at the rear of the train. I stop and turn back.

The guard is half-way down the first carriage and I walk up to her.

'Excuse me!' I say, once she finishes looking at the tickets of a young man.

'Yes?'

'Is this the Barrhead train?'

'No, this is the Cathcart Circle.'

'Really?'

'Yes.'

'I'm on the wrong train!'

'If you want to get to Barrhead, you are that, hen.'

'What station can I get off at to change for the right train?'

'You can't. You'd need to go back to Central.'

'How far is that?'

'Right around the circle.'

'How long will that take?'

'About twenty-five minutes.'

I let a lump of breath out that makes it sound like she's just imparted the worst news in the world to me.

'But I'm supposed to meet a friend in twenty minutes!'

'Sorry, but all you can do is sit and ride round. Can I have your ticket.'

'I don't have it. Lidia has it,' I lie. 'We were both running for the train and I lost her. I asked someone and they told me that this was the Barrhead train.'

'Then you'll need to pay for a new ticket.'

'I can't! I don't have my purse. Lidia has it in her bag.'

'No ticket and no money?'

I wonder how many times she's heard my story. It's hardly the most original fare-dodging excuse.

'There's a fine for travelling without a ticket,' she points out, fingering her ticket machine.

'I do have one,' I say. 'Just not with me, and just not for this train.'

'And you say you're going to Barrhead?'

'Yes.'

'Well, I tell you what. You walk with me while I check all the tickets. When I'm done, we can both sit at the back and have a wee chat. I'll keep you company back to the Central Station.'

Crafty cow.

'I'd rather sit on my own.'

'I'm sure you would, but it's either walk with me or I can always call the police.'

'What for?'

'Because I wasn't brought up the Clyde on a banana boat yesterday, Miss *My Ticket is With My Friend'!*

Don't you just hate smart arses.

The train pulls in at the first stop, Pollokshields East. I contemplate making a run for it but decide to wait. I need that fifty quid. I need to eat. And to do that I need to get to Mount Florida. I walk behind the guard as she checks more tickets. As we enter the second carriage I stop. The man with the dark suit and the sculpted beard is sitting facing us. As soon as he sees me he pulls the newspaper from his lap and opens it, covering his face.

'Tickets,' says the guard and the bearded man digs out his ticket and shows it.

'Hi,' I say to him, as the guard moves on.

The man ignores me, burying himself deep in his paper.

'I said, hi.'

More paper reading.

'Are you coming?' the guard asks as the gap between us opens up.

'Just want to say hello to my friend here.'

'Will he pay for your ticket?'

'I told you Lidia has my ticket.'

'Aye, well that's not legal currency on this train.'

'Excuse me!' I say to the man. 'Are you following me?'

He couldn't get any closer to the newsprint without poking his head through the paper.

'You see, I saw you on the bus earlier,' I say. 'And at the station, and now here. And every time, you've been looking at me. Do you fancy me or something?'

'Come on!' says the guard.

'Look if this man here pays for a ticket will you get off my back?'

'Darling,' the guard replies. 'If he will pay for a ticket, I'll also wipe the seat clean for you to plank your pretty backside on it.'

'Have you got fifty pence?' I ask the man. 'I'll give you it back.'

'Can you leave me alone?' he says.

His voice is deep, accent strange. He's not from these parts. Foreign for sure. Exactly from where, I couldn't guess.

'Well, here's a coincidence,' I say. 'If I get off this train before we get back to town the guard here is going to call the police. Now that's not good news for you, because if you don't give me fifty pence, I'm going to tell them that you've been following me.'

He looks up at me. He has an unruly swathe of hair that, combined with the beard and dark glasses, hides most of his features—all save a very prominent forehead. He reaches into his pocket and pulls out some coins. I lift one from his palm and give the guard fifty pence as the train pulls into the next station. The man gets up.

'Where are you going?' I ask.

He pushes me out of the way and leaves the train. I consider following. I've no idea what he is up to. It could all have been coincidence. At least it could have been, until he paid my ticket on the threat of the police. That changed things.

'Here!' says the guard handing me the ticket.

'My change?'

She drops some coins in my hand and I can almost smell the bridie they are going to buy. I sit down.

'Be careful. I've always told you to avoid strangers, haven't I?'

Mum's words on the phone the morning after she left.

'There are people out there that will want to find you.'

Was she talking about the man with the beard?

I chew on his presence. Is he following me? If so, why?

The train shunts on, and two stops later I jump off. The guard, now at the far end of the train waves at me from the platform before she signals for the train to leave, and leaps back on. I watch the train depart. Standing on the single middle platform, I'm alone. To my right there is the ticket office. To my left a set of stairs that leads up to a walkway across both tracks. Beyond the ticket office is another exit. I'm still thinking on the bearded man when a young boy runs up to me.

'Are you Catherine?'

He's ten, maybe younger, and is dressed in Glasgow dirty. Dirty trainers, dirty sweat top, dirty jeans and a dirty face.

'Who's asking?'

'Man back there told me y've to walk to Queen's Park an' staun' at the Pitch'n'Putt.'

'What man?'

'A man.'

'Where is this man?'

'Nane of your business! You've just to dae whit y'r telt.'

'Says who?'

'The man. Now am aff. I didnae sign up for blethrin' to some bird. A quid's no enough for that.'

He swans off and I'm starting to think that I've have been caught up in some bizarre treasure hunt. Queen's Park lies about ten minutes away. The Pitch'n'Putt was a place Mum took me to for the odd treat a good few years back. We missed the golf balls with our clubs more than we hit them, but it was a great laugh. I walk the length of the platform, past the ticket office, to the far exit.

'Don't turn around!'

The voice comes from behind. My knee-jerk reaction is to turn, and I start to whirl.

'I said don't turn!'

I stop. Whoever is talking will be hidden from anyone on the station platform by the steel fence next to us. I hear a couple of footsteps and the urge to look is almost uncontrollable.

'Package is behind you. Count to twenty before you turn!'

The footsteps retreat. I wait. When I turn there is no one there. Lying at my feet is a parcel about the size of a shoe box. It's wrapped in white paper and sealed with an industrial application of Sellotape. I look around but there is no one else to be seen. I kick at the parcel, moving it an inch. Alarm bells are ringing. Well not ringing, more clanging, if clanging describes the noise that deafened Quasimodo.

Walk away girl. Just walk away!

And then what? Somebody will lift that box and I'm not dumb enough to think that there's sweeties in it. Isobel and her brother won't be too happy if a stranger picks up that box. Or what if some kid opens it? The thought scares me. I check there is no one around once more and lift the box, tucking it under my arm.

And now, ladies and gentlemen, here come Glasgow's finest, springing their trap and capturing a notorious mule.

Isn't that what they call people like me? Mules? All of this now seems the worst idea since, well, since ever. I've done some dumb things in my life but nothing like this. I walk in the opposite direction to whoever delivered the parcel, clutching the box, certain I'm about to be jumped by police or an opportunist thief who just saw what went down.

Do I still go to the park? That's what the boy told me to do. More likely it was just a way to check if I was being followed. This whole trail thing has to be that.

There's an envelope attached to the parcel. I decided that the park is still a good place to head for and, a few minutes later, I'm sitting on a bench, partly hidden from passers-by under a low-branched tree. I sit, box on my lap, scanning the path for anyone taking an interest in me. That's a waste of time, everyone looks suspicious to me at the moment. After five minutes, I slit the envelope with my finger. A small sheet of note paper lies inside.

'Bar L. Visiting Time. Tomorrow. Cut off 9:00am. Take a passport and utility bill. You're visiting Paulo Rennie. You're his cousin. Leave the box in the visitor's locker. You get paid tomorrow.'

I read and re-read it and my initial thoughts are not that I'm being asked to smuggle the box into Scotland's largest prison. Nor are they about the risk involved. Nor are they about who Paulo Rennie is or even the dumb way the note is written. It's the simple fact that my fifty quid won't be in my hand today and, with a bus fare needed to get to Barlinnie in the morning, there will be little of the change from the bearded man's cash for food. Maybe a bridie and a Coke—that'll be it.

I sit back and, once the thought of 'no money today' passes, I consider what I'm being asked to do. For fifty quid I've agreed to ship drugs, for I'm sure it has to be drugs, into a prison. On the list of the foolish things to do in life this has to be in the top ten. Top five? Number one? The list of 'what could go wrongs' and 'what will go wrongs' unfurl in my head like cheap tablecloths. It would be better, by a country mile, to bin the box and tell my stomach to take a hike until Thursday when my Bru money is due. Even shoplifting seems easy meat compared to smuggling drugs into prison. What in the hell is the custodial sentence for a drug mule? Then again, what are the consequences for not following through? After all, Isobel knows where I live.

A thought occurs to me. Maybe it's not drugs. Maybe it's cash.

I know that the visitor's locker in the note refers to the cubbyhole where you leave anything banned inside the prisons, before you are allowed in to see a prisoner. One of Mum's friends had a brother who did some time for car theft, and I'd heard them talk about it. So, the only way I see this working is that I leave the box in the locker and when I finish visiting, I'll find the locker empty.

So, are the contents of the box a bribe to prison officers? Cash to make life easy for someone inside? As rooms that I don't inhabit this is one that I never thought I'd be making my bed in. What would Mum say? That's so easy to answer, it's ridiculous. Or is it? What *would* she say? Throw the box away? Inform the police? Open the box and see what's inside first? After all I'm short on cash. A shoe box this size could hold a fair amount of money, if it's not drugs. I lift the package up and bounce it a little on my hands. It feels solid. *Packed tight*. Easily the weight of a bag of sugar. Only it's not sugar, but the contents might be white… or they might be green. Either colour would ease my cash worries. Money would buy off the impending Warrant Officers, if they are on their way again. It would also get the house reconnected to the mains. And, if it's drugs? Well, you can turn drugs into cash? Can't you? But how would I do that? Jenny Meadows managed to source a little weed for Jimmy Roger's birthday party a year back. Her contact, someone she had been at pains to keep secret, is probably her brother, Francis. He quite likes me. Or so Jenny has said. He might know how to monetise the drugs.

I stop that train of thought. Slamming on the brakes. Come on girl. Asking your best friend's brother to sell some drugs for you. That's going to end well!

Jenny I'm thinking of taking up drug dealing—if your brother fancies earning a few spondoolicks on the side. No need for you to worry. Just a one-off thing. You see I stumbled upon this box in the park. Not sure what's in it. Cocaine, heroin? All white powder looks the same to me. But I'm sure your Francis could get a good price for it. I'll cut you in, Jenny. What do you say? Ten percent for you, ten for Francis?

And if it's cash in the box? How much would fit in there? Maybe I should have a look. The parcel is well taped up. Whoever wrapped it went to town. It wouldn't be possible to get into without it being obvious. We have a roll of Sellotape back home. I could open the box and re-wrap it once I know what's inside. If you're a prison officer in Barlinnie, are you really going to notice that the parcel is wrapped differently to the ones you've had before? Or maybe this is the first delivery. Paulo Rennie a new inmate and I'm his first mule.

'Hey, I'm doing you a favour here. It's no drugs and don't ever threaten to call the police on me again!'

That's what Isobel had said in the café. Or was she lying about it not being drugs? I mean I'd lie if I were her. Fifty quid seems a dirt-cheap wage if it's drugs. And if it is cash, well that's a different game. If I'm caught with it, I'll just claim I've been saving in a shoebox under my bed.

'Ten grand, Miss Day.'

'Sure, officer. The tips at the hair salon were to die for.'

But drugs? Dump them?

There's a bin a few yards down from me. Slit the paper, empty the contents and drop the box in after. Job done. If it's drugs, I might spill a little, but so what. A squirrel that gets high. I can live with that.

'Got ten pence?'

The voice makes me jump. And old man wearing a long dank Pac-A-Mac with shoe soles tied to the uppers by string, stands above me.

'Eh, no,' I say.

'What's in the box, lassie?'

His breath could stun a cow at twelve feet.

'Nothing,' I say, turning my head away.

'Doesn't look like nothing to me. But if you think it's nothing, can I have it?'

I realise that with the tree next to me, and the man standing in front, I'm all but invisible to the park-goers.

'Can you leave me alone?', I say.

'Why? Are you having a wee bit of a crisis here?'

'What?'

'You ken, one of those 'should I, shouldn't' I' moments.'

'What are you talking about?'

'I'm talking about doing the right thing. Not giving me the box for a start.'

'Why would I give you the box?'

'You shouldn't.'

I try and look around him to see who else is nearby.

'You picked a nice, secluded spot,' he says. 'Who knows what could happen to a wee lassie here?'

He smiles revealing a need for more dental visits than there are days in the year.

'I'll scream!' I say.

'What for?'

'If you touch me.'

A faint whiff of urine also floats around him. His eyes are bloodshot and he's shaking.

'Lassie, don't flatter yourself. I'm choosy when it comes to my ladies. What is it you're thinking there? That because I'm wrapped in old clothes and smell a bit that I'm not fussy on who I go with? What do you see when you look at me? Eh? A derelict? One of life's failures? Oh, look, there's a man who pissed his world away and now he's on the prowl. I'll have you know that I was the Regus professor of Physics at West Meade University. I know things that you don't even know can be known. I've presented papers to the educated, the good and the great. Okay, so my life went down the pan a little. I'm not the first, and sure as hell won't be the last to tread this path, but I have my standards. It might not look like it, but I do. So, calm it down to a rammy as my old mum would say. I'm only here to tell you to go home, not to open that box and just do what you were told.'

The last words mirror what the boy said to me on the station platform.

'Do you understand?' he says.

I nod.

'Good. Now you take care and, next time, don't judge a book by its cover.'

He shuffles away, leaving me feeling like I'm back at school, having just been given a dressing down by the headmaster. I watch him stumble along the path. For an instant, I catch sight of a man with a video camera, pointing it at me. He's standing at the park railings. He pockets the camera, walks away and I lose sight of him behind the tree. Meanwhile the old man staggers down the grass slope to the gate.

I figure I've been warned.

I tighten my grasp on the box, fingering the change in my pocket. First things first. Food. It's time for that bridie and Coke. I'll still have enough for the bus tomorrow to Barlinnie. Just.

I wait a few minutes before taking the same route the old man took. I can walk home from here. It's a good hour and half. I head for the butcher for the bridie. As I dodge a bus crossing the road, my bearded friend from the train appears in a café doorway, then dodges back out of sight, but too late for me to miss him.

I seem to be Miss Popular today.

10
THE BIG HOOSE

I RISE AT six-thirty the next morning to get the bus to Barlinnie prison. I know the bus number I need to get to the city centre, but I don't know the number I need to get to the prison once I hit town. I'm reckoning that it's a well-travelled path and that your average bus driver will know what bus I need to catch. After all, Barlinnie or, as the inmates call it, the Big Hoose, is the most famous prison in Scotland. Glaswegians knows it as BarL, a Victorian construct that houses a thousand odd prisoners in the east of the city. I've never been and it's scaring me so much that I'm struggling to think straight.

I've been awake most of the night. Waiting on a knock on the door, a ring from the phone or a full-blooded raid with *kitted up polis and rabid dugs*. I sat in the dark all evening, not even calling Jenny for fear the phone was tapped and I'd end up saying the wrong thing. If the man with the video camera, or whoever delivered the box, or my bearded friend, or anyone else followed me home yesterday, I hadn't seen any of them—and it wasn't for the lack of looking. My neck is sore from acting as the turning mechanism for the lighthouse that was my head. Before I leave I place the package in a 'What Every Woman Wants' poly bag and stuffed a couple of old newspapers on top. I sprinkle some of Mum's perfume on the paper in the insane belief that, should I encounter drug dogs, it'll throw them off the scent.

I wish I knew more about the whole visiting process at the prison. I've seen enough movies where cigarettes, drugs and weapons are smuggled in, but this is not a movie.

God, I so want to hand this box back to Isobel and be done with it.

I check the road outside for the tenth time by sneaking back the edge of the curtain in the living room. Still clear of whatever it is I think it should be clear of, I leave the house and take up my role as a walking lighthouse again. Head rotating like a good one.

The bus stop is busier than I'd expected. Thankfully there's no one I know in the queue. When my bus arrives, I wedge myself, plastic bag tight to my lap, in the seat nearest the exit door. Ready to make a run for it should I need to.

That almost makes me laugh. Run from what? Run to where? If this was a set up the police would have lifted me by now. Or maybe my bearded friend will pounce. Or what about the man with the video camera? Is he following me? Or what about the old tramp? Has he sussed what's in the box and wants a slice? Or has word got to 'Hair It Is'? The Chairwomen ready to alight. Lecture me on the evils of drugs. I peer out of the front window of the bus to see who is standing at the next bus stop. Trying to give myself a little time to react should the stop be full of police/baddies/weirdos/Chairwomen* (*delete as necessary).

We arrive at St Enoch Square incident-less. The driver tells me I need to catch a bus from Buchannan Bus station, a ten-minute walk north through the centre of the city. I set off at speed. I've wandered these streets for years. Often in the tow of my mum or buddied up with Jenny or as part of a gaggle of giggling schoolgirls on a Saturday afternoon—killing time and annoying the shop staff of the clothes stores and record stores that litter the area. I walk up Buchanan Street. When I was wee this was a road full of cars and vans, but it's now pedestrian only. Some of the posher shops that Glaswegians frequent lie here. I pass a bin lorry in full flow. As the men jump from the back to wrestle the industrial bins into place, I spot two policemen out on the beat and move to the far side of the street. Both look at me as they pass. I feel like the box in my bag has a neon light in it, and an air raid siren on full blast—both telling the policeman to come search me.

They don't.

When I arrive at the bus station, there's a double decker waiting. I jump on. This time, I'm only one of two passengers downstairs, the other being a fat man clad in an overall. There's so much oil on his clothes that he'll leave a slick on the chair. As the bus departs he opens a copy of the Daily Express, making straight for the sports pages. I read that Scotland's first ever football manager, a guy called Andy Beattie, has just died.

As we trundle through Glasgow's East End, I realise that I'm going to be early. There's been a bit of an Indian Summer this year so I won't freeze if I have to hang around outside, but I really could do with some food, any food. Even the sheer fear of what I'm about to do can't take my mind off eating. The oil slick man pulls a bar of chocolate from his top pocket and gets stuck in.

'Excuse me!' I say.

The man looks up.

'Please don't take this the wrong way but would there be any chance of a square of your chocolate? I'm off to see my dad in prison and things are a little tight. I've not eaten since yesterday.'

'BarL?' he asks.

'Yes.'

'What's your dad's name?'

That catches me stone cold.

'Eh, George.'

'George what?'

'Eh, George,' I hesitate, trying to think of a surname that isn't mine. 'George Express.' I say taking the name from his newspaper.

'Express?'

'Yes.'

'Your name is Express?'

'Forget it,' I say, regretting my actions. 'Just forget it!'

'I don't think I've ever heard of anyone called Express.'

The man is hefty, with a chin that probably needs shaving twice a day. His right hand's forefinger and thumb are stained with nicotine.

'Where is your dad from?' he asks.

'Just leave it.'

'Express?' He flips his paper over and points to the front page. 'As in this.' He points to the masthead.

I turn away.

'Here,' he says, holding out the chocolate. 'Have what's left, Miss Express.'

I can't help myself and reach over to take it. As I do, he grabs my wrist. What the hell is it with men? I yank away, and he lets go.

'Express?' he repeats.

I get up and slide forward a few seats. The driver sees me moving and thinks I'm wanting to get off. I wave at him to keep moving forward.

'I don't want off,' I say. 'I'm going to Barlinnie but the man back there just grabbed my arm. Can I stand here?'

The driver is in his fifties. A small compact man, hunched over the giant steering wheel.

'Do you want me to stop the bus?' he offers. 'There's a police station two stops up.'

'No, but can I stand here?'

'Sure. You're not meant to, so if my inspector comes on just make like you're getting off.'

'Thanks.'

'You're a bit early for visiting time at BarL?'

'I know. I've never been before so I don't want to be late.'

'Who's inside?'

'A friend.'

'That's a shame. I had a mate who did some time there. He doesn't talk about it much. But then again, would you?'

'Probably not.'

'He loved his cars,' the driver says.

I get the sense that chatting to passengers is a distraction he enjoys.

'Loved them too much, if you know what I mean? When he ran out of money to buy new ones, he decided that stealing them was easier and cheaper. He was a dab hand at it. Man, he nicked a lot of automotive metal in his time. Never arrived at my house in the same car twice. Got a caught a few times but escaped with fines and some community service. Except when his luck finally ran out.'

He stops talking to pull the bus over for someone wanting to get on. Once they've paid and he has the bus back on the road, he continues the story.

'He always fancied a Ferrari. A 365, if I remember correctly. Thin on the ground in Glasgow. But he got wind of some punter up in Bearsden that had one. Some rich guy with a big house. Well, my mate couldn't resist it. And would you believe it he rolls up to my gaff in a bright red Ferrari one Saturday morning, pleased as punch. I live out in Drumchapel, so you can imagine what the neighbours thought! Around my neck of the woods if you have a bicycle you're doing well. A Ferrari! It was like the circus had come to town. Within half an hour, there had to be fifty people crowded around the car. And there's my mate, stage centre, smile like a piano keyboard. The car as hot as the sun's heart and an arrest waiting to happen.'

The tale stops as he pulls in for some more passengers.

'What happened?' I ask as we move off again.

'It made the papers. That's what happened. Made the bloody papers. My mate starts to give people a ride. A quid a time. Five minutes around the block. A quid was a fair slug of cash for many, but he had no end of takers. All morning he ferried people down onto Great Western Road and back. Pound a time.'

'And', I say, drawn into the story, 'did the police turn up?'

'No. Not the polis. At least not when he was in our neighbourhood. I tell you who did turn up though. A local headbanger called Eddie Nicol turned up. That's who. A real piece of work. He knew right away that the Ferrari was hot. He jumped the queue and forced my mate to take him for a spin. Then the daft bugger pulled a knife on my mate, forced him into town and onto the M8. *'See how fast this thing can go!'* That's what he said to my mate. *'See how fast this thing can go!'* And all the while, he held the knife next to my mate's stomach.'

He pulls the bus to halt at another stop. My overall grabber gets off without a word. I have to squeeze into the corner to avoid him touching me.

As we start up again the driver keeps the story rolling, 'Well, my mate's shitting himself. But what can he do? A knife in his side, and Eddie has history for blades, if you know what I mean. *'See how fast this thing can go!'* Eddie says again. So, my mate plants his foot and they are away. Out towards Edinburgh. And man, did they go. Eddie claimed they got up to two hundred miles an hour, but that's a bullshit claim for his pub mates. Although not as bullshit as you'd think. The top speed of the Ferrari was supposed to be over a hundred and seventy, and my mate reckons they passed one fifty a few times.'

'Before the police stepped in?'

'Nope. They got all the way out to Harthill without a copper in sight. Weaving in and out of the traffic. Eddie yelling like a loon to go faster. My mate hanging on to the steering wheel for grim death. Every time my mate tried to slow down, Eddie would jab him with the knife and scream to keep up the speed.

'So, what happened?'

'They ran out of petrol.'

'Really?'

'God's truth! In the outside lane. Not far from the Livingston turnoff. Ground to a halt. My mate was so scared by then he didn't even have the nouse to move the car onto the hard shoulder. Just came to a stop in the outside lane. Well, you can imagine! A hot Ferrari, stock still in the middle of Scotland's busiest motorway. Eddie and my mate were both bang to rights and it was also bloody dangerous to sit there. Eddie decided to bale, and my mate followed. Two minutes later, a forty-foot artic ploughed into the back of the Ferrari. Carried it two hundred yards up the road. Thankfully, no one was hurt but the car was a write off and the truck driver was more than a little bit shook up.'

We stop again for more passengers.

'What a road-block that made!' he says, once we are up and running again. 'Shut the motorway down for two hours.'

'And what about Eddie and your mate?'

'Well, the polis did eventually turn up, but it took them time to get through the traffic. My mate hadn't gone far. Shock, I think. He was sitting on the embankment. Eddie ran for it, but they caught him on an industrial estate trying to steal a car.'

'And they both went to prison?'

'My mate didn't stand a chance. Six months in the slammer. Turns out the guy who owned the Ferrari was a hot shot lawyer. Had friends in court, if you know what I mean.'

'And Eddie?'

'Eddie got twelve months because the daft tosser still had the knife on him when they caught him.'

The driver flicks the indicator.

'Your stop,' he says. 'See that road over there?' He points. 'Just follow it up and the prison is six or seven streets up on your right. Just ask anyone, they'll tell you. You're well early, though. I think cut off is nine.'

'What's cut off?'

'After that time, they won't let you in. You'll have missed your slot and need to rebook.'

I get off, thanking him, thinking that that conversation is Glasgow in a nutshell. Ask a question, get a tale. People like to let their mouth run. Discuss most things. Give advice on most things. It's the Glasgow way. And all with a smile. 'Glasgow's Miles Better'. Isn't that what the slogan says?

I cross the road, eyes peeled for any of my new cohort, but if they are there, then they're doing a great job of hiding in plain sight. After yesterday, I'm sure Isobel must have someone watching me. There *are* a few people around but anyone of them could have been sent here to make sure I do what *'I'm telt'*.

I'm over an hour early. Normally, when I've never been somewhere before, I like to get there in advance. Scout the place out. Take in the lay of the land. Where's the entrance? How long will it take it get there? I'm not for that this time. Standing outside a prison with a bag full of drugs or money is just plain stupid. I'm still finding it hard not to turn tail and run. I walk past the road leading to the prison and keep going. I can hear a roar in the distance and soon stumble across the motorway slicing through the city beneath me. I look down, imagining Eddie and the bus driver's mate hammering along. I look back up. Across a bridge I can see green. I decide that some leaves and grass might soothe my soul a little.

Once over the river of flowing cars, the green turns out to border a golf course. There's a gap in the fencing surrounding it and, with a quick look around, I squeeze through. I crawl into some bushes. I'm soon hidden from the road and find a dry spot, not far from a putting green, to sit. My Mickey Mouse watch tells me that I've forty-five minutes to kill. It's quite warm. The trees and bushes around me have dulled the motorway noise to a distant hum. Almost hypnotic. I lean back on a tree trunk, the plastic bag with the box wrapped tight to my chest.

Crack!

The noise rips me from my sleep.

I'm disoriented.

Where the hell am I?

I sit up and remember what's going down.

I look at my watch.

I've been out for over half an hour. The lack of sleep last night catching up with me. I'm due at the prison in just over ten minutes.

'What are you doing here, trying to steal my ball?'

The golfer talking is wading into the bush near me. I realise that the crack was his ball hitting wood. I get up.

'What are you doing here?' he says.

I launch myself towards the fence.

'Is this yours?' the golfer shouts.

I ignore him and squeeze onto the road.

My bag. The box.

'Is this yours?'

Shit! I've left it behind. I must have let go of it when I fell asleep. I squeeze back in, shouting, 'It's mine.'

'You got drugs in here?'

I can't see him, but I can hear foliage being pushed aside.

'Give me it back,' I say as I clear some branches. I find myself on the edge of the green. Two men stand by their golf clubs, both wearing grey polo shirts and dark golf trousers. There the similarity ends. One is a tall, lanky streak of water with a nose that's modelled on Concord. The other is a tub of a man with a gut throwing shade over his bollocks. The lanky man has my bag.

'Give that back,' I say.

'What is it?'

I haven't time for this.

Cut off 9:00am.

'Please. I'm going to be late?'

'For what,' asks Tub Man.

'I'm meeting my…'

I stop. Suddenly I feel like the biggest fool on the planet. Here I am about to smuggle drugs into a prison and what have I done? Told a stranger on a bus where I was going. Told the bus driver where I'm going, and I am just about to tell the two golfers the same thing. I'm leaving a trail like a snail for anyone to follow. I change tack and race across the green.

'Hey, you can't be on the green with those shoes!' shouts Tub Man.

I feel my heels sinking into the grass as I run towards them.

'Look at the mess she's making,' yells Lanky Man.

I don't slow down. I aim straight at Lanky Man, grabbing my bag as I rush past. In surprise he lets it go. I wheel away, heading back to the bushes.

'The groundkeeper will go mental,' I hear Tub Man shout. 'Look at the green!'

'We'll get the bloody blame.' Lanky Man says. Then he screams, 'Stop, you wee cow!'

As if.

I rush headlong into the bushes, branches whipping my face and arms. I clutch the bag hard and ram myself through the gap in the fence. I start running. A horn sounds as I sprint across the road onto the motorway bridge. I keep my head down, running all the way to the road that leads to the prison, before slowing down.

I catch my breath as I walk up to the prison, feeling as conspicuous as a polar bear shitting in Fraser's department store.

The entrance to Barlinnie is a dark, foreboding place that oozes depression from the walls. I push into the reception, still catching my breath, I'm probably the guiltiest looking person in here—and in BarL that's some achievement. I'm sweating as if I've just run a marathon. I hope people put it down to the warm start to the day. At the desk I fumble out the required ID and I'm pointed to the lockers.

'Is that drugs you have in that bag?'

The prison receptionist says this without moving his lips. At least he does in my head. I'm dismissed as the next person moves forward to sign in. I stare at the wall of small boxes. With real haste, I ram the bag inside a vacant box and slam the wee door shut.

'Not mine, mister. Don't know who put it there. Wisnae me.'

I look up. I stare right into the lens of a CCTV. Is someone watching me right now? Wondering what I have just locked away. Maybe sending someone to check it out. I consider walking out now. After all, my job is done. Package delivered. But would I still get paid? Do I care anymore? Before I can run, we're called to go in.

11
STIMULATION

'CAN YOU SING?'

Paulo Rennie is a lot older than I'd expected. Although, in truth, I hadn't given much thought to him prior to this moment. I'd been so wrapped up in that bloody box, I'd pushed everything else to one side. I'm still focussed on it. A quick search of my locker and I'm going to be sitting on the same side of the table as Paulo in the near future. Well, not quite the same table. Barlinnie doesn't cater for women. Men only.

'Sorry? Can I do what?' I ask.

'Isobel wants to know if you can sing? And so do I.'

I'd guess he's in his early sixties. Head shaved to a shadow, a lard of a man, arms like Popeye and hooded eyes that never stop wandering. Mostly to my chest, We are sitting in a cavern of a room, spaced out from other visitors and prisoners. Everyone is head down, chatting. Wardens dot the perimeter.

'How long do I have to stay here?' I ask.

'Why? Am I not riveting company?'

'I just want to know.'

'Until visiting time is over. These things take a little time. Can't exactly go raiding your wee locker when everyone else is looking, can they? Anyway, you never answered my question.'

'No. I can't sing.'

'I don't believe you.'

'That's up to you. Now can I ask *you* a question?'

THE PRISON WAIT...

'About what?'

'Here.'

'BarL?'

'Yes.'

'Okay.'

'What's it like?'

'Being in prison?'

'Yes.'

'Like a holiday camp.'

'I'm being serious.'

'It's crap.'

'What kind of crap.'

He rubs at his stubble. 'What kind of question is that?'

'I know nothing about prison.'

'That's a good thing. Take it from me.'

'Is it violent?'

'Sometimes, but mostly it's a lot of waiting.'

'Waiting?'

'Waiting on the cell doors to open in the morning, waiting in line for food, waiting for exercise, waiting to get released, to go home but, on top of that, every day you are waiting for something to happen...'

'Like what?'

'Something to break the monotony.'

'And does that happen often?'

'No, but when it does there's a scale.'

'What kind of scale?'

'A scale of boredom relief.'

'Really?'

'At one end you have something like a riot, that'd be a ten and at the other end a wee dispute between two inmates, that's as common as muck—a one. That sort of scale.'

'What lies in between?'

'A right fracas amongst the boys. A wee bit of nonsense in the canteen. All sorts.'

'That all sounds violent.'

'Aye, it is. Take this. Visiting time. This can be right entertaining. It can get a wee bit tasty now and again.'

'How so?'

'Guys in here have a lot of time to think about stuff. And this place loves gossip.'

Who knew that Maggie Hamilton's hair salon and a prison had something in common?

He goes on, 'A guy gets to hear that his woman might not be keeping his side of the bed as empty as she should. That can gnaw at you. Especially in here. Whispers race around this place. What might start as some visitor saying they saw Agnes at the shops talking to Mary's husband turns into a full-blown affair by the time the gossip reaches Agnes's man's ears in here. Come visiting time, the accusations don't take long in surfacing. Ask the screws!'

'What is in the box?' I ask, flipping the subject.

'None of your fucking business.'

The change in tone is so sharp my bowels loosen a little. I sit back.

'Now,' he says. 'I don't believe you when you say you can't sing. And I'm bored. I need a little light relief. Let's go for a five on the scale. Here's what we are going to do!'

He leans back a little, scanning the visitor's room.

'What's your favourite song?' he asks.

'I don't have one.'

'Rubbish. Everyone has their favourite. I'm an American Pie man. You?'

Surreal is a word that I don't really understand, but I'm thinking that this conversation might be made for it.

'I really don't have one.'

'Well, I'll choose one for you.' He stands up. 'Mr Craig. What's in the Top 40 just now.'

One of the wardens walks over.

'Paulo?' he says. 'Sit down.'

'What's hot in the kids charts at the moment? Your Gemma must keep you up to speed.'

'The pop charts?'

'Aye.'

'Tons of stuff.'

'What's Gemma's favourite?'

'Why are you asking?'

'Just humour me, Mr Craig.'

'*Red, Red Wine* by UB40 is her go to, has been for weeks.'

'Perfect, Mr Craig. Thank you.'

Paulo sits down and the warden walks away, shaking his head.

'That's your song Catherine,' Paulo says. '*Red, Red Wine*. So, what about you give me a wee sing song?'

'Sorry?'

'A wee sing song. Let's hear those vocal chords. I think you're hiding your light under a bushel.'

'I'm not singing in here.'

He leans in again. 'Listen darling. You're going to get up and give us all a treat. And I'll tell you why. Remember yon box you brought in here. Well, a wee word in Mr Craig's ear and off you go to Glasgow Sheriff Court.'

'You wouldn't.'

'Why not?'

'Whatever is in it would be confiscated. That's why not.'

'So what? It's not for me.'

He takes up his leaning pose once more. Comfortable. In control. I wonder what he's in here for, but I'm not for asking.

'You see, Catherine,' he adds, 'As I said, it's boring in here. I need a bit of stimulation and you are it.'

The word stimulation comes out with the word letch attached to it.

'You're the *stimulation* today, Catherine. Either as an impromptu singer or as a little mule that gets caught. All the same to me.'

With his eyes roving all the time, I can't get a read on him. He can't be serious. Sing? Here? Now?

'I'll give you a wee hand to get going, then it's over to you.'

He stands up. 'Ladies and gentlemen, I'd like your attention please.'

'Paulo, sit down,' says the warden.

'Just give me a minute, Mr Craig. I'm not going to cause trouble. It's just that young Catherine here has a fair voice. She used to sing to me when she was a kid. I just want to hear her croon a few bars of something.'

'Stop the nonsense, Paulo and sit down, or visiting time is over!'

'Up you get Catherine,' he says to me. 'Mr Craig'll let you sing a bar or two. Won't you, Mr Craig?'

'Paulo, that's enough.'

'Two bars Mr Craig. Just two wee bars.'

Mr Craig shakes his head. 'Just…'

'Up you get Catherine!'

I don't move.

'Would you rather I talk to Mr Craig on another matter?'

He's not for backing down on this.

'I'll count you in and if you don't start, then me and Mr Craig will have that wee chat.'

What the hell can I do? I push the chair out and stand. The entire room looks at me.

Mr Craig moves over.

'Be quick, and nice and loud, now Catherine,' says Paulo. 'Belt it out! Ah one, ah two, ah one two three four…'

I open my mouth and the sound of escaping air hisses like a deflating tyre. I have no voice.

'Sorry, ladies and gentlemen,' says Paulo. 'A little stage fright I think.'

'Okay, Paulo,' says the warden. 'You've had your fun, now settle down.'

'Okay, Mr Craig, but can I talk to you first. In private.'

Paulo steps towards the warden.

'RED, RED WINE.'

I belt out the line and do a great job of stunning the audience.

Paulo grins, 'The girl has a voice.'

Two lines more and the warden shouts to stop it. Gratefully I drop to the chair.

'That's some set of vocal cords you have there,' says Paulo, returning to his own seat.

'Would you have really told the guard about the box if I'd not sang?' I ask, once the warden is out of ear shot.

'Aye. And to prove the point lift your T-shirt and let's see your tits.'

'What?'

'I can call Mr Craig for that chat if you prefer. Just a wee glimpse. A wee bit of *stimulation*.'

'Screw you.'

I stand up.

'Where are you going?'

'Away from here.'

'I'll tell about the box.'

'Do what you want. In fact,' I say. 'I'll tell.'

The warden looks at me.

'Mr Craig!' I say.

'What?'

'Can you come here? I need to talk to you.'

'Don't you fucking say anything,' Paulo spits under his breath.

The warden traipses over again.

'Are you two going to monopolise my day? What is it?'

'I want to leave', I say.

'Who's stopping you?'

'I'd like you to know something.'

'Mr Craig, how's the wife?' interjects Paulo, trying to head me off.

'Fine Paulo.' He looks at me, 'Now what is it you want to say?'

'This man here…' I begin.

'Fucking shut up,' says Paulo, rising to his feet.

Mr Craig swings around. 'What's going on?'

'The girl wants to leave,' Paulo replies.

I tap Mr Craig lightly on the cuff, 'Do you know that Paulo here also wants to sing?'

'Just stop this bloody nonsense, the pair of you!' he says.

'Honest Joe, he does,' I say.

'Leave it!' Paulo hisses at me, his nose flaring so hard I can see the forest of hairs up each nostril.

'You see he wants to sing really badly. When I was wee he would sing back to me. He used to sing *Little Boxes*. Do you know it Mr Craig? All about *wee boxes*, it is.'

'Right,' says Mr Craig. 'This visit is over.'

I do a little jig on the spot, 'I used to dance to it. Do you remember how it goes, Paulo?'

'We'll sit down, Mr Craig.' Paulo says.

'No, we won't, Paulo,' I reply 'Lost your singing voice? Well, maybe I'll sing to Mr Craig about Little Boxes unless, of course, you want to sing first. Then I might not feel like singing about *Little Boxes* so much.'

Mr Craig knows something is going down. Working in here must require a sixth sense. He just can't figure what it is in this case.

'Okay this is done,' he says. 'John,' he shouts to another warden at the far side of the room. 'Escort Paulo out! And you,' he says to me, 'come with me!'

'Sure,' I say. 'But do you mind if I sing a few lines as we walk?'

I turn my back on Paulo as the other warden approaches.

'Now,' I say to Mr Craig. 'About these little boxes. You see…'

'TWINKLE, TWINKLE, LITTLE STAR.'

Mr Craig spins. Paulo is giving it laldy.

'Will you shut up?' Mr Craig shouts.

The other warden steers Paulo away.

I walk away, a smile on my face, but it doesn't last long.

I'm escorted to the reception area where I open my locker. The plastic bag with the box is gone. In its place is an envelope. I whip the letter out, pocketing it quickly. I exit, looking neither left or right. I walk, head down, until I reach the main road. I spot a bus heading to the city and jump on, not caring exactly where it's going. I use the last of my money for the fare. Huddling into the corner of a seat I stare out of the window as the adrenalin in my system begins to sour.

This is not my world.

This is not my universe.

This is so wrong that the word 'right' has been banished from my dictionary.

I take a deep, deep breath, uncurl and check out the other passengers. I recognise no one, although if Isobel had me tailed then anyone on the bus could be following me. Except they would have had to have been psychic. I was the only one that got on at my stop.

Paranoia is an easy friend to make.

I can feel the envelope in my jeans pocket. Hot, wanting out, *needing* out. But I can't do that here. Not now.

The bus rumbles into the city centre. I jump off a couple of stops before the terminus at the top of High Street. I have no plan of action in my head, other than I have to walk home. A good two and a half hour march - but that won't be near enough time to clear my head. I touch the envelope, looking around me for a place to open it. A lane next to me looks inviting. As it would to a mugger. I walk on. I pass down through the town, out by the High Court.

Prophetic?

I know that Paulo was on a power trip back in the prison by making me sing. He couldn't possibly have risked whatever was in the box being found, but neither could I run the risk he was serious about dropping me in it. Until he asked me to show him my breasts, that was. Prick. For a moment, I really had thought about telling the warden all about the box. For a moment. Until common sense kicked in. Had I done so, I'd have landed myself in it and Paulo would have simply declared his ignorance. But I was so angry at him. So angry at the way I was being treated. So angry that Paulo saw it in my eyes and that's why he belted out Twinkle, Twinkle. He couldn't take the risk on me blabbing. Small revenge for both my humiliation and his misogyny.

I cross the River Clyde, looking down on the dank dark waters. A reflection of my soul at the moment. I wander through the remnants of the Gorbals and Hutchesontown. Basil Spence's Queen Elizabeth Square, the most notorious monument to atrocious design and slipshod building, staring me in the face. People are talking about it all being pulled down less than fifteen years after it was built. I enter the tenement canyons of Govanhill and think about circling back to my seat in Queen's Park. I dismiss the notion as stupid. Finally, I find a close and slip inside.

I slip the envelope from my pocket and open it. Inside is a note.

'Call.'

12
THE SECRET CORNER

I ARRIVE AT the Bru office early the next morning. I haven't called Isobel as instructed. I'm planning to face her one-on-one over my cash. She obviously signs on at the same time as me. To stave off my hunger, when I'd got home, I'd borrowed some milk, sugar, butter and bread from Mrs Carol next door and pigged out on pieces and sugar until I was nearly sick. She'd asked about Mum, and I told her she was at my uncle's.

I'd then spent the evening flip-flopping between calling Isobel to give her a piece of my mind or just trying to walk away from it all. It had been late on by the time I'd decided that I wanted a face-to-face with her.

When I arrive, I take up residence near the main entrance of the Bru office. A few of my fellow benefit claimants are already gathered, waiting on the doors to open. To a person they are all smoking. Each is dressed in low-end fashion. A mix of Chelsea Girl and Goldbergs. Fitted jeans and Baracuta jackets. Knocked-off upmarket labels from the Barras, seventies clothing being worn to death. Unemployment is on its way up and there's a sense of desperation and despair around me. The promises of Margaret Thatcher cut no ice in the face of the closing shipyards and mines.

The office doors open, and the hoards enter, but I hold fire. I haven't seen Isobel or her brother so far. They have thirty minutes to get here. With five to go, I spot them both wandering down the street. I move back, out of sight, behind the entrance porch, stepping out as the arrive.

'Isobel?'

'Catherine.'

'Where's my money?'

She screws her face up. 'Not here.'

'I want my money. You said today.'

'You'll get it, but if we don't get in the queue, we'll be late.'

'Just give me my money!'

'For f's sake, I told you. You'll get it.'

'I want it now.'

'That's not how it works.'

'I did what you said. You told me I that I would get paid fifty quid on the day.'

'I'm getting in the bloody queue.'

Billy and her squeeze by me. I have no choice but to follow. Once we are at the end of the line, I lean in and whisper to her, 'Money?'

'Later.'

'Now!'

'I haven't got it here. Just hawd y'r wheesht for twenty minutes.'

The line crawls forward and, as we reach the front, I step in front of the two of them.

'What are you doing?' says Billy.

'I'm signing on first, then I'll wait outside. If you go first, you could bugger off and leave me.'

Once I'm finished, I give them both a stare as I pass by. I take up station at the front door.

Once they have finished, they both exit without a word.

'Okay, where is my money?'

They blast past me. I need to move quickly to catch up.

I walk next to Isobel. She is moving fast.

'Money,' I say as we turn at the end of the street.

'What's your beef?' she replies. 'You've got your Bru.'

'And you owe me fifty.'

'When you pick up the next delivery.'

'What?'

'That's the way the system works. Your next package will have the fifty quid in the envelope.'

'You said I'd get it yesterday.'

'I lied. It's the way it works, makes sure that our couriers come back.'

'I want my money and I want out.'

'You can get out anytime you want, but if you walk you don't get your money.'

I grab her by the shoulder. 'I smuggled God knows what into prison for a lousy fifty quid, fifty quid that you're not going to give me. Is that it?'

'Fifty quid that you *will* get when you pick up the next package.'

'And the man in prison is a pig.'

She doesn't reply.

'He told me to show him my breasts.'

Zip.

'Are you listening?'

'No! Now if you want your cash, there's a pick-up in half-an-hour in George Square.'

'I'm not...'

Billy steps in and growls, 'Go get the next sodding package. Leave my sister alone!'

He's right in my face. I stop walking, but Isobel keeps going.

'Leave!' Billy says to me as he turns away.

124

I stand still, letting him go. It's not worth risking my safety. Billy doesn't look beyond hitting me.

I watch them walk away.

This isn't right, but I'm just plain dumb for getting involved in the first place. Down to experience. That's what I should do—put it all down to experience and leave.

But I can't.

I won't.

I let the two of them get a good lead on me before I cross the road and start to follow them.

Now we can witness Private Investigator Catherine Day in action. When I was wee, I always fancied myself a bit of a Nancy Drew. It was great escapism. And now and again I can summon my alter ego, PI Catherine. When I'd stood at the Bru office, I'd been holding my lightweight jacket in my hand. It was too hot inside to wear it. I pull it back on, pull out an elastic band from my pocket, and tie my hair back. Not the best of disguises, but better than nothing. I know this area a little, but not well. I've no idea what I'm planning to do.

What can I do?

Isobel and Billy vanish around a bend. I break into a jog to catch up a little. PI Catherine on the prowl.

As I reach the bend I slow down, catching sight of them a hundred yards ahead. They are lost in conversation.

'That's the way the system works. Your next package will have the fifty quid in the envelope.'

They expected me to go. My fifty quid, the magnet. In their world, that's how it works. Mules want the cash, so they always do the next run. So, what will happen to the package when I don't turn up? Do I care? A bit. I could do with the fifty quid. If Mum doesn't come back soon, binning the bills the way I am will have consequences.

Warrant Officers.

I pass the old Odeon cinema, not that long ago closed for good. It was a treat to go there as a kid. I saw Jungle Book and cried when Mowgli was sent back to the village. I keep to the opposite side of the road from Isobel and Billy. My eyes scan the road ahead. I'm looking for hiding spots if either should turn and look back.

The couple didn't know, couldn't know, they were being followed. PI Catherine was way too smart for that to happen. This was just routine. Another day, another dollar. A little more leather off the soles. A few more cigarettes smoked in shop doorways. A day-old paper in the pocket for covering her face when required. A FAR job, Follow and Report. Only Catherine knew that this was something more. Her gut could be trusted. It was her secret weapon. Her way of seeing into the future. Seeing things that others couldn't. She thought of it as her Future Specs. Just hold the course. That was what her Future Specs said. Hold the course and be ready! Always be ready. Never get caught napping. Act laid back, be alert. Natural cover is your pal. Look like you have all the right in the world to be there. Give the targets no reason to think otherwise. Out shopping. Making for the bank. A quiet stroll. And, of course, be flexible. Improvisation was Catherine's other super-power. Improv Woman. Whatever life throws at her, she's the chameleon that can react. The award-winning actress. Can't go left, go right! Can't run, fly! Can't be caught, escape! Gut and improv. Future Specs and Improv Woman— the dynamic duo.

Isobel stops at a shop window. I walk into the close next to me, as if this is my home. Nancy Drew used shop windows all the time to check if she was being followed. Is that what Isobel is doing?

'Got a fag?'

The voice from the gloom belongs to a young lad, dolled up in faux-leather jacket, white T-shirt and drainpipes. A George Michael fan of some sort?

'Sorry,' I reply. 'I don't smoke.'

'Got a drink on you, and don't tell me you don't drink.'

His slicked back hair must require a lot of product.

'I drink, but I don't carry it around with me.'

'There's an offie around the corner.'

'I'm sure there is.'

'Could you get me twenty Embassy Tipped and a quarter bottle of Whyte & Mackay?'

'Get it yourself!'

'I have the readies.'

'I can't.'

'You mean you won't'

He's dressed to look twenty but can't be more than fourteen.

'Smoking and drinking are bad for you,' I say. 'I need to go.'

I turn and look out the close. I just catch Isobel and Billy before they disappear around a corner.

'I can get you a pair of jeans that were worn by one of Status Quo's roadies on their last tour,' the boy says to me as I leave.

I exit. The last words I hear from him are, 'Genuine star material and real cheap.'

Maybe it's me. Catherine the nutter attractor.

I'm deep in the shopping area that borders Victoria Road, a sea of retail that runs all the way up to Queen's Park. I dodge a bus, heading for the corner that Isobel and Billy rounded.

Sometimes tracking your prey is all about working out where they are going. Know that, and things become easier. Sweeter. Their favourite bar. Their lover's home. Their secret corner. Everyone has a secret corner. It's a golden rule of private investigation. 'Where do you go to my lovely'?' as Peter sang. Find that out and you can light up, grab a cup of java and relax. Targets are homing pigeons, once you know their secret corner. Of course, you can always find them at home or at work but that, my friend, is dangerous. Strangers stand out in that territory. The prey feels safer in its secret corner—less aware. Easier to watch. It's not just the bad, the law breakers, the devious that have secret corners. The sweet old lady chewing her humbugs, the gentle giant tending his garden, the charity worker caring for others—all have a secret corner. It's a PI's dream.

Find the secret corner.

Isobel and Billy weave at speed through streets heavy on Asian shops and businesses. They have a destination in mind.

Secret Corner?

I duck into another close as they cross the road and enter a lane, Billy checking the road both ways before he enters.

A lane, not a street. Homes lie on streets, lanes less so.

Their secret corner?

I take a chance, breaking into a run, slamming to a halt just before the lane entrance. I pull myself up to my full height, stick out my chest and stroll past the entrance with confidence; the briefest of glances to check out what the couple are doing. I spot them about fifty yards down, picking their way through fallen masonry and rubbish. At a guess I'd say it's too far to circle the block and catch them at the other end. I double back, check once more. They are gone.

Okay detective this is the put up or shut up moment. Go in or go home.

My anger overrides my fear as I walk into the gloom of the lane. Careful not to trip and equally careful not to make any noise, as I work my way along. Either side of me red brick walls rise. Beyond them will be the tenements' back greens. Although the term green is a bit of a misnomer in my experience. Back browns would be a more accurate description of the spaces. I hear voices and slow down, creeping forward to a gate. I peer round.

Billy and Isobel are at the door of a brick shed, less than twenty yards away. The structure sits on its own in the middle of the back green. The door, a solid slab of sheet metal is open and there are a half dozen bodies standing around it. They are all focussed on Isobel, who is talking. Billy is pulling boxes from the shed.

The distribution point. *Their secret corner.* I turn and walk away, quickly, silently. I have only a moment to act. I pick up speed at the end of the lane, as I exit onto the road. I need a policeman. More than I've ever done in my life, I need a policeman. Isobel and Billy are bang to rights. There's no point waiting until they are gone to show the police what I'd seen. What would connect it to Isobel and Billy? I can't believe that Isobel would be daft enough to return, regardless as to what is in the shed, if she thought it compromised.

I need them caught right now!

I scan the road, coming up blank. How long do I have? Billy had just handed over a box to the first of the gang as I'd left. No-one will want to hang around for longer than they need to.

My heart leaps as a panda car appears. This is no time for subtlety. By the time I wave them down and explain what I've seen, the shed could be clear.

What would Nancy do?

Get them to follow you.

I rush onto the road. The police car slews to a halt, losing some rubber from its tyres in the process. I've caught the driver so much by surprise that he didn't even have time to hit the horn. I slam my hands down on the bonnet, feeling it dent. I repeat the action, screaming; 'Pigs, pigs.' I take off up the lane as the police car doors open. A quick glance back confirms I have two six foot plus coppers on my tail. I dodge the debris on the lane, aware that if I fall, I'm in for a night in the cells. As I run, I play the setting around the shed in my head. Billy at the shed door, Isobel back to me, the other six in a semi-circle around the door. I reach the gate and glance back down the lane. The police are barely ten yards behind. I dive through the gate, swinging hard left, putting the shed between me, Billy, Isobel and the others. I don't think anyone sees me.

I throw myself against the wall.

'What the fuck,' says a voice from the other side of the shed. It could be a policeman.

All hell breaks loose on the far side of the small building. Bodies appear to my left and right, none are Billy or Isobel. No one looks at me. They are all head down. Escape on their mind, and nothing else.

'Stop right there!' Definitely a policeman.

'Don't move!' policeman number one.

I count two bodies vanishing into closes on my side of the shed, and one through the gate I came in.

'Billy Caldwell' policeman number two. 'And Isobel Caldwell.'

There's a cry and I hear what sounds like a tussle.

'Billy stay right there! We know who you are,' policeman number one.

I can't stay here. I'm too exposed. Using the shed as a screen, I walk at right angles to its wall, heading for the far side of the green. There's another gate and, without looking back, I step through it, turning to my right, away from the shed. I break into a run, expecting a cry to go up at any second, but there's none. I make it to the end of the lane and slip onto the street, circling around the block to where the police car is parked across from the lane's entrance. Choosing a close that has a view of the lane and the car, I slip inside.

I watch. I wait.

A few minutes pass. No one emerges from the lane. I'm just beginning to wonder what is going down when a second police car arrives. Officers jump out and vanish up the alley. They are trailed a few seconds later by an unmarked car, from which two suited and booted men leap. Probably plain clothes police. When a third panda car arrives, I'm certain that whatever is in that shed has to be something of a coup.

Five minutes later and a police van appears.

It takes a further fifteen minutes before Billy, Isobel and two others from the semi-circle gang are led out of the lane and placed in the back of the van. Scared of being spotted, I duck back into the close, but not before I catch sight of Isobel's face. She has the look of cornered viper.

My Isobel and Billy problem may just have vanished. The only downside to this is that I won't be getting my fifty quid.

13
PLAY IT AGAIN, COMRADE

Friday, 25th August, 1989.

'THE WHAT?' says Davie.

'The Nieśwież-Szczecin Club.'

He pronounces it as the NiceWise Sisisin Club

'Easy for you to say,' says Daisy.

'And this club are offering us what?' I ask.

'One thousand pounds to play a gig tonight.'

'A grand,' whispers Daisy.

'A grand,' I repeat.

Davie holds up a folded envelope.

'Tonight?' asks Daisy

Davie nods.

'And given this is not April the 1st,' I say, 'And the most we've ever been paid to play is a hundred quid, why would someone offer us a grand?'

'An A&R man saw us and recommended us?' suggests Davie.

'For f…,' says Daisy. 'You and bloody A&R men. You see them the same way that my wee brother sees aliens. Do you know the wee idiot now claims that a friend of his might be an alien? Stephen Cassidy, Mitch's younger brother. My wee brother has known Stephen since he was five and now thinks he's an alien. And you, Davie McTierney are like him. Only you see A&R men in every bloody shadow.'

'And why,' I add, piling onto the Davie/A&R obsession, 'would a record label executive, whose job it is to spot talent and inform his employer before anyone else, decide, instead, to get us a gig at the… whatever that club is?'

'It's how they work, mysterious or what?' Davie replies.

'For f…' repeats Daisy.

Our band, Spread It Thin, have been on the go for two years. Me on vocals. Davie McTierney on keyboards and drum machine. Daisy Ali, also on keyboards and occasionally guitar. Our musical influences are early 80s electronic and, in the two years since we formed, there has only been one confirmed sighting of a real A&R man. A year back, at a small festival held in the Barrowlands. When we came on, fourth act in, four fifteen in the afternoon, the said A&R man wandered through the crowd of ten people to the bar after our second song and we never saw him again. Davie has been spotting other A&R men so often since then that Daisy has taken to calling him Davie Ar.

'Maybe they saw us at the gig the other night and liked us,' he says. 'Maybe my new look is attracting attention.'

Daisy and I sigh. Davie who, up until a week ago, had sported shoulder length hair tied in a ponytail, rubs at the frizz that now covers his scalp. He says the change of hairstyle is to reflect his new stripped-back style of song writing. As if. He's going bald and is just getting ahead of the wave, or lack of wave. The fact that his skeletal frame has recently sprouted a paunch has led him to wearing kaftans. His new look, he calls it. It also serves to make him look a lot older than his thirty-five years.

'Look,' I say, as I sip at my mug of tea, the café around us buzzing with lunchtime traffic. 'Forget A&R men and tell me who gave you the invite, Davie.'

'Hand delivered to my mum's flat early this morning,' he says.

Davie is living with his mother on a first floor flat in Shawlands.

'Hand delivered,' says Daisy. 'You mean the postie brought it.'

'No. Some guy in a black car rolled up at seven thirty this morning and handed it in. Mum said he spoke kind of foreign. I didn't see him. I was still in my pit.'

The fact that Davie is still living with his mother talks a lot to his lack of success in the music world.

'Let me see the letter,' I say.

Davie hands it over. Neatly typed it has a bright red letterhead that announces

'Nieśwież-Szczecin Klub'. 40 Old Castle Road, Cathcart.'

'Klub?'

'Must be foreign,' says Davie.

'You don't say, Sherlock?'

He scowls at me.

I know Old Castle Road, but don't remember any sort of club. It's a residential area.

'I don't get it,' Daisy says. 'Who books a band this late in the day? And what kind of club is it? We're not exactly Derby and Joan material, if the members are old crinklies. I think this is a wind up.'

'It's easily checked out,' I say. 'The address isn't that far away. I'm with Daisy. It sounds dodgy. I know the area and don't remember any club, but if there's the slightest chance that we can make a grand, then I'm all for checking it out.'

'When will we, will we, be famous,' sings Daisy, ripping off Bros.

'It never happens to me,' I sing back, ripping off Fergal and Vince.

It's Daisy and my in-joke. We are as far from success as it's possible to get, yet Davie is convinced we can make it big. I don't think we ever will, but we all live in hope. Davie more than Daisy and I. Daisy is a year younger than me. We met at a talent show. Me singing 60s hits and her playing the piano. Neither of us made the final, but we struck up a relationship that is better than anything I've had since Jenny Meadows and I were a duo. Daisy's mum and dad run a cash and carry in Paisley. She's second generation Indian, her family forced out of Kenya when it declared independence from the UK. Daisy's father had founded and run a successful manufacturing business in Kenya that was subsequently stolen from him. When he arrived in Glasgow he'd sold pots and pans door to door. He now owns one of the most successful cash and carries on the west coast.

The fact that Daisy is in a pop band doesn't sit well with her parents.

'I have one brother who is a doctor, another brother who is all but running the cash and carry, one sister that is an accountant and another that is studying forensics at university. You'd think that my parents would be satisfied with that and leave me alone.'

I like Mr and Mrs Ali, but they see me as the Devil that's stopping their daughter completing their full house of professional siblings. I'm officially 'that girl'. Daisy tells me that there are only a few worse insults in her family.

'What does the letter actually say?' asks Daisy.

'It simply asks if we would play tonight and states a fee.'

I hand it over and she reads it.

'And the person delivering didn't say anything else?' she asks Davie.

'Not that Mum said.' he replies.

Daisy turns the paper over. There's nothing on the other side.

'I'm going to check this out,' I declare. 'I'll see you back at your Mum's place in an hour or so, Davie.'

'I should go and check it out, not you,' he replies.

Davie is the de facto leader of our group but is as slow as a sloth on Mogadon when it comes to decision-making. In the late seventies he had a brief brush with fame when the New Wave band he was in, called The Ruggled, signed a deal with a small London label and produced an EP. It ran to a second pressing and a deal for an album was in the wind until the lead singer, a guy called Lee Dawn, quit to become a record producer. A highly successful record producer, as it transpired. Davie has been promising that he'll get Lee to produce our first album. So far that has led to nothing. The Ruggled disbanded years back—Spread It Thin is Davie's sixth band. In order, he was in a rock band just as seventies rock died a death followed by The Ruggled. Then, he was in a Ska band just after the early eighties Ska peak had passed. Next was a Power Pop band as New Romanticism took off, and he then flipped to a New Romantic band as that phase ran its course. Spread It Thin, with its Depeche Mode/OMD sound, is hardly cutting edge.

'Well Davie, if you are going to be the one to check the club out, go now!' I say.

'Give me a minute!' is his reply.

I shake my head and push the chair back. Daisy thinks our band should be called Give Us A Minute, as Davie uses the phrase so often. I think it should be called Catherine, Daisy and Who? as his lethargy means he doesn't turn up for stuff at all—and that includes gigs.

'See you at your flat, Davie' I say. 'I haven't got another minute to wait. At least not one of your minutes.'

As usual, this dig flies right past him and he just smiles.

I stand up and have to squeeze by a young boy wired into a Walkman. I can hear the tinny beat of *Ride on Time* by Black Box from the headphones. As I exit the café, I pull the letter from my pocket and read the short message again.

'Would Spread It Thin be available to play our club tonight? Fee £1,000.' The brevity takes me back to the note Mum left me when she bugged out.

Mum had come back briefly, the night after Isobel and Billy had been arrested. She never, *has* never, told me where she went. A few days after she returned, as if she had inherited a magic wand, all our money worries vanished.. Red typed letters stopped pouring through the letterbox. Warrant Officers were conspicuous by their absence. Food filled the cupboards and the fridge. I was even given an allowance.

Isobel and Billy got two years each at Glasgow Sheriff Court. I was tempted to pop in to see the trial, but my 'don't be stupid' head was on that day, and I avoided the place like the plague. It transpired that Isobel wasn't lying when she said it wasn't drugs I was smuggling into BarL. It was cash. The shed in Govanhill had contained over one hundred thousand pounds. All of it forged. My best guess was that the money in the locker at Barlinnie found its way into the pockets of some of the wardens in return for easing the life of selected inmates. I also heard that Paulo had served his time, was set free, duly mugged an old age pensioner and went back inside.

Isobel and Billy have to be out by now but if they suspected I had any involvement in their downfall, I've never been approached. For a while I'd feared that one of the gang from around the shed might have spotted me. Or maybe, while hanging around the close, I'd been seen. I'd waited for the knock on the door, the brick through the window, the cosh to the back of the head. I'd become a virtual recluse until I'd heard Isobel and Billy had been sent down. Now they are free from jail I'm worrying once more. In the wee small hours, my head wonders if they will ever find out what I did. Don't you hate the middle of the night?

THE MUM WAIT II…

The only other thing of note that happened in late 1983 was that Mum left again.

'Catherine, the house is yours and I've opened a bank account for you that'll see you through for a good wee while.'

Another note left on the mantlepiece. I'd called the police, but they said there was little they could do—it's still an open missing person's case, of sorts.

The first year was the worst. She didn't contact me at all. That was hell. I've talked a lot about waiting. But that was the worst wait of my life. My heart would race with every knock on the front door. Every ring of the phone. Every letter through the post box. I saw mum everywhere, The woman in the shop with Mum's hair who I rushed up to. The lady talking behind me in the bus queue with the same phraseology. I'd nearly decked her, I'd spun around so fast.

All I did was wait for Mum to appear.

Day after day after day.

I now know she's not dead. At least she wasn't dead a month ago. A year to the day after she left, I inherited a new friend who has kept me informed about Mum. Well, an old friend that is now a new friend. The man with the sculpted beard that followed me that day when I picked up the box for Barlinnie. The one that I took money from on the train. I've no idea who he is. Where he is from. What his connection to Mum is. I did see him talking to Mum the day before she left. The two of them buried in the local park, thinking they were hidden from prying eyes. I'd been following Mum. I did that a lot back then. Fearing she was going to take off again. *Correctly* fearing she was going to take off again. When she did leave, I had the guilt trip of all guilt trips wondering if my actions in trailing her around had been the catalyst to her exit. Me spotted—her thinking I've had enough. She never mentioned that I'd become a limpet mine back then— but she must have known. Must have seen me. She rarely left the house without me in tow.

PI Catherine—not as good as she thinks she is!

The man with the sculpted beard has appeared half a dozen times in my life since then. Each time he politely says hello, tells me Mum is well and leaves. Of course, I neither believe him, or leave it at that. I chase after him, every time, in one case screaming at the top of my voice. A black car always waiting. I took the registration and handed it to the police after his first appearance. They never got back to me.

I thought the man with the sculpted beard was lying to me about Mum. I wanted to believe him but all I had was his word. That was until he handed me the first letter from Mum—that would be three years ago.

'I know this is hard. It is for me, but I will come back to you. Just not yet. Please take care and forgive an old lady whose past won't leave her alone'

I have eight such letters. All a variation on the same theme. Last year the man with the sculpted beard handed me his mobile phone. Mum had been on the line.

'Hi Catherine.'

'Mum,'

I hadn't been able to say anything else. I'd burst into tears.

'I love you, darling. Please believe me, I will be home soon.'

Then she hung up.

There have been two calls since then. But still there's no sign of her. Each time, I've told the police and each time they told me that was good news. That she wasn't really a missing person—although they would keep it on the records.

But she is missing.

Six years missing.

I managed to scrape enough money for a private detective at one point.

PI Catherine couldn't cut it.

That got me nowhere.

A van horn drags me from this well-worn path. I weave towards the club's location, my head full of notes, calls and unanswered questions.

A thousand pounds.

Nobody pays that sort of money for a band like ours.

'Catherine why do you persist with that music group?'

A question that Maggie Hamilton likes to bring up when I need to leave early from 'Hair It Is' for a gig. After trawling the job market for ever and a day, I'd slunk back to Maggie after the Isobel and Billy affair, and proffered my olive branch, apologising for the Vosene incident to Wanda Craig—*soooo embarrassing*. But who knew I could cut hair, had a talent for it, enjoyed it? As Maggie's number two hairdresser, I now have some value in the salon. And Maggie's fake concern from my turn as an assistant's assistant turned out not to be quite so fake. It seems, that apart from an aptitude for cutting, Maggie quite likes me. Who knew? It's not the career I'd envisaged. Then again, I'd never envisaged any career. But it pays the bills, just, and I enjoy the banter of the chairwomen. I'm the preferred hairdresser for a few, including Lidia Todd, who still pretends to be ten years younger than she is.

I reach Old Castle Road. The River Cart flows along on one side of it for a stretch. They say there used to be fish in it. Maybe the remnants of the cod from the local chippie, by the colour of it. I check the address. The house number on the letter turns out to be an old tin shed squatting on the banks of the river. About the size of a couple of tennis pitches, I've always though it an

141

abandoned business or some storage hut. The corrugated sheeting that makes up its walls has rust dotting it like measles. The roof sags in the middle, and the main door is a slab of steel.

A thousand pounds?

If this is the club, they don't look like they could afford a thousand farthings. A small metal gate guards the path up to the door. I double check the number and open the gate. A small plaque sits to the right of the door. All but invisible to passers-by. I need to walk right up to it to read it.

Nieśwież-Szczecin Klub

Od 1961 roku

There's no doorbell. No handle on the door. I knock and stand back. Nothing happens. I knock again. This time, I hear some movement on the other side. A lock is thrown and the door is pulled inwards. An old lady dressed in a heavy knit cardigan and very sensible shoes appears.

'Yes.'

'Is this the Nies…nice…Sorry,' I say pointing to the sign.

'The Nieśwież-Szczecin Klub,' she says. She pronounces it NeeshVeesh Schteshin Cloob.

'I'm Catherine Day,' I say, handing her the letter. 'I'm the lead singer with Spread It Thin.'

She reads the letter.

'Ah, Catherine. It will be good to see you play.'

'Tonight.'

'Yes.'

'And there is a fee?'

'Mr Goleniewski deals with that. But if he said you would be paid, paid you will be.'

'Do you know what kind of music we play?'

'No, but I'm sure our members will love it. Do you need any special equipment?'

'Eh, no. And you are?'

'I am Lena. I help run the club. Now I need to go. Be here at seven! You are on at eight.'

She closes the door.

I look at the building, trying to discern any clues as to what type of club it is. Lena looks far from the dozen loyal followers that we trail to gigs. Most of them are south of thirty and still think that there is no such thing as too much gel in your hair.

A small path circles the building and I follow it, hoping for a glimpse inside or maybe to meet someone else. The building is windowless. The rear looks out onto the river across a small, neatly kept strip of lawn. A couple of bins sit at a back door made from the same metal sheeting as the front. If the building is one large hall inside it could hold a few hundred people, standing.

I walk back onto the road, taking a last look at the place. We were due to play at The Fotheringay pub tonight but it's not a paid gig, and there are four other bands on. We won't be missed, but I need to call to ask the pub to post a note on the pub door to say that we are not playing. Our fan base needs to be kept informed.

The grand for this gig couldn't come at a better time. I'm struggling to make ends meet. Mum's cash from when she left had dwindled quicker than I would have liked and the job at the hair salon covers the mortgage and bills, but not much else. I should really sell the house. There's now enough equity in it to let me buy a small flat and be almost mortgage-free. Mum's lawyer contacted me not long after she left and I'd signed a bunch of papers, including the deeds to the house, with which mortgage and all became mine. But I can't sell the house. I can't sell *Mum's* house. What would she say when she comes back? Where would she sleep? What would I do with all her stuff? Her bedroom remains untouched since she left, apart from the odd bit of hoovering and dusting. Her clothes still hang in the wardrobe, some shoes under the bed, ancient makeup and perfume lie on the dressing table. Daisy has told me on more than one occasion that it is creepy to leave it all like that. She's urged me to box it all up and store it in the loft. I can't bring myself to touch a thing. Now I just keep the door closed, the room ready for her return.

We split all earnings from the band 50/25/25, Davie getting the larger share. Two hundred and fifty quid will do nicely as a wee stash for Christmas. Not that I've any presents to buy, but nights out aren't cheap, and I'm praying that there might be a few that I'm invited to. I socialise a lot with Daisy, but rarely in the pub. Daisy doesn't drink. I don't socialise with Davie—and for good reason. He drinks too much and suffers from wandering-hand syndrome when he's had a few. Six weeks after we had formed the band—Davie inviting us to work with him after stumbling upon Daisy and I gigging as a duet to a backing tape in a local pub—he'd tried to grab my bum. I'd slapped him so hard he'd fallen off his seat. He's never tried it since, but Daisy has had to slap him once as well. We'd debated leaving the band, but he was so apologetic that we gave him another chance. But on the condition that we only ever meet up about the band, we never meet in a pub, and that any sign from him of his old ways and we're gone. So far he's kept himself to himself but I don't trust him.

I start to make my way to Davie's flat.

'Catherine Day, as I live and breathe.'

'Jennifer Marshall Meadows, a bad penny if ever I saw one.'

Jenny crosses the road to join me.

'Man, it's been a while!' she says.

'Looking good, sister,' I say.

And she is. As a kid, Jenny ran to fat the way your nose runs when you have flu. An inch taller than me, she now cuts a great figure in a thigh length, pleated skirt, a pair of heels and white blouse. Simple. Classy.

'How long, sister?' I say.

She sighs, 'Last time I saw you would be Karen Shields' birthday night out.'

'Three years back?'

'Try five!'

'Never.'

'At least.'

'God, what happened to us?'

'Well, you went all house-bound after your mum left and I found love.'

'How's Tim?'

'We're divorced.'

'Already?'

'Just the six shit years.'

'Sorry about that.'

Not a word had passed her lips about a new man back then, yet, out of the blue, without saying a blind word to anyone, she announced she was married. I've met Tim twice. He seemed dull to me. Nice but dull.

'What happened?' I ask.

'I found a better man.'

'And is that working out?'

'Not so much. It turned out that by better I meant worse. And you?'

'No one special.'

'Anyone non-special?'

'Nope.'

'Anyone at all?'

'Just call me Sister Catherine of the Perpetual Virgins.'

She laughs. I realise that I've missed that laugh.

'It's good to see you, Jenny!'

'And you. I hear you're still working for Telegraph Maggie.'

'Number two hairdresser at your service, ma'am.'

'And is she still the queen of gossip?'

'What do you think?'

'Do you know she goes through people's bins at night for info?'

I nod my head. 'I've heard all the stories, Jenny. I thought the bin one a crock of crap, but Lidia Todd assures me that midge raking is one of Maggie's night-time sports when she's on the trail of some real juicy goss.'

'She so does, Catherine. When she heard that Madge Reynold's daughter was up for that film part, she was desperate to know if she'd got it. It ate her raw. For days she pestered the life out of Madge, but neither her nor Jilly would say a word. And you know what? Suddenly Maggie knows the name of the film, the shooting schedule, co-stars—the works—even the salary. Madge and Jilly got real angry at that.'

'Maggie was telling anyone that would listen, Jenny. I listened to it for days. And you're saying that she got the info by rubbish diving?'

'Yip. Jilly said her mum dumped the offer letter in the bin by mistake one night. She went out to recover it and couldn't find it. Madge swore she'd seen Maggie on the street corner earler.'

'Do you know something, Jenny?'

'What?'

'Madge came around to the salon one morning. She lamped Maggie upside her head with a copy of the Yellow Pages?'

'I'd heard it was a first edition of War and Peace.'

'Definitely the Yellow Pages. I was there. And there was more.'

'Do tell!'

'When Madge later found out that Maggie had also told everyone what Jilly was getting paid, she returned and would have worked her way through an entire series of Britannic Encyclopaedias if we hadn't stepped in. To top it all, Jilly sneaked round one Friday night and filled the salon keyholes with superglue. Back and front door. Come Saturday morning Maggie had to smash the lock to get in.'

'Didn't Madge also set fire to the bins out the back of the salon.'

'We think so. What a stink. Burning hair isn't the best. The café still complains that the smell lingers in the back lane.'

Jenny smiles.

'Why did we drift apart, Jenny? It's so good to see you.'

'I didn't drift anywhere. You just stopped answering the phone.'

That's not strictly true. Tim had taken over Jenny's life.

'Why are you down here?' she asks.

'We have a gig tonight and I was checking out the venue.'

'Gig?'

'I'm in a band.'

'Get away!'

'Excuse me, Miss Meadows, you are talking to the lead singer of the electronic superband Spread It Thin.'

'Seriously?'

'We may even cut a single soon.'

'And where are you playing?'

I point to the tin shed.

She looks at the building, 'In there?'

'Yip.'

147

'Is that not a storage dump'

'No. It's a club.'

'What kind of club?'

'The Nieśwież-Szczecin Club.'

I screw up the pronunciation.

'Never heard of it,' she says. 'When are you playing?'

'Tonight.'

'Can I come?'

'It's a private club.'

'Call me your roadie. It's been an age. I could do with a good night out.'

'Are you serious?'

'I go to the gym.' She throws a pose. 'Slim, fit and able to lift the heaviest speakers.'

'Do you know what?'

'What?'

'You're on.'

'What time?'

'We need to be here at seven.'

'It's a date.'

'You have now been recruited as the new gopher for Spread It Thin.'

'Is the pay good?'

'That depends on what you mean by good.'

'Is there any pay?'

'No.'

'That good?'

'That good, now do you fancy a coffee?'

'I can't. I'm meeting Dad in half an hour. He's helping me decorate my new flat.'

'Where's the flat?'

'Shawlands. Are you still in your Mum's place?'

I nod.

'I need to go,' she says. 'Let's catch up tonight, but I'll tell you now I play a mean triangle if you need a new member.'

'Have you been to music school.'

'But of course,' she laughs. 'I was voted the musician most likely to succeed in *'the band where my microphone is turned off'* category. See you later!'

As she walks away, I realise how much I've missed her. She's also lying about her voice. Jenny can sing. As she walks away I realise that the chat also has a downside. It raises the 'special one' spectre from the depths. My single lack of 'another' in my life. A scattering of soul-searing one-nightstands and the odd second date have been the only nod to male company in the last few years. A small litany of drunken fumbles, regretful mornings. Daisy says I'm now actively avoiding men. She asked if I was gay, but I'm not. If mum was here, I'm fairly sure the subject of grandchildren would be on the menu. But she forwent that right when she buggered off. Daisy thinks that's my real problem.

'Catherine, you think that when your Mum comes home the world will be all smiles and you'll meet the perfect partner. Dear, it's not worth waiting for that day. Get on with it.'

She is closer to the truth than I'd like to admit. With the exception of joining the band, my life has moved on a couple of inches at best. Same home, same bed, same workplace, same same-old. Life on hold.

Waiting.

I contemplate running after Jenny and offering to help at her flat, but I have a shift this afternoon at the salon. Corrina called in sick, and Maggie needs help. And I need the money.

On the way to the salon, I nip by Davie's Mum's flat and let him know that the gig is on the up and up.

'I've got someone coming along to help tonight,' I say as I'm about to head off. 'An old girlfriend who wants to see the band play.'

'Will she be allowed in?'

'We'll say she always helps out.'

'Who is it?'

'You won't know her. An old school friend.'

I head off to breathe in more setting lotion. To swallow more bullshit.

14
THE REAR OF AN ELEPHANT

'CATHERINE, I'M RUNNING late. The van is all packed. Can you take it to the gig?'

I look at the home phone. 'Davie have you ever thought of setting your watch an hour ahead.'

'I'll be there in time for the gig. Have I missed one yet?'

'Plenty.'

'Have I missed a WHOLE gig yet?'

'Three.'

'They weren't my fault.'

'Davie they never are. And yet you are the only one that's ever late for a gig. And I'll repeat that—the *only* one that's been late. Any normal person would think on that, maybe change their ways.'

'Hang on, Catherine! Give me a minute, Mum is calling.'

I hang up. He is the proverbial wall that isn't worth talking to on this subject. I nip back to my bedroom and open the wardrobe. When the band first formed, I was a jeans and T-shirt girl. Then Davie pulled Daisy and me aside and said that he thought the band needed an image. He fancied leather as our theme. Daisy said he was just going to perv out on the two of us in leather trousers. I'd pointed out that I couldn't afford a leather thong never mind an entire pair of trousers. Davie passed the baton back to us. What did we want to wear? After an hour in Flip on Queen's Street, Daisy and I had to admit that leather looked good and, second hand, the price was good too. I now have two pairs of leather trousers that I rotate. Both black and both designed to cut off my circulation. Black T-shirts, black shoes - we are a funky funeral crew. But we do look the part.

I dress and, as I pass Mum's bedroom, place my hand on the door, pausing for a few seconds. I do this every so often. It connects me back with her, but I can't linger. It's easy to break down. I've spent more than a few hours lying against the door running myself dry on tears.

Where are you, Mum?

I take the bus to Davie's place, and he throws me the van keys from the first-floor window.

'I'll be there by eight,' he shouts

'And what if we are supposed to be on before then?'

'Do a few holders.'

By holders, Davie means play a backing tape to encourage a sing along.

I arrive at the club at ten to seven. Daisy is standing by the fence chatting to Jenny. I pull up, parking near the gate.

'Daisy, have you knocked the door?' I ask as I get out.

'No. I was waiting on you.'

'Jenny, this is where you earn the price of your entrance. Davie's running late. We three need to hump the gear in.'

Daisy swears. 'Why do we put up with him, Catherine? He doesn't lift a bloody finger. What's the betting he needs to 'nip off quick' after the gig?'

'High,' I reply.

If the police ever fingerprinted our gear, they'd struggle to find Davie's dabs on anything.

'I'll get us in,' I say to them both. 'Start lifting the stuff out of the van!'

I walk up to the sheet metal door and knock. There's no waiting this time, as Lena appears almost immediately. She's changed out of her cardie into a full-length black dress. She looks good enough to join our band.

'Hi Catherine.'

'Do we bring our stuff in here or around the back.'

'The back. You'll need to wait a little though to set up. Bingo is running on.'

Bingo? Okay, so the audience might be a tad older than I'd hoped. Maybe the Daisy and Catherine sing-along will be closer to the mark after all.

'I'll open the back door,' Lena says. 'You can stack your stuff in the kitchen until the bingo is over.'

She closes the door.

'Everything goes around the rear,' I say to Jenny and Daisy.

It takes us fifteen minutes to move our gear into the kitchen which is surprisingly modern—as clean as an operating theatre. Through a serving hatch we can hear a monotone voice calling numbers, but with the hatch closed we can't see the room beyond. There are no seats in the kitchen, so the three of us slump onto the boxes that hold our gear.

'*House!*'

A combination of moans and a small smattering of applause accompanies the call. We hear the numbers being checked and chairs and tables being moved. By the sound of the chat going on it's busy.

'Okay,' says Lena coming in. 'Everyone is going to eat, then you are on at eight. Is that okay?'

'Lena,' I say. 'Can you tell me a little about the club?'

'Maybe later, I need to make sure that the food service is up and running. The members can get very testy if they don't get fed promptly.'

For the first time I notice the tang of an accent in Lena's words. A lot of Glaswegian, but with a hint of something more exotic, more guttural.

She comes back a few minutes later.

'Okay, follow me.'

We leave our equipment in the kitchen to have a quick shufty at the venue.

The tramp back in the park, before I did my BarL trip, had said to me that I should never judge a book by its cover. The phrase could have been written for this place. I had it firmly in my mind that we were about to play a shit hole. As we walk out of the kitchen I couldn't be further from the truth if I tried. I'd guess the room we step into takes up about three quarters of the entire building. Low level lighting shines down on a deep-pile red carpet. The walls are adorned with cityscapes and bronze tinged mirrors. At one end, a small stage rises. Ceiling mounted speakers talk to a built-in, quality sound system. On the far wall, a trestle table, draped in a purple tablecloth, is struggling not to collapse under the weight of food. A well-stocked bar is recessed into the wall opposite the stage. Draught fonts and all. The tables that dot the floor are draped in pristine white cloth, each surrounded by satin covered chairs—all facing the stage. The place has the smell of money that, I suspect, a private club in London would love.

Our audience is lined up in a queue at the table, loading up on grub. I'd feared an average age of eighty, but it's a mix—all are dressed for a night out. Some are the same age bracket as us, some Lena's age, and a few look like they've been on the planet since Napoleon quit.

'You can plug into our system,' says Lena with a small grin.

I get the feeling we are not the first people she has pulled this reveal on.

'We have our own speakers, thanks,' I reply.

Lena shuffles away as we start to set up. When Davie is here, we can do this in twenty minutes, but even with the help of Jenny, it's ten to eight before we are ready.

'Where is our leader?' Daisy asks, as she sound checks her mic.

'He said he'd be here by eight,' I reply.

'Jenny, can you sing?' Daisy asks.

'She can,' I reply. 'We used to sing in the school choir together.'

Daisy dives into the keyboard box and pulls out a sheaf of paper.

'Lyrics,' she says and hands them to Jenny.

'What do I want with lyrics?' Jenny asks, leaving her mouth slightly open.

'We need help.'

'In the band?'

'Yip.'

Jenny looks like a deer caught in headlights. 'You're kidding. I'm only here to watch!'

'Just stand at the back,' Daisy says. 'Use Davie's microphone. I've already set it up.'

'I can't.'

'Of course, you can. Hide the lyrics behind the drum machine. Catherine will call out the next song.'

'I can't' she repeats. 'I…'

'And don't worry if Davie comes in! He'll need to make do. He's the one that's late. I can cover his keyboard parts, if you can work the drum machine.'

Jenny doesn't know what to say. Daisy can be a force of nature when she wants something.

'The three of us make a better unit than two,' she states. 'You'd be helping out. Catherine here needs all the help she can get with her crap voice.'

'This is insane,' says Jenny, backing off. 'I can't just *join* a band.'

'You'll stroll it,' says Daisy.

'Are you nearly ready?' Lena asks, walking up to us.

'Yip,' says Daisy. 'One of our band is late but it'll be fine. We've done loads of gigs with just the three of us.'

'Well, I'll intro you at eight. What do you want me to say?'

I dip into my backpack and hand Lena a scrap of paper. 'Use this.'

She reads it and nods.

'Five minutes,' she says to us before lifting my mic.

'Ladies and the gentlemen!' she announces. 'The band will start in five minutes. So, grab your drinks, or go for a whizz, or settle down, or all three—but be ready in five.'

This kickstarts a frenzy of activity as plates are loaded up, drinks are ordered, and crockery and glasses are heaved back to tables.

'Do you have many bands on here?' I ask Lena.

'Oh, yes,' she says. 'Last week we had a country and western band. *Dollar In Your Pocket* they were called, and the week before it was heavy metal—they were called *Forged with Fire*, and we had a punk band a month ago. They went by the name of... darn!'

She turns to the room, 'Mike what was the punk band called?'

A stout man, sitting at a front table, shouts back, '*The Boot In.*' 'That's them.'

I swallow hard. I've heard of them all. All of them have had hit singles.

'We had Jason Donavan a while back,' she adds. 'He was sorry that Kylie had to cancel on us. Next month we're trying to get Dexys Midnight Runners.'

I can't tell if she'd kidding. I swallow harder. If she's for real, then this audience is used to watching pros. Daisy doesn't looked fazed, but Jenny looks terrified.

'Nearly time!' says Lena.

I turn to Daisy. 'No sing along for this lot. A full gig is on the cards. I'll take the sequencer; you have all the keyboards. Jenny, are you okay with the drum machine?'

'No!' she squeals.

'It's easy. It's pre-programmed. We need it for each song. The buttons are numbered. When I shout out, just hit the number. Then kill it at the end of each song.'

'I can't, Catherine. I just can't!'

'Too late,' I say. 'You'll be fine. Just press the buttons and sing the lyrics. We only have a few of our own songs to start with. After that you'll know all the others.'

Jenny looks like she might run.

'Daisy are you set?' I ask.

She gives me the thumbs up. I push Jenny to the rear before she can exit. I can feel her trembling.

'Okay, good to go,' I say to Lena, who steps up onto the stage.

'Ladies and gentlemen' Lena says, before reading from the piece of paper I gave her. 'They have been called the next Human League by the Southside Post, the 'one to watch' by the East Bathgate Observer, and the hottest thing to emerge from Glasgow since Marmalade—or so says Jazzy Whack on Radio Serpentine. Can you please welcome… Spread It Thin!'

We're six songs in when the man with the sculpted beard appears. I'm cranking out the chorus of *A Little Respect* and stumble over the lyrics when I see him. Daisy throws me a glance. As I get myself back together, the man slides to the rear of the hall and sits down. A few people nod to him as he passes and, as soon as he is seated, the barman brings him a glass of something, as if this is a regular thing.

What the hell is he doing here?

We finish off the song, next up is *Enola Gay*. I fire up the sequencer and, on cue, I whisper back to Jenny to hit button three. The required beat starts, and Daisy takes up the keyboard intro. I spot a small smile on Jenny's face. I think she's beginning to enjoy herself. Now we are onto songs she knows she's stopped miming, and I can hear her singing. I twist up the volume on her mic a little, as she's gelling well with Daisy and I.

The audience are far from the dead pool I expected. As soon as we stopped our own songs and played the opening chords of *Don't You Want Me?*, a few were on their feet dancing. *Enola Gay* has even more up. There's still no sign of Davie. We normally take a break after forty-five minutes, if we are flying solo. He's been known to appear then. But even if he turns up now, he can take a hike. He's not getting five hundred quid for doing next to bugger all. I've already decided we'll spit the fee three ways between Daisy, Jenny and me.

When the fight breaks out, my thoughts of splitting the cash vanish.

It starts innocently enough. An elderly couple who had been sitting near the back, paying scant attention to us, rise to stand at the bar. They turn their backs to the stage, talking to each other, while leaning in to be heard over our sound. The man with the sculpted beard turns to look at them a few times. When it's clear that they are not returning to their chairs he gets up and approaches them.

It's a strange fact of playing a gig that you notice the oddest things in the crowds watching you. Who's chatting, picking their nose, slopping their drink, off their head, wearing a rose, eating a burger, mouthing the wrong words, flicking you the vicky. I'm hypersensitive to the crowd. Wanting them—*willing* them—to enjoy themselves. Needing them to go home singing our praises. Truth is, few ever pay us the sort of attention I want. After chatting with other bands, I find I'm not alone in my obsession. Daisy reckons I have the same disease as every other act. She thinks that even Prince is a 'crowd worrier'.

The man with the sculpted beard taps the elderly man and woman at the bar on their shoulders, pointing to their seats. The elderly woman shakes her head and returns to the conversation. The man with the sculpted beard isn't for being dismissed. He taps the elderly woman on the shoulder again. She doesn't turn this time. The man with the sculpted beard changes tack and grabs the shoulder of the elderly man, spinning him around. As he turns, the elderly man surprises the man with the sculpted beard by using the spin to put welly into a punch that, with the balletic grace of a scene from Rocky, connects. The man with the sculpted beard tumbles back, crashing into a table behind him, knocking the four occupants to the floor.

From here it goes south in the way only bar brawls can. That we are playing a gig to a crowd that reek of middle class, is of no odds. Bar fights are bar fights. Fuelled by drink, dark and devilry—people redirect their energy quickly in such situations. Some aggrieved at the violence they are subjected to. Some too quick to their own violence. Some seeing a chance to settle scores. Some just drunk, looking for any excuse to jazz up their evening.

A glass flies by my head as a wave of fighting flows towards us. I keep singing. An instinctive reaction born of a naïve belief that people will soon realise the folly of their actions and quit.

As if!

Lena, with a step far sprightlier than I'd have given her credit for, leaps onto the small stage and grabs my microphone.

'Stop this,' she shouts.

Daisy ceases playing. Jenny, eyes wide, doesn't kill the drum machine. For a few seconds the audience slug it out to the sound of snares and tom toms.

'Stop this right now. Jane, get the lights!', Lena shouts.

I reach back, powering down the drum machine as the hall lights flick on, dousing the fighting spirit in most. Another shout from Lena, and the fighting all but ceases. The exception being the man with the sculpted beard who has the elderly man in a headlock, while his partner is beating the man with the sculpted beard across the head with a plastic ice bucket. Lena runs the length of the hall, yanks the bucket from the woman's hand and undoes the head lock.

We huddle together on the stage.

'What the heck was that about?' asks Daisy.

Jenny leans in, 'Wow, is this normal?'

'No,' I say. 'But it happens now and again. Although I'd have bet my house not with this crowd.'

'You can never tell,' says Daisy. 'Best to just stand back and let them sort it out.'

'So, we just do nothing?' Jenny asks.

Daisy and I nod.

Lena has calmed the bar brawl to a quiet hum. A few people are still looking shifty, contemplating a last act of retaliation. Lena walks back to the stage, throwing out glares left, right, and centre. She steps back on the stage to take the mic.

'I'm going to give everyone fifteen minutes to sort themselves out. Then the band will come back on. You have been warned! We'll have no more of this nonsense in here. Does everyone understand?'

Like schoolkids, they nod.

Tables are rearranged, chairs righted, debris gathered. A brush and pan is brought out to clean up smashed glass. An orderly queue forms at the bar to refill spilt drink. The way this all happens speaks of a track record here.

'What do you think that was about?' says Jenny.

I explain what I saw, and Daisy says she saw it as well.

'Is that your man with a beard?' Daisy asks.

'Yes.'

'Oh, very mysterious,' she whispers. 'I think he has a thing for you. Protecting your honour and all that. That old couple turning their back on you was too much for him.'

'Maybe he's here because he's heard from Mum again,' I say, ignoring Daisy's dig.

'How would he possibly know you were here?'

I step off the stage, wind my way through the room, and approach the man with the sculpted beard, who is standing near the exit.

'Have you heard from my mother?' I demand.

'I am sorry about that,' he says, referring to the fight. 'I should have been more circumspect, but you deserve better than to be ignored by such people.'

'Mum?' I say, ignoring the apology.

'She is fine.'

'You've heard from her.'

'No, but I know she is okay.'

'Where is she?'

'Safe.'

GORDON J. BROWN

'From whom?'

'Safe.'

'Look, you can't keep doing this! I need to know where my Mum is.'

I've had this conversation before. It never goes well.

'She is safe.'

And it's not going well again.

'Just tell me where my Mum is!'

'I need to go.'

'I'm going to the police.'

'Do as you please!'

I reach out and grab at his arm.

'You can't do this to me,' I say. 'Just tell me where she is? Why is she doing this? Why are you doing this? Why are you here? What is going on?'

The dam which had previously broken in his presence, breaks again.

'Tell me now!' I shout. 'Just tell me where she is!'

He turns away.

'Don't you dare walk away again! Who the hell are you?'

I'm screaming.

He walks out of the door. I take after him, but he slams the door in my face. I bounce off it and stumble back. I rush forward to leave. Lena appears, hand on the door handle.

'Let him go' she says.

'Out of my way!' I bellow.

'Catherine, just let him go!'

'Why? What has it to do with you? Get out of my way. Right *fucking* now!'

Lena reacts by placing herself between me and the door.

'Let me out, let me out!' I howl.

'Catherine,' says Jenny, running up to me. 'Stop this!'

'I want to know who he is.'

'Calm down, Catherine,' Jenny says.

'Who is he?'

Jenny reaches out for my hand, 'For crying out loud, calm down!'

I look around. I'm stage centre for everyone in the room.

'Just take a breath,' she says. 'Come back to the stage.'

I let her lead me away.

'Why is he doing this, Jenny?'

'I don't know, but you acting like this isn't helping. Let's get a drink and sit down for a moment.'

When we get back to the stage, Daisy hands me a can of Coke.

'Well, Catherine,' Jenny says. 'You sure know how to show a girl a good time.'

I yank the ring pull from the can and slug at the liquid, spilling most of it down my T-shirt.

'I just want my Mum back, Jenny. That's all.'

'I know,' she says.

Lena walks up, 'Are you okay to carry on?'

'Who is that man?' I ask.

'Mr Goleniewski.'

'The man who will pay us?'

'Yes.'

'Did he also book us?'

'Yes.'

'Why would he do that?'

'He books all the bands. He owns the club.'

'Owns the club? What do you mean? Who is he?'

'He is an old friend who opened this club many years ago. He had a little money and chose to spend it here. What else do you need to know?'

'He knows where my Mum is?'

'I know nothing about that.'

'Where does he live?'

'It is not for me to tell you that.'

'Either tell me, or we don't play another note.'

'And if you do that, you will not get paid.'

'I don't care. Just tell me where he lives! I'll keep coming back here until I find out.'

'That is up to you, but I'm not going to tell you where he lives. So, are you going to play again?'

Daisy steps in, 'Yes, we will.'

I go to open my mouth. She raises her finger. 'Catherine, I need this pay day. We can find out where this guy lives afterwards.'

I'm all for walking out, when Jenny chips in, 'Catherine I was having fun. Why don't we finish off, and I'll help you find the man. I promise.'

'So, will you play?' Lena asks.

Everyone stares at me. I look at the audience, most now back in their chairs. My heart is still racing, but the hothead in me is starting to cool. Like Daisy, I need the money, and walking out won't get me any closer to Mr Goleniewski. Maybe someone else in this room can help. If I walk out, I may never be allowed back in here.

'Okay,' I say. 'Give me a few minutes to get myself straight.'

Give me a few days and I'll not have this straight.

'Catherine,' says Lena. 'Can I give you a bit of advice?'

Another Maggie Hamilton moment?

'Sure.'

'Mr Goleniewski is a good man. An *important* man in some people's eyes. Not in all, but in those that count. I know he is looking out for you, but he walks a fine line. He cannot be seen to *help* too much.'

'What does that all mean?'

'Do not ask anyone else in here about him!'

'Why not?'

'It is not in your interests.'

'You're not making any sense.'

'I am, but you just don't know enough to realise it.'

'Is that your advice?'

'Partly.'

'And?'

She sits down next to me, dropping her voice, to prevent Daisy and Jenny hearing.

'What do you know about your mother's past?'

'Mum?'

'Yes. I think that you don't know what you need to know. I think your mother kept things from you.'

'And how could you possibly know that?'

'Because your mother is better known amongst some of our members than you would credit.'

She stands up. Before I can ask anything else she says to the three of us, 'Ten minutes and you can start again!'

She walks away.

The rest of the gig passes with the audience, most who stay seated, spending as much time glancing at each other as at us. I'm wondering if fighting is a bit of national sport in here. We finish with *Gold* and, as soon as the lights go on, the crowd thins quickly as people exit. It's not yet ten. We treat ourselves to a drink at the bar, but we are persona non grata. Usually, we are buttonholed by some of the audience. No one talks to us. Lena comes up.

'I am sorry about earlier,' she says.

'And I'm sorry about blowing up with Mr Goleniewski,' I reply.

'Tylko ktoś, kto niczego nie żałuje może uśmiechnąć się na widok zadku słonia,' she says.

That brings a moment of silence.

She grins, 'It is an old Polish saying that means: 'Only someone with nothing to be sorry about smiles at the rear of an elephant.'

'Oh,' says Daisy.

'It makes no sense, no?' she says.

I shake my head.

'In the 70's we had a TV programme in Poland called Banacek. The detective in it would just make up sayings, but the programme was so popular some people started to use them.

'Are there other sayings?' asks Jenny.

'Chociaż hipopotam nie ma żądła w ogonie, mędrzec wolałby zostać przygnieciony przez pszczołę. That means 'Though the hippopotamus has no stinger in his tail, a wise man would rather be sat on by a bee.'

I laugh.

'Or Kaczka z trzema skrzydłami i bochenkiem chleba jest bratem indyka,' she says.

'Go on,' says Daisy. 'What does that one mean?'

'A duck with three wings and a loaf of bread is a brother to the turkey.'

We all laugh.

'Lena,' I ask. 'What is this club?'

'A private members club.'

'I get that but what does the Nieśwież-Szczecin bit mean.'

'It is the name of two towns. One in Belarus and one in Poland. At one time both were in Poland. We are a Polish club.'

'Why name it after two towns.'

'Mr Goleniewski started the club. He is from Nieśwież, as is his family. The other town has a connection to you Catherine!'

'It does?' I say with surprise in my voice.

'Your namesake was born there.'

'Who?'

'Catherine the Great.'

'The Russian empress?'

'In Poland?'

'Prussia back then. She was not Russian.'

'Is that why Mr Goleniewski hired us, because I have the same name as a Russian empress?'

She laughs. 'Some in the town of Szczecin are proud of the connection. Catherine was the longest serving empress of Russia. A great woman to many.'

I look around at the cityscapes on the walls.

'Are these the towns?'

'Yes.'

'And you are still not going to give me Mr Goleniewski's address?'

'I cannot. Now I need to go. I need to tidy up.'

With this she leaves.

'Okay,' says Jenny. 'I'll give you this, Catherine Day, you have just given me one of my top ten most memorable nights.'

'Only top ten? Surely number one,' I say. 'When else did you get to play in a band, witness a bar brawl and see me lose my rag.'

'Well, apart from the band bit, the rest is quite common.'

Daisy slides her glass onto the bar, 'Catherine, what in the hell is this really all about?'

'In what way?'

'Why are we really here? This isn't a normal gig. Given the names they bandied around as having played here before, we are from a much lower division.'

'Maybe they see out potential.'

'I doubt it and what is it with your bearded friend? The whole fight started over you.'

'Me?'

'Yes, you! You definitely have connection to this place. Mr Beard took exception to that older couple standing at the bar with their backs to us. I'm guessing he was telling them to return to their seats, and they wouldn't play ball. That's how I saw it.'

'And why would he do that?'

'The bigger question is why would the older couple turn away?'

'Maybe they just wanted a drink.'

'No one else went up while we were on.'

'Everyone else was lost in wonder at our amazing sound. Maybe the old couple think we stink.'

'As if! And with Mr Beard's connection to your Mum, I think this is all ultra-strange.'

She has that nailed to mast.

'If he knows where your mum is why won't he tell you?', Jenny asks.

'I've no idea. It's been going on for years.'

'Years?' says Jenny.

'That's why I got so angry tonight. He's been appearing, off and on, for what seems like ever. Always blanking me when I ask where Mum is.'

'Well, you know what you need to do, Catherine?'

'What?'

Jenny smiles, 'Find out where in the hell this guy lives and see if that leads you to your mum. After all, maybe Mr Beard and your mum are an item.'

GORDON J. BROWN

15
DOES THE JOB JUST AS WELL

Thursday, 24th December, 1992.

I NEVER DID find where Mr Goleniewski lived back then. I've not seen him since that night. Nor did I ever track down Mum. A couple of letters through the post should have kept my hopes up, but in truth they really kept them down - providing just enough evidence that she was alive to prevent the police from doing anything more. I'm fairly sure that Mum is in the USA. The letters gave that away, and the last call I had was so full of crackles and pops it told me that she wasn't phoning from next door.

It's strange how you normalise such things. I've read, probably more than I should have, about the families of missing people. For a while, I bought every newspaper going if such cases featured. I became obsessive to the point that the few friends I had would avoid me on the days when some high-profile missing child or adult case hit the headlines.

I'm sitting in my flat, glass in hand, Christmas Eve of 1992 on my own. The memory of that gig over three years ago—*three years (really?)*—rising in my head as a result of a photo on my lap. Sent to me a few days ago, it was forwarded by Lena's son. Lena died a couple of months back and, when clearing her stuff, her son had found the photo in an envelope that was addressed to me, along with an explanation of where the letter had been

170

found; he had also included a note that Lena had never sent. Why she had never done so is unclear. I suspect that the note was written not long back. Maybe she had been about to send it when she died.

'Catherine, I hope your band found fame and fortune.'

No, we didn't Lena. Not even close.

'I found this photo. It was taken by Mr Goleniewski that night. He gave me a copy a few days after your show. I thought you should have it, but I also thought that you should know that Mr Goleniewski recently lost his father.'

And that's the extent of the communication. The photo is a shot of Daisy, Jenny and me in full flow. We look rather good, if I do say so. I've read the note a dozen times, and PI Catherine is back to the fore. All the old questions bubbling around. Who the hell is Mr Goleniewski? Where is Mum? Why did she leave? What does it all add up to? Are Mr Goleniewski and Mum squirrelled away in America? Lovers? And if so, why America?

I push the letter to one side and sip at my G&T. Nine twenty, and I'm a few G&T's over my usual. I'd called Jenny this afternoon when I finally accepted that there was going to be no surprise invitation to her family Christmas. She told me that she is seeing her mum and dad, promising to catch up on Boxing Day. Daisy and her dad are in Pakistan. Her dad had a business trip, and Daisy has never been to his hometown, so they are doing a father/daughter thing. Davie phoned me, but I'm not that desperate. At least I didn't think I was, until I caught myself lifting the phone with his number open in my diary.

I'm off the back of a late shift at the salon. Tending to the chairwomen desperate to get their hair done before they do the whole turkey and trimmings gig. As I'm now the lead hairdresser, I was expected to cut until the death. I've been asked frequently when I might be setting up on my own. A scary thought that I park every time I'm asked.

Robbie Taylor also called, just after I got home. Robbie is an electrician who works down at Weirs. He's Marianne Taylor's son. Marianne is a chairwoman of note. She started coming to the salon a year or so back, gaining her notoriety through her brief, but seemingly productive stint as a movie star, of sorts, back in the day. She had minor parts in major films, although the way she talks you'd believe she'd been Oscar-nominated for every role. I've seen her on TV once. A western called 'Saddle Sore' about a family making their way west with nothing more than the clothes on their back. Marianne plays a brothel keeper in a small town along the way. She has three lines.

'This is no place for children.'

'We only sell hard liquor.'

'One of the girls could make you forget your worries for a while.'

I'd mentioned I'd seen it, wondering whether she'd be a bit embarrassed at the role. I was so wrong. For the entire time it took for her cut and set, she regaled me with a level of detail about movie making I never knew, or wanted to know, existed. Right down to what was on offer for breakfast, lunch and dinner every day of the shoot. Even the colour of the toilet seats (bright green).

Robbie had popped in one day in early August, telling his mum that he would be outside in the car when she was finished. I'd smiled at him. Two days later he popped back in to ask if I fancied seeing *Teenage Fan Club* at King Tut's Wah Wah Hut. I did, and we've been on a couple of dates since. But he's keener than I am and, as with all my other relationships, I'm waiting on Mr Right and Robbie is Mr Almost, But Not Quite, Right. That happens a lot. I'd told him I was having an early night tonight.

I'm twenty-seven. That answer belongs to someone nearer seventy-seven.

Laurie Mayer is currently telling me that George Bush has pardoned some people that are involved in the Iran-Contra affair. 'Sea of Love' with Al Pacino will be on BBC1 in a moment. Whatever happened to 'It's A Wonderful Life'?

I kill the telly.

I play with the gin bottle lying on the carpet next to me. A glass bottle of tonic clinks as I spin the gin bottle into it. I'm out of ice. With the tiny ice box in my fridge, I'm always out of ice. Warm gin and tonic does the job just as well.

John Grisham's Pelican Brief is waiting to be read on the coffee table. It'll wait a wee while yet. I pour a home measure of gin coupled with a thimbleful of tonic. At one point I used to add lime juice. Not anymore. Tonight is shaping up to be the same as most others. The only upside is that I don't need to work tomorrow.

Eating mints doesn't hide it, Catherine.

Lidia Todd's words this very morning. I didn't ask her what that meant. I knew. It's far from the first time she's said it. I could be sponsored by Trebor Extra Strong Mints. So what? It's good customer service not to breathe alcohol on the clients. And let's not beat around any bushes here, our customers drag in as wide a variety of post booze-night smells as can be imagined. Saturday mornings can pong like a pub carpet. Maggie keeps a ready supply of aspirin and IRN-BRU. A few of the cups of tea are also laced with an exotic variety of drink, supplied by the customers, of course; heaven forbid Maggie would spring for such an indulgence.

And it doesn't end there. Take a week past on Saturday when Wilma Hunter, her of the toy boys and self-made money, announced she was getting married (fifth time). Her intended's name is Geoff or Gerard or George, Wilma seems a little unclear on her betrothed's actual nomenclature. The wedding is to be a 'do' of enormous proportions. A marquee in the grounds of Pollok House the centre piece. An impressive achievement given the grounds are Glasgow Council owned, and the city is not given to granting such requests easily. Money talks. Wilma has been a generous supporter of many causes over the years. She even sponsored her own slice of the Glasgow Garden Festival, back in '88. That won her some Brownie points at Glasgow City Chambers. Hence the marquee's approval.

The wedding announcement in the salon was accompanied, with West End stage timing, by the arrival of a dozen bottles of Moët & Chandon's finest fizzy grape juice. That ended well. The four incumbent Chairwomen: Lidia, Wilma, Mary-Beth Andrew (a newspaper journalist) and Tilly Spencer (one-time Commonwealth team swimmer for Scotland) had taken to the champagne as if it were going out to fashion. Of course, it would have been rude not to join in when asked, so I did. By eleven o'clock that morning the salon was no longer a salon. It was, to all intents and purposes, a pub in full Friday night swing. Newcomers arrived to find their slots were running late. They either joined in the drinking and merriment, as most did, or left to find an alternate solution to their hair problems.

The police were called at just after two o'clock. A second delivery of champers had been supplied by the Oddbins across the road at twelve. Not chilled—but warm fizz is still fizz. By then, there were thirty people in the salon and any attempts at haircutting had ceased. It was the conga line that convinced the café owner next door to call in the authorities. Thirty drunk women holding up traffic by, hands on each other's hips, dancing down the main road. At the front was Wilma who had found a tambourine from somewhere (no one seems to know where she got it). I was mid-line. Maggie took up the rear. The real money shot occurred when Wilma, giddy with the whole shebang, decided to take the conga into John Menzies. Already a busy place with Saturday shoppers, the conga epitomised the phrase 'brought chaos to...'. The resultant damage included three broken shelves, a trashed newspaper rack, half a dozen smashed bottles of lemonade and a collapsed counter—the latter the direct result of the conga line utilising said counter as a bridge to the exit.

A semi-cohesive conga line emerged from the shop. Wilma was considering the next emporium that might benefit from a line of crazed women when the panda car arrived. Promises to pay for any damage, plus another promise to disperse with immediate effect, avoided arrests and incarcerations. The salon was closed for the afternoon. The hastily scribbled sign on the door said: *'Closed early on account of personal issues.'*

So, when Lidia Todd complains about my breath, she'd do well to remember that she was the number two to Wilma in, what has now been christened, the Hair Cut Thirty.

I sip at the gin before lying back. If I'm not careful I'll spend another night on the sofa. Since finally selling up Mum's old house—a financially driven necessity—I'd found myself more often than not waking up on the sofa of my flat. Why not? It's comfy. Saves all that hassle of getting ready for bed.

The phone rings. It takes me a moment to rise. I cross the living room, not quite in a straight line, and lift the receiver.

'Hi darling.'

There's a ghost on the line.

'M...m... mum?' I stutter.

'How are you, Catherine?'

'Mum?'

'Been a while darling.'

'Mum?'

'Sorry I've not been in touch.'

'Mum?'

'Is that all you have to say, Catherine?'

'Mum?'

'Are you okay?'

I shake my head, trying to clear the gin fug. It doesn't work and only succeeds in making my head spin more.

'Mum?'

'For heaven's sake Catherine, yes, it's me, your mother.'

'Eh?'

'Have you been drinking?'

'Mum?'

'Oh, for crying out loud, stop saying that. Yes, it's your mother - now can we move on from that?'

'Where are you?'

'At last, some sense. I'm coming home. That's why I'm calling. Isn't that good news, Catherine? You and me will be back together.'

'Coming home?'

'Yes. Isn't that wonderful?'

'Coming home?'

'Are you going to repeat everything half a dozen times, Catherine?'

'Coming home?'

'Yes!' the exasperation in her voice is crystal clear. *'I'm coming home. I thought you would be excited.'*

'When?'

'When what?'

'When are you coming home?'

'Tomorrow. I'll be back for Christmas. Isn't that great?'

Is it? Shouldn't it be? God, I wish I'd laid off the gin tonight. I'm trying to process the information, figure what to say, while clearing my head at the same time.

'It's wonderful,' I say, but sound less than convincing.

'Well Catherine, I'm not sure what I was expecting from this call, but it wasn't this.'

'Mum you've been gone for over nine years.'

'I know, but things happened.'

I stutter, 'Things happened. Is that it? After nine years you're coming home and all you have to say is 'things happened'?'

'We can chat when I am back. Is my room useable?'

'Mum, you don't have a room!'

'What do you mean?'

'I sold the house.'

'You did what?'

'Sold it.'

'How could you do that? It's our house!'

'Mum, you said it was my house, remember, you signed it over to me. Anyway, who has been paying the mortgage for nearly a decade? For all I knew you were never coming home.'

'Of course, I was coming home!'

'Nine years. Who stays away for nine years and doesn't say why? Who?'

The gin is ramping up both my anger and my bravery.

'Don't use that tone with me, miss.!'

'Tone, Mum? You're lucky I don't slam the phone down on you.'

'Don't you dare!'

'Or what Mum? You'll spank my arse? Ground me? Or maybe you'll walk out on me.'

'Catherine Day, stop this at once!'

'I'm stopping nothing Mum. You're the one that did the stopping. Stopped being a mother, a provider—stopped doing your duty.'

'My duty?'

177

'Yeah Mum—you don't get to have a child and then just fuck off when things get tough.'

This last sentence is an Exocet. One that has been locked and loaded for years. There is more ammunition under my wings. I've had this conversation in my head a thousand times. I should pull back as it never ends well. I boil my blood every time.

But I'm not stopping anything.

'Catherine…'

'Mum don't, just don't! Whatever your excuse is it can't be enough. Not to let you drop me like a piece of rubbish.'

'I never did such a thing. I provided for you before I left.'

'How Mum? How? Enough money to last for how long? A mortgage I couldn't afford, bills I struggled with—and all at the age of seventeen. Aye, you provided alright. For yourself.'

I slam the phone down and immediately regret it. I down the rest of my drink, re-fill, fuming both at my mum and myself. Over nine years and she just made it all sound like a long weekend in Ayr. And she's coming back tomorrow—*tomorrow?* Christmas Day. Why would she come back on Christmas Day? And how will she do that if she doesn't know where I live?

Mum, back, here.

What am I thinking? Why am I not delighted? Mum is back. Isn't that what I've dreamed of for all these years? Cutting her off on the phone was an act of fury.

Haven't I wanted her back in my life?

I drop into the sofa, staring at the phone. It's lucky I kept the same phone number when I moved. If she really wants to come back, she'll call again. After all she didn't know I'd moved, so she won't know where I live.

The phone stays quiet. Did I hang it up properly? If I pick it up to check will that be the moment she calls back? Will she think I've taken the phone off the hook? I leave it alone. I'm sure I hung it up. I can't phone her back. I've not got a number.

She'll call.

She won't call.

She *might* call.

Of course, she'll call.

Only I wouldn't. After nearly a decade she'd announced she was coming home, and my reaction was to heap abuse on her. Why did I do that? How many nights have I cried myself to sleep pleading for some unknown power to return her to me?

Mum, please call back!

The phone rings. I pick it up so quickly that it slips from my grasp. The receiver takes the phone with it. Both crash to the floor.

'Mum!' I shout into the mouthpiece, once I've retrieved it. 'Hello, Mum.'

'Not your Mum. It's Jenny.'

'Oh God, Jenny, Mum just phoned: she told me she was coming home, and she told me it would be tomorrow, and I said that she had a duty, and I said that she left me to pick up the pieces, and she said that she hadn't expected me to react like this, and I said that I... and I... and I... hung up on her.'

Whoa, Catherine, take a breath. Back up!'

'I hung up on her, Jenny. After more than nine years of wanting her back and she says she's coming back. And what did I do? I hung up on her. And I insulted her. Shouted at her.'

'Breathe, Catherine, please breathe.'

'If I phoned BT would they tell me the number she called from? Can they do that? Or can they call her for me? Tell her I'm sorry and could she call back and...'

Jenny jumps in again, loud, *'Breathe for heaven's sake, Catherine, just breathe! Calm down!'*

'I can't. I hung up on her. Angry, I hung up on Mum.'

'I know, but you need to take it down a little. She said she was coming back. When?'

'Tomorrow. Christmas Day, Jenny. She's coming back on Christmas Day.'

'To your flat?'

'I don't know. She didn't know I'd sold the house. Sounded angry at the fact I had. But you know I couldn't afford to keep it going, Jenny—I just couldn't. The interest rates got too high. I couldn't pay the mortgage anymore. I had to sell. You know that, don't you Jenny? And I didn't even mention the interest rates to her. I just told her that I'd sold her house. Then I hung up.'

'Catherine, listen to me.'

'I hung up.'

'Listen to me.'

'I hung up.'

'Catherine, listen to me!'

'Hung up.'

'Catherine Day, will you shut up and listen to me?'

Her shout stops me.

'Are you listening?'

'Yes.'

'Put down your gin and tonic!'

'How do you know I have one?'

'There's a letter d in the day.'

'Ha, ha. Funny.'

'I wish it was.'

'What?'

'Nothing, now pay attention. Just calm yourself to a whirlwind, okay. If your Mum phoned to say she is coming back, after all this time, then a little shouting on your behalf is not going to change her mind.'

'You think?'

If you had decided to come home after, what, nine years? Do you think you'd do it on a whim, or would you have thought it over, planned it, committed to it?'

'Mum drinks. She can be all over the place.'

'She drank back then. Who knows what she does now. So do yourself a favour, put the booze away, grab a coffee and wait for her to call back!'

'How do you know she will call back?'

'Simple, she doesn't know where you live.'

'She might.'

'And if she did, she'd have known you sold the house, but you said she didn't.' Look I'll be round on Boxing Day to catch up, so just sit down and wait tonight. I was only phoning to arrange a time on Boxing Day. Dad can drop me off at midday, does that work?'

'Yes.'

'And if your Mum comes back tomorrow you can tell me all about it, but do me a real favour!'

'What?'

'Lay off the sauce, at least until she arrives! Now I need to go.'

'Okay and thanks.'

I hang up, making sure that the receiver is firmly in the cradle. I sip at my drink. I'll call it quits after this one. Or if Mum hasn't called maybe one more.

Or a couple. After all, it's Christmas Eve.

16
HELL'S TEETH, I FEEL CRAP

HELL'S TEETH, I feel crap.

I sit up, pushing myself upright, slowly. Another night on the sofa. I rub at my forehead. I need some painkillers, but that'll need to wait for a wee while. Standing up is an act too far at this moment in time. My foot kicks a bottle over. I reach down to right it. I must have spilled some last night, as the gin bottle is empty. I flop my hand around on the carpet but can't locate the wet patch. I sit back up.

The conversation with Mum last night comes back. She never called again. I give it ten minutes before heading for the toilet. Things are going to be slow. I'm thinking I drank that last gin a little too quickly. As I sit on the toilet seat, I consider the day ahead. Christmas Day. No tree this year. I just never got around to it. No presents for me. Not that I gave any to anyone. Christmas dinner will be beans on toast. The flat could also do with a tidy. That'll need to wait. With the way I'm feeling, I'm going to lie down for a bit.

I finish off, flush and strip; throwing my clothes in the wash basket.

It needs emptying.

I could do with a shower, but that'll have to wait as well.

In the bathroom mirror, I look on a body that lacks the fat it had grown used to over the last few years. I knew I was losing weight. I'd pulled on my best leather trousers for a rare gig a couple of months back. When I'd bought them, they had been so tight that Jenny said she could read my fortune. Now they are loose around my waist and my legs have room to breathe. I could also do with a haircut. If I didn't feel so bad that would make me laugh, given my job.

I creep to my bedroom. My bedclothes could do with a wash. That'll wait. I pop open the aspirin bottle on the bedside cabinet, tipping out three. I swallow them dry, then add a fourth for luck. I crawl into my bed. As soon as a I lie down, I feel like vomiting. I focus on keeping it down and win that small battle. I wait for the aspirin to kick in, hoping that if Mum *is* coming that she won't arrive just yet.

When I wake up again, I'm not feeling much better. Maybe I had more than I thought last night. The alarm clock tells me it's one thirty. I need to get myself together. As a minimum, I have to wash, dress, and try to sort the flat out a little.

Just ten minutes longer.

Three minutes to three and I wake again.

I need to pee.

I stagger to the toilet, then back to bed.

Ten minutes.

Six fifteen.

I shower before plodding to the living room.

I could kill for a G&T.

Hair of the dog and all that.

Then I'll clean.

The clear liquid makes me gag but I force it down.

I sit.

Better.

Now to clean.

Where to start?

What needs done?

The hoovering. The polishing. The dusting. The windows. Empty the bins. Tidy away my clothes. Wash my clothes. Wash the bed linen. Clean the kitchen surfaces. Clean the cooker. Mop the kitchen floor. Mop the bathroom floor.

Another G&T first.

The Only Fools and Horses Christmas special is on in ten minutes.

I'll watch that first, then clean.

Where's Mum?

Okay it's Birds of a Feather next on TV. I'm not a fan, so time to clean.

After one more drink.

Shirley Valentine is coming on. I've never seen it.

A drink to go with it.

I wake up.

On the sofa.

Morning.

Hell's teeth, I feel crap.

17
EVERY DAY IS CHRISTMAS

MUM NEVER CAME home. It's the phrase that permeates my Boxing Day hangover.

And you never cleaned the house.

I check the phone, in case it's off the hook. My foot kicks the gin bottle. I must have spilled it again last night. It was full when I started and is all but gone now. I drag myself around the house, making a half-hearted attempt to tidy up. After an hour, I slump on the sofa to survey my work. I'm struggling to see what I've done.

Jenny will be here in a couple of hours.

Where's Mum?

If she had come home, what would she have found. Me in bed? Me watching TV? Me asleep on the sofa? A flat needing a gutting? I get up again. This time I move the hoover around before cramming all the clothes I can into the washing machine and setting it off. I open the windows. An ice-cold blast of air whistles through the rooms. I look for polish, but I have none. I make do with a damp cloth. I traipse down to the bin shed and dump my rubbish. The sound of clinking bottles loud in my ears.

I return to the flat and use the damp cloth to wipe at the kitchen and bathroom surfaces. I pull out the bucket but can't find the mop. I rinse out the cloth for use on the kitchen and bathroom floors. After I clean I pour away the water. It's as black as sin.

Twenty to twelve.

I shower, after which I pull on what clean clothes I have.

The doorbell rings.

Mum or Jenny?

I open it.

'Hi,' says Jenny. 'Is your Mum back?'

I shake my head as she squeezes by me.

'It's Baltic in here!' she says.

I close the window.

'And it smells like a distillery.'

'I spilled some drink on the carpet.'

I haven't found the spills yet, but they have to be somewhere.

'How much did you spill? A whole bottle? And, if you don't mind me saying, you look like shit and your flat...'

'What about my flat?'

'Can't you tell?'

'Tell what?'

'Catherine this place needs an industrial clean.'

'I've spent the morning doing just that.'

'You're kidding. If this is it after a clean, what was it like before?'

'Do you want a drink?'

'No thanks. Too early for me.'

'It's never too early.'

I pull a gin bottle from the table.

'Do you think Malky's will be open today?' I ask.

'Malky's is always open. Why?'

'I need some more tonic.'

'What you need, Catherine Day, is *less* gin.'

'Who are you, my mother?'

'No. I'm your friend.'

I slump into the sofa, bottle in hand.

Jenny places one hand on her hip, 'Jeez Catherine, what in the hell has happened to you?'

'Nothing a good drink won't fix.'

She perches on the arm of the chair. 'Can you hear yourself? Do you really need more drink?'

'What? It's Christmas.'

'Catherine, every day is Christmas with you.'

'I've no idea what that means.'

'Yes, you do. You're holding that bottle as if it's a baby. Why don't you just swig straight from it? Wouldn't that do the trick?'

I look down on the bottle. Her suggestion would work. I unscrew the top.

'Catherine!' Jenny exclaims. 'I wasn't being serious.'

'With no tonic, why mess up a glass?'

'No way, darling,' she says, as I raise the bottle to my lips.

She jumps across the room, slamming the bottle from my hand. It goes spinning into the air and crashes to the floor near the TV. I leap from the sofa.

'Look what you've done!' I shout, yanking the bottle up to stop it emptying. 'It's my last bottle.'

Jenny sits back down. 'Catherine, I wish that were true.'

I take a slug. There's barely enough left for another mouthful. I finish it off.

'I'm going to Malky's for another.'

Jenny sighs. 'It's just as well your mother didn't come home yesterday.'

'Why?'

'The fact you have to ask should tell you why.'

'Is that supposed to be some clever statement?'

'No, Catherine, it's supposed to be a helpful one.'

'Look, if I just get another wee bottle, we can do the cryptic thing all night.'

I stand up, grab my handbag, open it and root out my purse. It's empty.

'Have you got a fiver you could lend me, Jenny?'

'No.'

'You must have!'

'I don't.'

'Let me see your purse!'

I cross the room. Jenny backs away.

'Come on,' I say. 'A fiver. A lousy fiver. I'll give you it back when I get paid. I've done a shed load of overtime this week. You'll get it back before New Year.'

'I said no.'

'And what do you want me to do for the rest of the day? You spilled the last of my drink.'

'Try going dry for the rest of the day!'

'Just give me the money!'

'Not going to happen.'

'Jenny, just give me the money!'

She keeps backing away and I follow her.

'Catherine, stop this!'

'A fiver, a crappy fiver. You can afford it.'

'Catherine, just stop this!'

'God what kind of friend can't lend a five-pound note?'

I reach out and try to grab her hand. She keeps drawing away.

'Catherine, stop this now. Look at yourself!'

'Just give me the money! I'll only be gone five minutes.'

She dances to her left and heads for the front door.

'Where are you going?'

'I can't watch this. This is so sad. What in the hell happened to you, Catherine Day?'

'Nothing. I just want a drink. Is that a crime?'

'I don't know what to do here. I really don't. You need help.'

188

She opens the door and vanishes, but not before I spot tears in her eyes.

What the hell? I start scouring the flat. Down the back of the sofa, the nether regions of cupboards and closets, pockets turned out, old purses raided, my porcelain piggy bank smashed. I gather up two pound thirty-eight pence in coppers and silver. Not enough for a whole bottle of gin, but enough for a half bottle. I pull on my jacket.

Malky's store is busy. Malky's store is always busy. The owner, Malky Iqbal waves at me as I enter. I stand in the queue. Three people are ahead of me. I recognise none of them. All are doing that post-Christmas Day emergency shop thing. Milk, bread, sugar, booze and chocolate. When I'm second in the queue, the man in front of me complains that his favourite magazine isn't in. Malky explains that it'll be in later in the week.

'But it's due on the 26th,' the man says. 'I've been collecting them since last January and it is always here on the 26th of the month.'

'I know Mr Cochrane,' answers Malky, 'but the wholesaler doesn't deliver on Christmas Day or Boxing Day.'

'And why not? Do you celebrate Christmas Mr Iqbal?'

'I am a Muslim, Mr Cochrane. I am happy for those that want to celebrate it and knowing that they are happy makes me happy.'

'Well, I'm not Muslim but I don't celebrate Christmas either. So, why should everything come to a halt? I can't even see my favourite TV programmes. They have moved University Challenge to later in the week, and One Man and his Dog is off air for two weeks. Do they think farmers take Christmas off, Mr Iqbal, do they?'

'I'm sure that farmers celebrate Christmas in their own way.'

'But the cows still need milked, and the milk truck still turns up. If a cow is sick the vet will be available. So why don't they deliver magazines?'

'Mr Cochrane, cows do not know it is Christmas. They cannot look after themselves. That is why the farmer and the vet work. Much as you like your magazine, I don't think that Steam Train Extravaganza is seen as an essential item.'

'Do you know the new issue has a special pullout section on the Flying Scotsman? It will fly off the shelves.'

'Ha, ha, Mr Cochrane, that is funny!'

'What is?'

'An issue with the Flying Scotsman that will fly off the shelf!'

'Is that funny?'

'Okay Mr Cochrane, there are other customers waiting, can I ring up your messages?'

'I need a bottle of Blue Nun and a bottle of Green Nun as well.'

Mr Iqbal chews on the inside of his left cheek.

'Green Nun, Mr Cochrane? We have Blue Nun but I have never heard of Green Nun.'

'I read they were doing it as a special for St Patrick's day.'

'St Patrick's day is not until the 17th of March.'

'I know, but these companies always send stock out early. Don't you already have Cadbury's Creme Eggs for sale?'

I stamp my foot in frustration at the wait. Mr Cochrane doesn't notice or doesn't care.

'Mr Cochrane, I do not have any Green Nun,' sighs Malky. 'But I will ask my cash and carry.'

'Can you phone them now and ask when it will be in?'

'No, Mr Cochrane, they are closed today.'

'Why?'

'Why are they closed?'

'Yes.'

'Because they are always closed Christmas Day and Boxing Day.'

Mr Cochrane slaps his hand down on the counter and I notice that, under the black bunnet and grey Macintosh, he is wearing striped pyjamas. I glance at his feet. Slippers.

'Why is everywhere closed, Mr Iqbal?'

'We have had this conversation Mr Cochrane; now can you give me your shopping so I can add it up.'

Mr Cochrane obliges, handing over ten glass jars of baby food and a loaf.

'Do you still want the Blue Nun, Mr Cochrane?'

'Make it two, and do you have any Christmas Cards?'

'No.'

'You had some on Christmas Eve.'

'I have put them away.'

'So, you still have some.'

I stamp my foot again and this time let out a 'humpf'.

Mr Cochrane still blanks me and asks Malky, 'Can I see the ones that you put away?'

'It will take me a minute or two. Can I serve the other customers first, then I will fetch them?'

Mr Cochrane looks like he is going to argue over this point. I give him a nudge in the back.

'Oops, sorry,' I say. 'I'm in a bit of a hurry. I want to see the film on telly.'

He turns to me, 'What film?'

I have no idea what is on.

'Eh, The Great Escape.'

'You mean Escape to Victory?'

Do I?

'It is not on until ten minutes past two,' he says. 'You have plenty of time.'

'I need to cook first.'

'What are you cooking?'

'Sorry.'

'What are you cooking?'

'I'm not sure, now could I get served?'

'My wife is making turkey curry,' he says, turning to Malky. 'I assume that you are having turkey curry, Mr Iqbal.'

'No, Mr Cochrane. For a start I am a vegetarian and secondly, although I like curry, it does not follow I have it every day.'

'Really?' Mr Cochrane says. 'But your shop always smells of curry.'

'So you tell me every day, Mr Cochrane. Now please stand to one side and let me serve young Catherine here.'

I step forward, elbowing Mr Cochrane on the way. 'Can I have a half bottle of gin.'

'Only a half-bottle, Catherine? Are you cutting down?'

I laugh. A cold sound. Malky fetches the gin saying, 'No tonic?, Catherine,'

I nip to the soft drinks shelf and lift a bottle. When I get back to the counter, Malky takes my money. He counts out all the coins. I wince as he plucks some fur from one coin and chewing gum from another.

'And another thing,' says Mr Cochrane to Malky as I leave. 'Why are half bottles of alcohol in your shop not exactly half the price of a full bottle?'

I walk back to the flat as quickly as I can. I have already broken the seal on the bottle's cap by the time I enter. I land on the sofa, crash a large gin into my glass, let it sniff the tonic, and swallow.

'That's better,' I say as the gin slides down my throat.

I stand up once the first drink is gone, and wander over to the window to look down on the street. Mr Goleniewski is standing under the lamppost that sits at the corner of my road. He's looking up at my flat. When he sees me, he makes no attempt to hide. Emboldened by the fresh influx of booze I storm from the house, glass in hand, and march across the road.

'What are you doing here?' I ask, as I walk up to him, my face inches from his.

'We all have to be somewhere, Catherine.'

'Well, you don't have to be here.'

'That is true. I don't *have* to be here. But I choose to be here.'

'Where is my Mum?'

'Is she not in your flat?'

'Is that why you are here? Did you know she was coming home? Well, you're out of luck! She's not here.'

'That is sad news indeed.'

'So, you can leave.'

'I will leave when I am ready.'

He is oozing a quiet confidence that rankles me, as if I needed much reason to be irritated by him in the first place.

'Maybe your mother will arrive later.' he says.

'It's none of your business.'

'Maybe she got delayed.'

'I'm not talking about this anymore.' I turn away.

'Catherine, you are drinking too much!'

That stops me and I spin around, 'How would you know? What is it to you?'

'You prefer a life with a bottle to one without. That never ends well.'

'Keep your observations to yourself!'

'I am worried about you.'

'Is that so?'

'It is why I am here. I blame myself for this. I have been negligent. I should have been around before now.'

'What are you talking about?'

'The way your mother behaved when you were a child has told you that it is okay to drink so much.'

'I can't do this.'

'Do what?'

I swing away spilling some drink, as I try for a diva exit.

Back in the flat I refill on gin, and stand in the living room, Mum on my mind. I wander to the spare room. I'd humped a lot of mum's stuff in here when I moved. The wardrobe is full of her clothes. Three suitcases lie under the bed and, in one corner, a stack of boxes full of assorted knick-knacks are threatening to fall over. I'd tried to sort the good from the bad when I'd moved but, in the end, had taken the easy route and binned all but Mum's clothes, the suitcases from her wardrobe and the stuff in and about her dressing table. I sit on the bed, my heels kicking one of the suitcases under the bed. I've never opened any of them. Couldn't bring myself to. Just pushed them out of sight when I moved in. I reach down, pull the handle of the case I'm kicking, and drag it out. I stop for another mouthful of gin before dropping to the floor. I undo the case's latches.

Clothes.

Mostly mine from when I was wee. I root around, find nothing worthwhile, and close the case. I fumble for another case, an old brown leather affair. I have to push my head under the bed to get to it. I've no idea what I'm looking for. I'm just looking. The case takes some extracting, but it comes free. I open it.

More of my kid's clothes.

I reach for the last case. I need to wriggle under the bed to grab it. I haul it out and know it will be locked. It's a sturdy black vinyl affair. Mum used to keep all the important documents in it but cleared them out long back. It's light. I'd tried to open it before I moved but couldn't find a key.

I lift it onto the bed and stare at it. I try the latches. Locked. I rise, staggering a little and fetch a carving knife from the kitchen. Conscious my hands are not the steadiest, I place the tip of the knife under the latch and press. The latch flies open with ease. I repeat on the other side. I lift the lid. Inside is a metal box, the size of small cash box. I extract it. It too is locked. I stick the carving knife into the lock and twist. The knife snaps off at the tip and I swear. I have a screwdriver and a hammer in the kitchen, my only tools of note.

I fetch them. Placing the screwdriver against the box's lock, I swing the hammer hard. The box flies across the bed, the lid bursting open. A small clutch of papers breaks free. They land on the floor as the box crashes into the wall.

I crawl around for the papers, swigging the last of my gin. I contemplate a refill before examining the contents. I decide against that, for the moment. I lift the papers up and spread them on the bed. The box now lies empty at my feet.

There are only four sheets, all of a similar style and layout. Each is A4 in size, faded yellow, and all are typed on – the type-face a throw-back to an earlier time when typewriters ruled the office world. All carry dates, and I quickly shuffle them into order. They are official documents of some kind. Redacted in parts and, once I've read through them, I go back and read them again, gin a forgotten thing for the moment. I'm careful with each sheet, they are worn at the edges, old and look like photocopies, or maybe pre-photocopier. What did Mum call it, Gestetener?

The first three papers are dated 1961. The fourth is from 1964.

AB: 2361/(A) - LAVINIA (SNIPER)
January 4th 1961, Location ███████████

Subject: LAVINIA IN TRANSIT

LANGLEY request we release LAVINIA with immediate effect, but LAVINIA may know the ID of USSR mole(s).

Suspected of being a UK resident(s).

We are aware that the US reception committee in LANGLEY are at odds over the debriefing process and have rejected our involvement.

Recommendation: hold LAVINIA in the UK for limited time period.

We <u>NEED</u> to know ID of mole(s).

Signed

███████████████████████

AB: 2361/(E) - LAVINIA (SNIPER)
January 5th 1961, Location ██████████

Subject: LAVINIA BEING HELD

LANGLEY are threatening to sever all links unless we hand over LAVINIA. LAVINIA knows that only LANGLEY can give him what he really wants. We cannot ignore LANGLEY much longer, but we need the name of the mole(s). PM has ruled out any strong-arm tactics. He believes we will get the name(s) once LANGLEY gets to work. I don't hold with the PM's faith that LANGLEY will hand over this information. At least not easily or quickly. I wouldn't. We are banking on DAYLIGHT. She has been told to concentrate on nothing but the ID of the mole(s). LANGLEY can have LAVINIA once we have that. It's our best bet.

Recommendation: hold in UK for as long as we can.

We NEED to know ID of the mole(s).

Signed

██████████████████████

AB: 2361/(G) - LAVINIA (SNIPER)
January 8th 1961, Update

Subject: LAVINIA RELEASED

LANGLEY now have LAVINIA. We have ID'd GEE, KROGERS, HOUGHTON and LONSDALE. All arrested yesterday but DAYLIGHT thinks there is one more. So says LAVINIA. The missing mole is not at the Admiralty Underwater Weapons Establishment. They may be in WHITEHALL. Imperative we ID them. We do not know the identity of the new mole. The PM is no longer convinced that LANGLEY will help us. He has just heard that they are planning to overthrow CASTRO and is of the opinion that this will trump any requests for intel from us for a while. Equally we cannot let LANGLEY know we have another mole. They already think we leak like sieve.

It may be worth sending DAYLIGHT to Washington as she seems to have earned LAVINIA's trust, but we cannot let LANGLEY know.

Signed

AB: 2361/(Y) - LAVINIA (SNIPER)
September 8th 1964, Update

Subject: LAVINIA (Addendum)

As we know LAVINIA never revealed the 'other' mole, but we suspect that he was referring to Blunt. Blunt confessed to MI5 on 23 April of this year. Langley are still wary of us. Reference their red flag status on UK intel. We also know that DAYLIGHT visited LAVINIA in Queen's, NYC a month ago. Note LAVINIA is now calling himself Tsarevich Alexei. The claims he makes with reference to his new name are discredited but LANGLEY are still watching him. We did not authorise DAYLIGHT's visit. A debrief has since been undertaken with DAYLIGHT and no new intel noted. LANGLEY are upset at DAYLIGHT'S actions and have asked we keep an eye on DAYLIGHT. They have given no reasons for this other than a cryptic reference to an interest in LAVINIA and DAYLIGHT by WARSAW. We know WARSAW have been watching LAVINIA. Our NYC contact informs us that WARSAW's local station has an ongoing 'watch and report' on LAVINIA. For this reason alone, we will monitor DAYLIGHT - who is leaving the service with immediate effect.

Additional Note:

We have had direct communication from WARSAW. It is connected to LAVINIA's new claims, not his role as LAVINIA. LANGLEY are unhappy that we have been contacted but that indicates that WARSAW think there may be something to LAVINIA's claims.

Signed

█████████████████████████

The last paper has something attached to the rear. I turn the paper over. A faded photograph has been taped to it. The setting is unmistakable. A black and white background as iconic as any. New York; Empire State Building and Chrysler framing midtown Manhattan—the edge of the United Nations building just visible on the right. There are two people stage centre. Either side of them a river flows. One of the subjects has me transfixed. The other, dressed in a fedora, a four-button, nip-waisted suit and spats, is a man sporting a familiar style of beard. On the left, holding hands with the bearded man is a woman. She's wearing a bright white Marilyn Monroe dress, blowing out in the breeze, a small pillbox hat on her head; her hands are wrapped in forearm-length white gloves. Her smile is dazzling. His grin infectious. A happy photograph.

And none of that really matters. Not the clothes, the stunning cityscape, the smiles, the glistening river. The only thing that matters is the identity of the woman.

My mother.

Younger.

Much younger.

But my mother.

In Manhattan.

In the sixties. At a guess.

My mum.

I stare at the photo.

Mum.

Mum looks heavy on makeup but good with it. There are no photos of Mum when she was younger. At least none that I know about, but this can't be anyone else.

The man next to her is a stranger, but a stranger with a touch of familiarity about his face. A ghost of Mr Goleniewski in the forehead and eyes. The beard sculpted into the same squared off shape, moustache trimmed to match the angular cut.

I stare at the photo and then read the papers again. To the photo and the papers, but always drawn back to the photo.

To Mum.

To a Mum that had never mentioned being in New York, ever. To a man that has the same pronounced forehead as Mr Goleniewski.

What in the hell?

I leave the room to fetch the last of the gin, necking it as I read the papers once more. The words make little sense to me. What is the connection with the photo? My head is spinning a little and I feel tired. I decide to leave the papers and photo 'till later. Morning will do to work out what this all means. I wish I had more gin, but there is none left.

I enter the living room, fire up the electric fire and push the sofa a bit closer to it to catch the warmth. I lie down, the photo in my mind. I yank up the blanket I keep on the sofa for snuggling in.

I doze.

18
SMOKE GETS IN YOUR EYES

I WAKE UP, coughing and confused. The world is cloudy. I rub my eyes. They sting. I cough again. An acrid taste in my mouth. The fog doesn't clear, and my eyes are watering. An electric shock races up my toes as I stretch out. I scream. I yank my foot back and that's when I see the flames

I've just stuck my foot into them.

I leap up, my head spinning from the booze. Instantly wanting to vomit. I sway and realise that the far side of my sofa is alight. A burning cushion rests against the bars of the fire. I must have kicked it off as I slept. The flames have leapt from it to the sofa. My blanket is alight. I stagger back. The smoke is so thick that my coughing is constant.

On the floor!

The fire advice from school kicks in. I drop to the ground where the smoke is a little thinner. I crawl away from the flames towards the front door. For a moment I think about filling the bucket in the kitchen with water to tackle the blaze.

For a moment.

A short moment.

I keep crawling, my eyes streaming, my lungs burning from lack of air. I reach up and open the front door, tumbling onto the landing. I lie for a second as the cool air outside slides down my throat as sweetly as the first G&T of the day.

'Catherine?'

The voice comes from below. It's Mr Goleniewski.

'Fire!' I croak. 'My flat is on fire!'

He climbs up and pulls at me.

'We need to get out,' he says. 'Can you stand?'

'Papers, photo,' I gasp.

'We need to move, Catherine.'

I cough and try to rise, but the smoke and booze have turned my legs to rubber. Mr Goleniewski grabs me under the oxters and drags me down, my backside thumping each step as we descend. When we reach the ground floor, he drops me to the stone floor before battering on one of the two doors that flank the close's entrance. I think the owner is called Mrs Hutchinson, but I'm not sure. He gets no reply and tries the other door. I can't even guess the name of that owner.

Mrs Hutchinson opens her door.

'There's a fire,' Mr Goleniewski says. 'In Catherine's flat.' He points to me. 'Call the fire brigade quickly, then get out!'

'A fire?' she says.

'Please call the fire brigade, now!' he snaps.

Smoke drifts down and she yelps before vanishing.

Mr Goleniewski tries to haul me to my feet. Fails. Makes do with half-dragging me out of the close and onto the pavement. He dumps me to run back in.

I lie on the cold concrete, looking up. With the curtains to my flat open I can see the flicker of red against the cloud grey that blankets my windows. I struggle to stand as people begin to emerge from my building. Every one of them looks up at my flat, then at me as they exit. I step back onto the road. There's a crack as my window explodes. Glass showers down on the pavement. People scream as flames flick from the broken window. More people exit the close, now running. There are four floors in my block, eleven homes. I don't know any of my neighbours well enough to do much more than nod at some as they pass. They all seem to know me. Eyes jumping from me to the flames and back.

'Where's the fire brigade?' one says.

'I need to go back. My stuff…'

'You can't. It's too dangerous…'

'I had to grab my baby when the man came to the door…'

'I thought he was a nutter…'

'God, look at the flames…'

'The whole place could go up…'

'It's her flat…'

'No doubt drunk again…'

'Always drunk…'

'This was just waiting to happen…'

'Where are the fire brigade…?'

'God, look at the flames…'

I move away from the crowd that's now standing on the far side of the road, looking up. Every so often, a head turns in my direction. The wail of a distant siren forces their gaze from the conflagration towards the end of the street. As the first fire engine grinds to a halt, hurling firemen onto the street, Mr Goleniewski sprints from the close, a woman in tow, and a young child in his arms. He runs up to the first fireman.

'I've checked all the flats bar the top left!' he shouts 'They aren't in or don't answer.'

'Thanks, sir, we'll take it from here.'

Mr Goleniewski hands the kid to the woman and spots me. As a second fire engine roars in, he walks over. I look back at my flat. The fire is raging hard, flames licking the lintel above the window, the sound of cracking and popping like machine gun fire on a battlefield. The firemen rush into the close, one dragging a hose, while the new engine uncurls its ladder, swinging it towards my window.

'What happened, Catherine?' Mr Goleniewski asks.

I can't speak.

I really can't speak.

A crowd from other tenements is gathering. Rubber-neckers.

The next hour and a half pass with a brief examination of me by the ambulance crew that have arrived, a talk with a policeman, a talk with one of the firemen as, with some small relief, I watch the fire brought under control without spreading to the other flats.

All the while I can hear my neighbours and the rubber-neckers talking.

'That'll stink...'

'She should pay to clean up the mess...!'

'Can we claim her insurance...?'

'Did it reach our flat...?'

'Will she be charged...?'

'She *should* be charged...!'

'Should be in an institution...!'

'Who's the man with her...?'

'She'll not be staying here for a while...'

'Can't even look at us...'

I stand up to find the fireman that I talked to. He's directing the clean up as they prepare to leave.

'Is it safe to go in?' I ask.

'It's a mess. The fire investigation officer is in. When he's finished you can go in, if he says it's okay.'

'Did the fire reach all my rooms?'

'No. You were lucky that we got here so quick. The big bedroom will smell although the fire didn't reach it—but your living room, the smaller bedroom and most of your kitchen are gonners. We got it before it could spread to the other flats, but it's still a mess.'

'What happens now?'

'You need to contact your insurance company and take it from there. We'll provide a report, but it won't look good.'

'Why? Will I be charged?'

'I doubt it. Looks like an accident to me. A bit stupid to have the sofa so near the electric fire. It was a blaze waiting to start. You'll also have a problem with your neighbours directly below you.'

'Why? I thought you said the fire didn't spread.'

'It didn't but they'll have no end of water in their flat from the hoses, probably the ground floor flat as well.'

I rub at my forehead. A headache is building. I could do with a drink.

Mr Goleniewski comes over.

'You cannot stay here,' he says to me.

'I need to contact the insurance company.'

'Are you insured?'

'I think so.'

'That is good. We can call from my house.'

'My neighbours below will have damage. I should apologise.'

'The state you are in, I would leave that until later.'

'I want to see the damage in my flat.'

'Okay, I will ask how long that might take - but then we go.'

Once the firemen have wrapped up, my neighbours begin to file in. After an age the accident officer gives the all-clear. Mr Goleniewski escorts me into the building. As I pass the ground floor flat that lies beneath mine, I hear swearing. On the next floor up the swearing is a lot fiercer. Mr Goleniewski leads the way, and we reach my door, which is wide open. The hall carpet is saturated. The smell of burnt material makes me gag. The door to the living room hangs from its hinges, and beyond is a scene from a post-apocalyptic movie. The walls and ceiling are black. My sofa is a melted hulk wrapped around the TV. Probably thrown there by the firemen as they tackled the blaze. In one corner, the remains of the electric fire and what might have been my coffee table are making love. The small sideboard that supported my CD player is now under the window. I back out and check the bedrooms. Mine is okay but the fireman was right—the smell is a killer. The spare room is a dark, burnt shell. The papers and the photo are gone, the bed they sat on little more than a brown lump melting into the floor. The kitchen is a disaster area, but it looks like the firemen caught the conflagration before it could take full hold of the wall cupboards. I pull open a cupboard door. A small stack of plates slides out and crashes to the floor.

'Leave it!' says Mr Goleniewski. 'We should secure the place and make that call to your insurance company. Do you have your policy and maybe a change of clothes?'

I return to my bedroom and pack what I think I need, not even sure why I'm agreeing to go with a man who has done nothing but haunt me for years. But where else would I go? Jenny's? Is she even talking to me after last night?

Fortunately, I keep all my home documentation under my bed. As I close the front door, surprised that it locks, I'm led downstairs by Mr Goleniewski.

'My car is around the corner,' he says.

We leave as the last of the fire engines finishes packing up. We walk to Mr Goleniewski's vehicle. He drives a battered black BMW that has more dinks and dents than a dodgem car. The interior smells of fish and, as I sit down, I wonder again at the prudency of this action. I don't know even Mr Goleniewski's first name. He starts the car and U-turns.

My head is hangover central, I could kill for a gin. As we cruise through the city, in silence, I lie my head against the side window. I'm wondering if I can ask for a quick stop at the off licence. Except I have no money. A little later we pull up at another tenement block. I know where we are, not that far from my old home, but hopefully far enough away that no-one I used to know should be hanging around.

As we exit the car I think on the papers and the photo.

Gone.

What did they mean?

I try to remember the typed words but my head is full of fuzz.

Mr Goleniewski guides me to a close. We climb two flights of stairs to enter another world. An older world. One of candles and gold framed mirrors. The hall wall is dark, the ceiling darker and the carpet black. The sole light above does little to illuminate safe passage. We enter the living room, and the dark theme continues. A large, chocolate leather suite, spiderwebbed by cracks, dominates the room. There's no TV that I can see. A monumental oak sideboard is loaded up with framed photos centred around a three-prong candelabra. The candles are stubs on their last legs. Floor length, velvet plum curtains are closed tight across the main window. Above the ornate wooden fireplace sits a colossal painting. A panorama of the Kremlin in oil. Dark brown at the edges. Maybe the victim of years of tobacco smoke, but not from here. The tell-tale stench of a smoker's home is missing. Mr Goleniewski bends down to straighten a circular rug emblazoned with a faded roundel of a golden, double-headed eagle on a claret background. He points to the sofa.

'Sit down, I will make some tea.'

I'm left to my own devices. Maybe he has a drinks cabinet? When he returns, I'm on my feet examining the cupboards that lie within the sideboard. I quickly stand up and pretend I'm studying the forest of photos.

'I have no alcohol in the house, Catherine. I prefer my club for that sort of thing.'

I stand up. 'I wasn't looking for booze. I was looking at the photos.'

Most are sepia tone portraits; people dressed in their fine and best from an era long ago.

'Take your tea! Then I'd suggest you might want a little nap.'

'A nap?'

'You look tired.'

I am, but a wee glass of something would sort that out.

'Look Mr Goleniewski, I appreciate the help, but I'm not a kid.'

'I never said you were. I was simply making an observation. If you don't want to put your head down, then you might want to call your insurance company and inform them of what has happened. The phone is in the hallway.'

I sip at the tea. Strong and sweet. Just the way I like it. How did he know? Or is builder's tea his go-to drink.

'Mr Goleniewski...' I start.

'Later, Catherine. Later with the questions. Finish your tea, call the insurance company and then a little sleep. I have some things that need to be done. After that we can talk.'

'About Mum.'

'Later.'

He drains his teacup and stands. 'I am going now. You can use the spare bedroom. It is the one on the left. The bathroom is next door. Please do not go into my bedroom!'

With this, he leaves me to my tea.

The call to the insurance company is an epic. I have to pause it after ten minutes to hunt down some paper and a pen to take notes of what is required. The agent on the other end of the line witters on about the need for me to fill in claim forms, allow insurance assessors access to my flat, obtain fire reports and police reports, take photographs (where possible), and list damaged goods. When I ask about payment, I'm blanked. That will come once my claim is processed. How long will that take? A few weeks, if all is okay. When I ask about cleaning the flat, I'm told the it would be better to wait until the assessor has been.

After near on an hour on the phone, I'm thinking that Mr Goleniewski's idea about a nap is looking good. I enter the spare bedroom. It's no lighter or cheerier than the rest of the flat. I'm about to plank myself on the bed when I give a little thought to the last thing that Mr Goleniewski said.

Please do not go into my bedroom!

A not unreasonable request. But I need to know more about the man. I make for his bedroom, stand at the door, resting my hand on the handle, looking towards the front door before I turn the brass knob. As the door cracks open, the first thing that hits me is a strong scent: Parma Violets, a sweet from my days when the general store was a must-stop on the way back from school. I push the door. More darkness. This time so dark that the little light that comes from the hall doesn't penetrate more than a foot or so. I fumble around on the bedroom wall and locate the light switch. I throw it. A dark red ceiling shade lights up. I could still do with a torch. The twins of the curtains in the living room prevent any outside light disturbing the scene. The room has three pieces of furniture. A double bed from Bedknobs and Broomsticks, a wardrobe from The Lion, the Witch and the Wardrobe, and a blood red Chesterfield armchair from any movie set in the Victorian era. The carpet has even thicker pile than the one in the living room. You could lose a herd of kids in it. Except none of this really registers until later. Much later.

I've stopped, frozen still, halfway into the room, my eyes fixed on a picture that hangs above the bed.

I've seen this picture before. Recently. Very recently. It's a giant version of the photo from the lock box that was in mum's suitcase. The one lost in the fire.

If you want to define creepy, try discovering a three-foot by three-foot photo of your mother above a stranger's bed. Pride of place. No other pictures in the room to detract. To add to the creep factor a mirror is placed on the opposite wall. It's not flush, the top hanging away from the wall, supported by a cord. When I look into it, I can only see my feet. I sit on the bed, adding another notch to the creep factor. The bed is marshmallow soft. I stare at the photo and then look over at the mirror. I know what I'll see in it if I put my head on the pillow.

More creep.

I shuffle along the bed and swing my feet up. I lay my head down and there, on the opposite wall, is Mum smiling back at me. Strategically placed, the mirror provides the perfect reflection of her. When Mr Goleniewski lies here, he is looking through a time window. Every night and every morning of his life the last thing and the first thing he sees is my mother next to a man with a vague, but obvious connection to Mr Goleniewski.

On the pillow the smell of Parma Violets is even stronger. Mum introduced me to them when I was wee. She always had a packet in her handbag. Mystique and Parma Violets are the smells of my mother.

I stare at the picture. So young. So happy. So, what is she doing on Mr Goleniewski's wall? I lose myself in the picture.

Hunting for answers.

Bang.

I hear the front door. My eyes snap open. I'd fallen asleep. I try to get up, but I'm not quick enough. The bedroom door opens and in walks Mr Goleniewski. I'm halfway to upright.

'What are you doing?' he says.

I swing my feet off the bed. 'I could ask you the same thing.'

'Is this how you repay my hospitality? I specifically told you not to come into this room. And here I find you lying on my bed.'

'To discover that you have a picture of my mother on your wall with some creepy guy.'

'It is not what it looks like.'

'What does it look like?'

I get off the bed. We are in awkward land. Me in an old man's bedroom, him blocking the door.

'Why the hell have you got a photo of my mother on your wall? What is that photo?'

'Did I not tell you that I would talk to you when I got back?'

'You told me to take a nap.'

'Not in my bed.'

'This is way too weird,' I say, pushing past him.

I return to the living room. He follows me in.

'So, tell me about it!' I say.

'I do not know if I want to. You are clearly in a bad way, Catherine Day. You drink too much; you have set your own house on fire and now you disobey me.'

His clipped method of speaking combined with his accent just serves to, unjustifiably, rile me.

'Give it a rest!' I spit. 'You talk as if you're my dad. I only came here because…'

'Because you have nowhere else to go, is that not right?'

'I have plenty of places I could go.'

'Name one!'

'I don't need to.'

'You don't *want* to, you mean. Because you have no other place to go.'

I open my mouth and he shuts me down, 'Oh, I'm sure you can tell me that your friend Jenny would have taken you in. Maybe Mrs Hamilton from the hairdressers? What about Davie McTierney? Or what about none of them?'

'How do you know who I know? Why are you stalking me? Some sort of bloody voyeur on the prowl? Is that what all this has been about over the years? Are you obsessed with my mum and, because she's not here, are you perving out on me?'

'Do not insult me, Catherine! I have been watching you for all these years for good reason. But you always do your best to undermine my efforts. You are, in my humble opinion, and do not take this the wrong way, pissing your life away – I think that's the right phrase.'

'How dare you? Who are you to talk to me like that?'

He turns away, looking at me side on, eyeing me up, 'Me, Catherine? I am no one. No one at all, but I'll tell you this for the price of a cup of tea, you have potential to be much more than you are. Yet you've found every way possible to bury that potential under barren soil in the last few years. Trust me, nothing will grow from that.'

'You have no idea what is going on in my life. None. So don't stand there and lecture me!'

'Where do you want me to stand? On the chair? On the dining table?. On the window sill?. What if I stand naked on the number five bus while singing the Hallelujah chorus and reciting the list of mistakes you have made? Or,' he continues. 'I can stand here and tell you a few home truths.'

'I don't need this.'

'You are wrong, Catherine. You *do* need this. You needed this a while ago, but I was remiss. You need to stop feeling sorry for yourself and, as our American cousins would say, step up to the plate.'

'You try walking in my shoes, smartarse!'

'What? Shoes that are young, pretty, talented, with the world to be grabbed. I'll take those shoes any day you feel you can give them to me.'

He's getting under my skin. Right under. 'You are clueless about my life.'

'Why? Because the baby's mother rejected her?'

'How dare you?'

'Is it not true? Is that not what you think?'

'Well, you'd know all about my mum. Do you play with yourself when you look in that mirror? Imagining her naked? Eh. Is that it?'

'You really are a decomposing woman.'

'A what?'

He crosses to the curtains and runs his finger along the material. 'See this?' he says, holding the material. 'Made in my hometown by people with real craft and care. In a market where cheap is the norm, they sell this material at twenty pounds per yard. That takes attention to quality. An eye for what people want, and a desire not to sell out. Not to take the easy path.'

He lets the curtain go and picks up a photo from the sideboard. It's a picture of an elderly man wearing a full frock coat. He's crowned with a top hat. Standing erect, body at an angle to the camera, head straight on, he's sporting a similar beard to Mr Goleniewski.

'This,' he says, 'is Bartlomiej Goleniewski. He lost both his parents when he was six years old. A bus crashed off a cliff. He was the only survivor, spent the next ten years in institutions whose conditions beggared belief. He was thrown out on the street on his sixteenth birthday without shoes on his feet. Can you imagine? Poland, in the middle of winter, and he was left staring at the closed doors of his last institution, wearing a cotton shirt, canvass trousers and little else. He could have laid down there and died. He could have joined the men down at the River Oder, huddled around a fire drinking Spirytus Rektyfikowany. But he did not. He chose another path. He begged for work, and a cobbler took pity on him. He worked for years for nothing more than a bed, some bread and a pair of shoes but the man for whom he worked taught him everything. It took Bartlomiej a long time to learn. Even in his late thirties, Bartlomiej was still an apprentice, earning fewer zlotys than a man of his age required. But do you know what Bartlomiej became?'

I ignore the question. I'm seething at the way this is going.

'He became the cobbler to Maria Augusta Nepomucena Antonia Francisca Xaveria Aloysia. The rightful heir to the throne of Poland. This photo was taken much later in life, by which time he had built a shoe empire that still stands to this day. And,' he adds, 'he did not use the absence of his parents as an excuse to waste his life. Every one of the people in these pictures made something of themselves.'

I shake my head, 'So what?'

'So what? So what? You have potential. You have much to give. Yet you drown it in a bottle.'

'I do not.'

'Denial is a common thing in one that drinks too much.'

'I do not drink too much.'

'A bottle of gin a day is too much.'

'I don't drink that much.'

'You buy a bottle a day from the corner shop.'

'That's rubbish.'

'It is easily proved. Ask the owner of the corner store you frequent.'

'I don't need to. This whole conversation is a pile of crap! You are just some weird creepy man who is keeping me from seeing my mother because… because you want her for yourself.'

He laughs. A tinkling yet guttural sound that comes from deep in his stomach.

'If that were true then how, may I ask, have I kept her from seeing you?'

'Maybe you have kept her prisoner.'

As I say the words, I realise how dumb they are and, at the same time, how scared I would be if they were true.

'In this flat, Catherine? For all these years?'

'Just tell me where she is! Just tell me!'

I've never wanted something so bad. It gnaws at my core. Sours my soul.

'And that will solve everything, Catherine?'

He plays with the curtain again.

'Is that what you believe, Catherine? That the return of your mother will somehow set you free? Stop you wasting your life?'

'Just tell me!'

'You have the power to change your world, but you use your mother as an excuse to do nothing.'

'Just tell me!'

'Ask yourself this, Catherine Day. Ask yourself: are you seeking your mother because you want to see her, or because you want out of the prison you have created for yourself? A prison whose only bars are in your head. What if your mother is never coming back?'

I shudder at the thought. 'Mum will be back.'

'When? How hard has it been to come back to you over the years?'

'Obviously, for some reason, she couldn't come back.'

'Or she didn't want to.'

'She said she was coming back yesterday.'

He throws his hands out wide, 'And where is she?'

'You know where she is. You bloody know!'

'Believe it or not, Catherine, but I do not know.'

'Then why the creepy picture? Why follow me? What the are you up to?'

This is like the thickest brick wall ever. I could bounce a wrecking ball off this and not make a dent. I want to lash out. I slam my foot down and scream. A loud, deep wail that comes from far inside my heart. 'Just *fucking* tell me where she is!'

'Do you want a mug of coffee?'

At that moment I can understand why some people are driven to murder. Why violence rises and explodes in situations like this. No pre-meditation. Simple frustration the driving force. A primordial reaction to a situation that you cannot deal with. A way to remove pain and exert control. The red mist. I leap forward with no other intention than to inflict pain on the thing that is inflicting pain on me. Mr Goleniewski catches me by the arm and, with no small skill, takes my forward momentum, using it to catapult me back into the centre of the room. He does it with such gentility that I wonder, for a second, if someone flipped the room around me.

'Catherine, sit down!'

His action has not only spun my body but spun my head. My anger turns to confusion. I was really going to try and hurt him. I mean deep down and dirty hurt him.

'Look at yourself!' he says. 'Just take a look at yourself!'

I stand like a lost sheep in a strange field with strange thoughts.

'You need to move on, Catherine Day.'

'Mum.'

'Just stop that and stop it now. I do not know where she is and, even if I did, it is not my place to tell you. I am, and always have been, trying to help you. But you need to help yourself now. Take your finger off the pause button! Put away the gin bottle, quit the job at the hairdressers, get out of this backwater alley and get onto the main road!'

I sit down. On the carpet. Crossing my legs. I put my head in my hands.

'You have a special place in people's lives, Catherine and you don't know it,' he whispers. 'You have a *responsibility* to act differently to this.'

'What are you talking about?'

'You are heading for an early grave.'

All I want to do is ask him where Mum is again and, as Mr Goleniewski leaves the room, I giggle. A stupid sound that arises as I remember the story of the spider and Robert the Bruce, King of Scotland. Six times he had led his men into battle against the English. Six times he had been beaten. Lying in a cave he watched a spider try to throw her thread to the far wall and six times she failed.

'Poor thing!' Robert the Bruce was supposed to have said. 'You, too, know what it's like to fail six times in a row.'

On the seventh time of asking the spider succeeded and Robert cried, 'Yes. I too will try a seventh time.'

That's what I need. The inspiration to ask Mr Goleniewski about my mum, one more time. Only this time he will answer.

When he comes back into the room, two coffee mugs in his hands, I stand up, 'Look where is my mother? I...'

'Catherine, how would you like me to become your band manager?

19

THE EVENING SESSION STAGE

Sunday, 13th July, 1997.

'OH MY GOD, Daisy!' I exclaim, a squeal accompanying the words. 'T in the Park. We are about to play T in the Park!'

'It's only the Evening Session stage, Catherine, and we are first on. It's barely lunchtime.'

'There are a few people out there,' says Jenny looking at the crowd through the pile of equipment that litters the area.

'But Radio 1 are recording this,' I say. 'Bloody recording it!'

The three of us are standing just off stage in a tent in the middle of field. Admittedly there are a lot of other people standing in the same field, and admittedly there are other tents. And stages, and food wagons, and drink stations, and booze stations and, well just and... We are the first up on the Radio 1 Evening Session stage on the second day of T in the Park—a massive Scottish music festival that moved this year to Balado; halfway between Dunfermline and Stirling in the heart of Scotland. Spread It Thin, now renamed The Chug, consists of Daisy, Jenny and me. I'm still on vocals, although I now have a keyboard in front of me for the few notes I know. Jenny is on drums, Daisy on guitar and keyboards. Mr Goleniewski, our manager, stands next to us. Our instruments are set up on the stage. We are under strict instructions as to when we have to go on, and when we have to be off stage.

We have put out a few singles in the last two years but our last one, 'Check That Back' has gained some traction on local radio. Enough to warrant an appearance at Scotland's largest music festival.

I'm nervous. Not because of the crowd. We've had larger, but the scale of the festival that surrounds us is mind blowing. I'd looked back at the line-ups for previous T in the Parks and it's scary how many big bands started out, like we are, low on the bill on a smaller stage.

'Are you ready?' asks the stage manager.

We all nod.

Mr Goleniewski gathers us all around, 'And what do we say at this point?'

This makes us all smile. We stretch up our arms, bashing our hands together in the air, making a crooked pyramid.

'Chug, Chug, Chug,' we all shout. 'Let's Chug!'

We spring away from each other, pumped up and ready.

Then we are on stage.

THEN WE ARE off stage.

The gig flew by and there is no time for congratulations as we need to get our stuff clear. Our sole roadie and sound tech, Daisy's brother, Umar, helps us clear everything as the next band sets up. I wish them luck, before we make our way to the front of the tent, a few T-shirts in hand. We sell them all to the waiting few, and I wish we had brought more. Once we've packed our stuff away we head for the back-stage area.

'Who is driving tonight?' I ask.

'It will be my pleasure,' says Mr Goleniewski.

Mr Goleniewski rarely drives. Umar smiles; unlike his sister he is fond of a glass or two of beer, and, as designated driver, he has just been given a free pass.

'I'll see you all later,' he says and sprints away.

'Where is Umar going?' I ask.

'Off to see his new friends,' says Daisy.

'Again?'

'They've asked him to be their sound tech.'

Umar had met up with a guy called Terry a few months back. Terry fronts a post rock band called Diligent Twice. A seven-piece group that were gifted state of the art equipment by Terry's dad, a rumoured multi-millionaire. They are to support The Lang Ones on a European tour. Umar thinks that touring the continent is the dog's bollocks.

'Did he say yes to the tour?' I ask.

'What do you think?' replies Daisy.

'Well, we'll need someone else.'

Jenny chips in, 'Forget Umar for the moment. We just played T in the Park.'

The four of us enter the hospitality area, flashing our wristbands at security. We approach the bar, a few blagged beer tokens in hand.

'Well, Catherine, what is your poison?' asks Mr Goleniewski.

I scan the bar, reaching deep inside for the resolve that I need. 'A diet Coke, please.'

He smiles.

Jenny orders a glass of red wine, Daisy a water, and Mr Goleniewski declines anything. We exit the beer tent, looking for a spot on the grass outside to sit. With the sun beating down, the hospitality area is buzzing. Space is at premium, but we find a slice of free lawn near some portacabins. A small white fence surrounds the temporary structures, and a smattering of people with multiple passes dangling from their necks lounge around on garden chairs, some sipping booze.

'Well, glasses up!' says Mr Goleniewski, and we all raise our drinks. 'To us!'

'To The Chug!' says Daisy. 'A small crowd, but virtually no one left and quite a few came into the tent while we played.'

'I'd guess we had over a hundred by the end. Given it's lunchtime, we were first on, and most of our audience would have been on the juice last night, I'd say we didn't do too badly.'

'Well,' Mr Goleniewski chips in. 'I have a surprise for you all. Please wait here, it may take me a little while to find who I need to. So please do not move an inch.'

We all look at each other wondering the same thing. What's the surprise?

When Mr Goleniewski had offered to manage the band that day in his flat, I'd thought it so ridiculous that I'd laughed at him. With no money and no place to sleep, Mr Goleniewski had also offered to put me up. Only he banned drink.

Three days later, when he told me that Daisy and Jenny might be up for a more serious attempt at making the band work, I was going through withdrawal hell. I had been caught by Malky trying to steal a bottle of gin the night before, Mr Goleniewski had convinced Malky to let it lie. But it was my fifth attempt to obtain booze in less than twenty-four hours. I'd targeted four different stores plus Malky's twice. In each case I'd been caught. Mr Goleniewski persuaded each shop owner not to call the police. Mr Goleniewski then took to watching me like a hawk, confining me to the bedroom, calling Maggie Hamilton to tell her I was ill.

I wasn't ready to quit booze. I hadn't accepted I had a problem. I hadn't hit rock bottom. Yet, against the odds, the cold turkey treatment worked. After a fashion. There have been a few falls from the wagon since, but the angel's patience that Mr Goleniewski has showered on me has seen me through. While I cried for a drink and soiled myself, he sorted my burnt-out flat, taking care of the insurance company, and taking care of the nightmare of getting it back into fit shape. He also dealt with the irate neighbours, the workers, the whole gambit.

I moved back in three months after the fire. I'd love to say that I stayed sober, behaved myself and became a model citizen. None of that happened. What did happen was that Daisy and I discovered we could write a half-decent tune. That Davie McTierney was never invited to join The Chug. That Jenny *was* invited and learned to play drums. That Daisy and Jenny stuck with me as I struggled with achieving any level of sobriety. That we spent six months working up material. That we debuted in Glasgow to an audience of six, including Mr Goleniewski plus three of Daisy's family. We had six songs in our repertoire that night; three were covers.

The haul to today has been a long and painful one. Personally, and professionally. We are all the wrong side of thirty and people are not slow in telling us we started too late. Youth is the key. So you would think. But that's not true. The keys are talent, drive and sheer luck. The latter being the bucket that needs to be the fullest. We've met plenty of talented people who have got nowhere. We know individuals with the drive of the devil that still feel they are at the bottom of the mountain. And then there are those pain in the arse, fly-by-night, lucky bastards that have minimal ability, sod-all work ethic, and yet are the talk of the steamie. Does the green of my envy show there? Take Walky Rocky—dumb name to start with. A harmonica player and an electric violin aficionado. Less than a year since their first gig, and they've just been signed a two album deal with one of the monster labels. The oldest of the duo is seventeen years and three days old. They are playing the main stage here today.

I spot the lead singer of another band, CrissNotKross, standing on her own.

'Hi Sam!' I shout, standing up.

'Hey Catherine, made it big yet?'

'Tomorrow.'

'Us too.'

We both laugh. Sam went to the same school as me, but a few years below. CrissNotKross are a rock band of old school vintage. A Cream/Stones/Kinks covers band that recently cut their own music. NME have them on their Ones-to-Watchlist. We've been on that list as well. It doesn't count for much.

'Are you playing, Sam? I didn't see your name on the running order.'

'Main stage, headline act. Didn't you know?'

'That's our slot!'

'Sorry, it's already taken.'

'And seriously? Why are you here?'

She drops to the grass, and I join her.

'Our manager tried every trick in the book to get us a gig this weekend, but old school rock isn't *de rigeur* at the moment. Spice Girls. Blur. Oasis. Pulp. The Charlatans. All okay. Fans of long hair hippy sixties rock—not so much.'

'I thought the last single did well.'

'Well enough, but we won't be on Top of the Pops anytime soon. You?'

'Same but one step behind you. So why are you here?'

'Geoffrey Tadcaster.'

'Sorry?'

'You've not heard of him?'

'Nope.'

She swipes at her long, dyed-blonde hair. Sam could cut it as a model. A lot of her band's fan base are teenage guys with fantasy in their eyes.

'Seriously Catherine, you need to get on the train.'

'Okay, enlighten me!'

'Have you heard of super agents?'

'Is that like a comic book thing?'

'No. It's the agents that rep some of the big bands. They have a stable of the high, the mighty and, importantly, the 'yet to be'. They are always on the hunt for the next, next, next thing. Geoffrey is a great white in those waters.'

'Not an A&R man.'

'No, as I said, an agent. No affiliation to any label. Has a gold-plated history when it comes to unearthing talent.'

'And you have a meeting with him?'

This brings out a gale of laughter from her. Some snot flies from her pretty button nose.

'God, no! I wish we did.'

'Is he here?'

'So it is said, but I haven't seen him yet.'

'But if you aren't playing and you're not here to see him, what's your game?'

She turns around. 'See that man there? The one in the black polo neck?'

A man, so skinny he's almost see-through, stands near the entrance to the bar. A gentle breeze and he'd be airborne.

'Yes.'

'That's my cousin, Luke. His band, Lady Lay, just signed with Geoffrey.'

'Don't tell me! He's promised you an intro.'

'It seems our Geoffrey is a big fan of his band's recommendations. He's signed quite a few artists that have been bigged up by his own stable. We're playing the Arches tomorrow night, supporting Lady Lay. Geoffrey will be there. I want to say hello to him before the gig. Do a little glad-handing.'

'Can you intro us?'

'How much is it worth?'

'I've got three quid and a copy of this week's Melody Maker.'

'Sorry but my minimum price is a fiver and six classic copies of Sounds'

'Well, I'm screwed! Now I think on it, I *do* think I've heard of Geoffrey. Is he the guru behind The Band Plays On?'

'That's the very man.'

'Whoa! He's big time.'

The Band Plays On is a music night held in London across a range of changing venues, where no end of bands have been discovered. It's a massive deal just to get on the gig list.

'You were good today,' Sam says.

'You saw us?'

'Wouldn't miss it.'

'Thanks for doubling the crowd.'

'I heard a lot of good words out there. Those four tracks before you did the oldie stuff are killers.'

'They're the new ones. We only wrote them a few weeks back. We weren't even sure we should include them all. It meant dropping a few favourites.'

'Are you cutting them soon?'

'Maybe.'

'You really should.'

'It all comes down to money. Studio time isn't cheap.'

'Faint heart never won fair lover, Catherine.'

'Try telling that to the bank!'

'Look, I need to go. My cousin has the memory of a goldfish, and I've just spotted him wandering to the exit. If I don't catch up, he'll end up in the dance tent, forgetting all about his promise to me.'

She gets up and I rise as well.

'See you later, superstar,' I say.

'Catch you in the spotlight,' she replies.

With this, she skips away, turning more than a few guy's heads and a couple of girl's heads too.

I return to Daisy and Jenny.

'Well, what did Sam have to say for herself?' asks Daisy.

'She says that Geoffrey Tadcaster is in town.'

'Really?' asks Jenny. 'Now that's one dude I wouldn't mind taking us in tow.'

'Where is he?' asks Daisy.

'I've no idea,' I reply. 'I wouldn't know him, if he walked right up to me and said hello.'

'Hello.'

I look up at the owner of the voice.

'Hi. Geoffrey Tadcaster.'

My jaw swings open.

'I saw you play earlier and wondered if you had a minute. Your manager asked me to come see you. He can be a very persuasive man.'

Mr Goleniewski stands behind Geoffrey. Both men are suited and booted. Geoffrey draped in upper-class Saville Row. Mr Goleniewski in middle-class St Michael.

'Could we find somewhere for a quick chat that doesn't require me sitting on the grass?' he says.

I nod, still speechless, but have no idea where to suggest.

'Paul!' he shouts to a man standing in the little fenced off area next to the portacabins.

'Yes.'

'Could we use your office for five minutes?' He points to one of the cabins.

'Sure, Geoffrey. Just let me check there's no one inside.'

Paul pops his head in the cabin and waves us over. Geoffrey leads with Mr Goleniewski behind. The three of us follow—the dwarves behind Snow White—in awe, acting like kids, prodding and shoving each other. Sam is ten yards away, and the look on her face is a dirty mix of surprise and jealousy. She's not the only one watching us. I'd guess most of the turned heads are band members, in one form or another.

We enter the cabin, a spartan affair, stuffed full of cardboard boxes with the T in the Park logo plastered across most of the contents. Geoffrey pushes a few of the bigger boxes to one side to reveal a couple of tables. He perches on one and encourages us to sit on the other. The four of us squeeze on.

It's hot in here, but Geoffrey must have air conditioning fitted to his suit. He looks cool enough to freeze ice poles.

'Okay team,' he says. 'Time is tight. I have a meeting in ten minutes at the main stage. Do you all know who I am?'

We all nod.

'Well, that saves time. I'll be brief. I like a lot of what I saw on stage. I hate the covers crap. Dump that. Love the original stuff. I take it you write them?'

We all nod like idiots.

'Ditch the leather look,' he continues. 'We can work on a better image. I hated your name but now I'm now thinking it's cool. I'd like to take you on, and the way I work is simple. You keep your manager, but he's demoted to looking after the day-to-day. You listen to my advice. You don't have to take my deal—but you'd need a bloody good reason not to. You won't get better. I look to rep you, get your exposure up. You give me twenty-five percent off the bottom line. You sign with me for three years, but I get to break it when I want, and you don't. If that doesn't sound fair, it's because it isn't. But I've not walked away from a band in ten years, and I don't intend to start with you. I love the Glasgow vibe, but I need you in London for six months. I'll find you accommodation, but you'll pay me back for it. My job is to get you a record deal. I get a quarter of the net on that as well. If you need references, I'll let you chat to any of my artists. I'm fair, but also a bastard. And I don't mind who you say that to. I'd love to get to know you better and trust me I will, but just not now. It's up to you whether you want this deal. The offer is open for twenty-four hours. Non-negotiable. Take it or leave it. For info some have walked away at this point. I can give you their names as well. Trust me, you won't know any of them. I know I sound like some pompous prick, but that's me. I tell it as I see it. Oh, and you need to ditch your sound tech. He screwed up on half a dozen occasions. I have a guy that covers my new bands until they can get things sorted. Any questions?'

Well, that sorts out Umar's future.

I find my voice, 'This is all a bit to absorb but do you really think we have what it takes.'

'Good question, and the answer is simple. I only take on talent that I think can make it. And by make it, I mean really make it. Top ten, albums and singles. No less. Does every band I take on succeed? Hell, no! I trail failures like a fishing boat trails seagulls. But none failed because of lack of effort on my part. I can open the right doors. I can get you in front of the right people. I can help you avoid the wrong ones. Any other questions?'

'Is there a contract?' asks Daisy.

'Another good question. Yes, there is. And it's a swine, biased in my favour. Your lawyer will hate it and advise you against signing it. I would. But it is what it is. As I said, talk to any of my people and they'll tell you I'm fair. A money grabber, but fair. Your manager has a copy already. Any other questions?'

Jenny puts her hand up, as is if she's back in school.

'Yes,' Geoffrey says.

'Why us?'

'Third good question in a row. I like you lot. Easy answer. Combo of music, looks and timing. Girl bands are in and only going to get bigger, but you're not just five singing heads. You can play. That makes you a double win. Girl power with instruments. I think that combo is pixie dust at the moment. We need to move fast though. And that's something I'm good at. Anything else, as I need to go?'

He jumps off the table, shakes our hands and leaves. The hush in the room speaks to that observed in a rarely used mausoleum.

'Bloody hell!' says Jenny, finally breaking the silence.

'For f's sake!' says Daisy.

'What in all that is holy?' I stammer.

Mr Goleniewski stands up, 'Well girls, have a chat and let me know what you think. I need to see a man about a dog.'

'Oh my God!' Daisy screams after he leaves. 'Did that just happen?'

The three of us leap to our feet and huddle.

'Chug, Chug, Chug,' we all shout. 'Let's Chug!'

20
THE MORNING AFTER

I'M OUT FOR a walk. I was up at five this morning. Unable to sleep, I'd spent the night tossing and turning, running the conversation with Geoffrey Tadcaster over and over. I've no destination in mind and it's still too early for most of the nine-to-five brigade to be out. I treat myself to a bacon roll and a mug of tea in a cafe—something my purse usually stays closed for. Cash is still tight, but I need to celebrate is some way. I'd watched Jenny fill up on cheap wine, and Daisy smoke her fair share of wacky baccy last night. I'd stuck to Diet Coke but have to admit that, as the evening wore on, my resolve was tested in a way that it hasn't been for a while. Finally, when Daisy and Jenny announced they were off to the Slam Music Tent to watch Carl Cox, both high as a kite, I managed to convince Mr Goleniewski to give me lift to Glasgow and come back for the others later. I had a feeling that the girls were in for the long haul, no doubt finding someone's house to take it all the way to the morning. In fact, I wouldn't put it past them to be still at it now.

There is a copy of today's Daily Record on the café table. I flick through it.

'Catherine Day?'

I look up and don't recognise the person talking to me.

'Do you not ken me?'

Something clicks. I do a classic double take.

'Isobel?' I stutter.

'Long time no see, Catherine.'

It dawns on me that subconsciously I'd wandered back to the area of Glasgow where I'd seen Isobel and Billy dolling out the cash all those years back. Isobel is barely recognisable. She was skinny before, but is now as thin as a razor blade; her face is transparent tissue tight to her skull. Her hair is an army crewcut and her clothes, a worn old mohair jumper and a pair of army fatigues, hang from her like a bad bag of washing. Her eyes are rose pink, sunk deep.

'What you doing here?' she asks.

I stutter, 'Eh, just grabbing some food. You?'

'I live nearby.'

There is no conversation with her that I can imagine that I want to have. My roll is only half-gone, and my mug of tea still near-full. Even so, I stand up.

'Where are you going?' she asks.

Her words are one long slur.

'I'm meeting someone. I just realised I'm late.'

'So, you're not going to finish that roll.'

'No.'

'Can I have it?'

'Be my guest.'

She sits down, drawing a scowl from the waitress.

'I hear you're in a band,' she says, as she wolfs down my bread and pig.

'Yeah.'

I start to walk away.

'The Chug,' she says to my back. 'I saw you.'

I don't want to stop but can't help and ask, 'Where?'

'At the Queen's Park bandstand.'

We'd played a small pop-up festival there last summer.

'You were good. Not brilliant, but good.'

I grimace and leave. But, before I can reach the door, she shouts out; 'Catherine, when you're famous, you can pay me back for me not grassing you up back then.'

I push the door open and step onto the pavement.

In all this time it had never occurred to me that Isobel and Billy could have dropped me right in it when they were arrested. After all, why would they? They were in enough shit without telling the police that they were bribing guards at Barlinnie. Especially Billy. He'd likely served his time in BarL. He would know who was on the take. That would have made his residency a lot easier than most. Isobel would have been sent to Cornton Vale up near Stirling.

I was just so relieved when the police arrived and arrested Isobel and Billy, even more so when they were sent down, that it never once occurred to me that they might grass on me. After all, I'd done only one job. Hadn't even been paid. Not that that would matter if they had squealed. I'd been on the visitors list at Barlinnie for that day. CCTV would have caught me. I remember looking up at the camera. Wondering if my image was being burned into the memory of some guard watching me placing the package in the locker—my fingerprints all over it. Occasionally the memory of that day rises like an unwanted pluke. Less now than it used to, but every so often, it pays me a visit. And never once did the thought that Isobel could have ruined my life with just a few words feature.

The whole incident with Isobel in the cafe kicks me in the gut. I mean, could she still go to the police? Surely not. After all this time what evidence would there really be? The money will be long gone. The guards won't open their mouths and the CCTV shows what? A woman placing a parcel in a locker and never retrieving it. But it would show *someone* retrieving it. A warden. Is that enough to start an investigation?

Just dumb, Catherine Day.

Just plain dumb.

No one is going to check CCTV footage from back then. It won't even exist anymore.

Will it?

'Could it?'

I say that out loud, catching a young lad by surprise as he walks by. He gives me a look that needs no words to indicate what an idiot he thinks he's just encountered. I speed up, looking back on the café door in case Isobel has decided she wants a longer chat. I break into a small run. A stupid thing to do. A useless thing to do, but it makes me feel better when I reach a bus stop and jump on the first bus to arrive. I keep a watch on the street corner where the café lives until it's lost from sight, vowing never to return to this area.

The bus is heading away from town, back to my old house. I don't really want to go back there, but then again what's the harm. I can hardly see Isobel tramping all the way out there, and if I get off early and walk up the back way, then there's little chance of meeting anyone else.

So why not?

The bus trundles on. I can't park the chance meeting with Isobel. Here I am, finally on the edge of success. A better life in the offing, if things go well with the band, and a stupid action from a desperate time rolls back into view. I can't see how my trip to Barlinnie can rip my chance away from me, but I'm unable to shake the feeling that it could.

When the bus reaches my stop, I skip off and take a quick look-see for any familiar faces. I hear that Maggie's salon is still on the go. I wonder if any of the chairwomen still hold court. I could always take a wee peek, for old time's sake. But no! That would be inviting back my old world. I've no reason to avoid it, other than the same nagging feeling that I have over Isobel. What went on in the past should stay in the past. Congas down the High Street, an alcoholic mother, bad-mouthing teachers. They would all make for good grist if a journalist went digging, and maybe Geoffrey might not take to such antics well. Then again that's a crazy thought. The world of rock'n'roll is full of excess. My little misdemeanours wouldn't warrant a column inch on an F list celeb magazine.

House, then back to my flat. That's the plan for me.

I trudge up the hill and ponder why I'm back here. Simple. I'm curious. A last glance at my old life, before I embark on a new one. I've been itching to return, have a peek. It's been a good few years since I last walked this road. What am I expecting to see when I get there? A blue plaque?

'Rock Star Catherine Day Lived Here.'

Or

'Mega Rock Star and Hall-of-Famer Catherine Day Graced this Humble House With Her Presence.'

Or

'Her Royal Highness the Princess Day of the Day, Rock Queen and All-Round Legend Passed Through these Portals.'

I reach my old house, *our* old house. For an instant, I'm back, school bag in hand, Mum opening the door, me rushing in for tea. Mum's smile lighting up the street. Lighting up my heart. I grin. The house looks the same. White, although maybe a bit whiter than when I lived there. Windows look similar. Well, maybe not. The door looks new. I look up and the slates on the roof, once grey, are now a light red—again new. The garden out front is show-ready. Neatly trimmed lawn, flower bed in perfect condition, plants orderly. A garden that used to be an ugly sister to the others is now a Cinderella. The driveway, once red chips, is paved and shining.

The thought of Mum vanishes. This is not *our* house. It's someone else's. Someone who has put their stamp on it. It still looks like our house, but it isn't.

I want to go around the back, but I know what I'll see. A pristine strip of grass. A new conservatory. A curated path of slate leading to a polished pond with golden Koi gliding among sea green fronds.

The curtains in the front room move. Snow white curtains. A head appears. A woman. Not much older than me. Tight brunette curls from a posher hair salon than 'Hair It Is'. A silver necklace shines above a lilac top. Her eyes screw up. I've one foot on the small stone wall that marks the garden's boundary. I'm fifteen feet from her. Staring.

What have they done inside? Is my room still a bedroom? A study? A sauna? Is it even there? Knocked through to make way for some American style kitchen diner.

The woman at the curtain turns.

Calling someone?

A man appears next to her.

Equally coiffured.

'Who is that, Murray?'

'Why, Madeleine, I don't know.'

'Should we call the police?'

'She does look shifty. I heard the Farquharson's were broken into last week.'

'Dreadful wasn't it? Tanya lost her Gerrard and Co tiara.'

'Findlay had his Oyster lifted.'

'She looks like the sort of person that would do that. What do they call it, Madelaine? Casing the joint?'

Both are wearing a scowl that would sour ice cream.

I shake my head. Our home has gone. What am I doing here? It takes some restraint not to flick the couple a vicky. Although why would I do that? I don't know them. All I know is that our house was perfect when Mum and I were there, and now they've ruined it.

I walk away but can't resist an obvious peek to the rear. The angles defeat me. I can't see anything, but my action looks as suspicious as hell.

'See, Murray, she is *casing the joint.'*

I smile as I walk away, wiping away some of the nostalgic hurt that was welling up.

You're going to be a success, Catherine Day. No need to look back. You've waited long enough for this moment. It's time to shine! To wipe your feet on the mat of this place. To not look back.

Save that this is the place where I last saw my mum. And that's really why I'm back here.

Mum, look, your daughter is doing good. She's not a screw-up. She's been given the chance of a lifetime. And she's going to grab it with both hands.

'Well, look who's back in town!'

I look up to find Maggie Hamilton standing in front of me. A few more wrinkles, a little more tan to hide ageing skin, hair higher than ever, heels as tall, pant suit just as out of date.

'Hi, Mrs Hamilton.'

'Oh, for goodness sake, it's Maggie. I'm not your boss anymore and you're not a girl.'

'Sorry, *Maggie.*'

She can't help but look over my shoulder towards the old house. Maggie doesn't live near here. She bought a swanky home up where the better people live, not long after I started working at the salon full time.

'A mortgage to choke an elephant and a lifestyle to bankrupt a queen.'
Lidia Thomas said that often, and insisted that someone should
engrave those words on Maggie's forehead. I know the house
purchase caused Maggie no end of stress in the early days, which
explained her obsession with every ha'penny that she could grab.
So, if she's on this street, I'd like to know why.

'And how are you, Catherine?'

'Fine.'

'Your mother?'

Never one to dodge the hard questions is our Maggie.

'I don't know.'

'Still missing?'

You know fine well she is.

'I hear from her now and then,' I say.

'Ah well. I'm sure she has her reasons. And the band? I hear
you were playing at T in the Park thing this weekend.'

'Yes, we were.'

'And I hear it went well.'

How do you know that?

'The audience seemed to like it,' I reply.

'And did anyone spot you and sign you up?'

'What do you mean?'

'Well, you know these music things. People always looking
for the next big thing. Isn't that what they say?'

First Isobel and now Maggie. First a threat and now what?
Clairvoyance? Maggie couldn't know about Geoffrey. Or could
she? The hospitality area was rammed when he'd taken us to one
side and, to be fair, none of us were slow in telling anyone that
asked why he'd done so. Even so, who does Maggie know that
would have been there? More to the point, it's barely nine
o'clock the morning after. Did someone tell her? Did she spot
me? Rush to catch me? She *is* a little out of breath.

I might be making it big. Maggie would want a slice of that.

'It's been nice seeing you again, Maggie. I'll pop into the salon. Maybe I'll get my hair cut.'

'You're always welcome, and I'm sure we can do some 'mate's rates'.'

As if.

'That would be good,' I say. 'Bye.'

I leave her bemused. I've not provided sufficient quantity of gossip for the chairwomen. And that will lead Maggie to a necessary bout of invention.

I met Catherine Day near her old house. I wonder why she was up there.

Cue the conspiracy theories.

'Maybe she came back for something.'

'What?'

'Who knows?'

'Isn't it odd that no one has seen her mother for all these years?'

'Didn't the Wests bury bodies in the garden?'

'You don't think she killed her own mother…?'

Bloody hell, Catherine Day, what are you doing? Stop this right now! I speed up and hit the main road singing *Don't You Want Me* to stop the thought train heading further into that tunnel.

It takes me a couple of hours to walk back to my flat. I give Isobel's area as wide a berth as possible. I make myself a cup of tea when I get home, and realise I have no milk. I pull on my coat to nip down to Malky's. I reach the bottom of the tenement stairs. I change my mind.

Hi Catherine, how was the gig?

I don't want that conversation. For all I know Malky is a member of the music super-agent fan club, life president, and knows Geoffrey intimately. He's probably waiting at his shop, info on The Chug hot from Geoffrey's mobile.

Catherine, did you know my son, Mo, could sing? You'll need another singer as a backup in case one of you gets sick. You know, a substitute, like football. Is that not a good idea? Ten percent would be a good wage...

'Ahhhh!'

The scream echoes around the close. I storm back upstairs, telling my stupid brain to just shut the fuck up.

The phone is ringing when I get back in the flat.

21
THE PHOTO

'TONIGHT?'

'Tonight, Catherine,' says Mr Goleniewski.

I twiddle with the phone receiver.

'You want us all to go to London tonight?'

'I had a call with Geoffrey not twenty minutes ago. There is a Band Plays On gig tomorrow night in Fulham. Some pub called The Player's Card. Six bands, six songs each. It's how it works. We are second to last. That means he likes us a lot. The nearer the end of the night the more we are his favourite. There will be a slew of record execs and radio people. I'm told there always is.'

'We haven't even signed his contract, Mr Goleniewski. We haven't even *read* the contract.'

'Are you saying that you don't want to sign?'

'No. It's just that...'

'Just what, Catherine?'

I can hear the deep note of frustration is his voice. It's quick to the surface when it comes to me.

'Just nothing, really. It's just so fast.'

'And why is that a bad thing, Catherine? Some bands wait a lifetime for a chance like this.'

'But our equipment?'

'We are taking the van.'

'To London?'

'Of course. How else will we get all our gear from place to place when we are down there.'

I twiddle with the phone cord, wrapping it around my index finger, pulling it up before sliding my finger free and watching the cord bounce up and down.

'I've never been to London.' I say.

'All the more reason to pack your bag and be ready for me to pick you up. I'll be around at six. I still need to talk to Jenny and Daisy, neither are answering their phones.'

'You called them first?' I say, before I can stop myself.

'No. I called you first but you didn't answer either.'

Paranoia Catherine, paranoia.

'How long are we going for?'

'You heard the man. Six months. Or more, if things work out. Far less if they don't.'

'He didn't like our look,' I add.

'How do you fancy a little military style?'

'In what way?'

'You like your cargo pants, and the new songs have a sort of military aggression to them. I've a friend at the club that supplies the Polish army. He has some stuff that might just do the job.'

'Interesting.'

'I thought so. I'll ask the other two, but we'll need to see what Geoffrey says.'

The hint of regret in that statement is a sign of what he sees coming. Geoffrey had made it clear it was his way or no way. The *day-to-day*. That's what Mr Goleniewski is relegated to. The VG man, as Daisy calls people like Mr Goleniewski. Van and Gear. I'm sure that he'll make a great VG man, but today is the first day of his new subservient role and he can't hide the disappointment.

'Okay,' I say. 'Can I ride shotgun with you?'

The van, a beaten-up old Transit Mr Golenweiski bought when he'd started managing us, has room in front for three. In the rear there are two old cinema seats bolted to the floor, lifted from a skip outside the Hillhead Salon cinema when they were refurbing it. With no Umar, two of us will sit in the back, the other will ride up front with Mr Goleniewski.

'It's Daisy's turn. You blagged the good seat last time, when we went up to T in the Park.'

Comfy as the cinema seats are when stationary, it's a different game when on the move. Years of movie fan's backsides have worn the burgundy cloth smooth. Any sudden acceleration or swerves, and you fly off them. Umar nailed a wooden bar across the rear of the van to give those in the cheap seats something to brace their feet against. It helps, a little.

'Six o'clock, Catherine, he says. 'And by six, I mean six, not ten past six, not one-minute past six. Six.'

'Okay.'

'Six.'

'Got it. Six.'

I hang up.

This is a bit of whirlwind. London for six months. Who knew that was on the cards yesterday morning? There is a dawning realisation that this really is the make or break for the band. Maybe even for me. If this all pans out, then life will be a whole different shape. And if it doesn't… I leave that alone. There's a lot to be done. Mothballing the flat needs a bit of attention. Letters will need redirected. *To where?* Neighbours will need informed. *Will they?* Oher people will need informed. *Who do I mean?* Bags need packed. *Twenty minutes max!* Hair needs cut. *Priority!* Maggie's place. *No way!* Buy some essentials. *Urgent!*

Okay, Post Office first on redirecting mail. See if I can blag a hair appointment at Curly Sue's on the way, then get a shop on.

'FILL IN THIS form and return it to me!' says the man behind the Post Office grill.

I've just spent half an hour waiting in line only to discover that the form I needed was lying on a table all the time—to be completed before standing on the queue. Curly Sue can't see me until four. That means I'll be tight for the pick-up at six. I scan the form and curse. Forwarding address required. I don't have one. I leave to track down a phone box to call Mr Goleniewski.

'I've no idea where you are staying other than for the next three nights,' he says when I ask about our address in London. 'We are booked into a hotel just behind the Albert Hall, Catherine.'

'What are you doing about your mail?'

'I'm getting it sent to the club.'

'And what?'

'They will send it to me in batches.'

'Can I do that as well?'

'If you want.'

'That would be great. Could you let them know? I doubt there will be anything other than bills, but you never know.'

Maybe a letter from Mum.

Before he hangs up, he repeats the word 'six' at least four times.

CURLY SUE'S IS busy. I don't drop into a chair until gone four thirty, but at least I got my shopping done.

'What will it be, Catherine?' asks Sue.

'The usual. Nothing drastic.'

'You could do so much more with your hair.'

'And I might be going for a new look, but not just yet. So, leave them enough to work with!'

'Them? You are going to another hairdressers?'

'I'm off to London for a wee while.'

'And you'll pay triple what you pay here.'

'If I knew what the look was, I'd get you to do it, but we have a new manager and he wants us to change it up a little.'

'No more Mr Goleniewski?'

'No. He's still our manager; we just have another manager as well.'

'How does that work?'

I tell her the story as she cuts but, as I'm her last customer of the day, every time I chat, she pauses to listen. By the time I'm done it's ten to six and I still haven't packed.

'SIX,' I SAID.

Mr Goleniewski is standing in my bedroom as I throw my clothes into my case.

'Was I speaking Swahili, Catherine? Six.'

'I'll be ten minutes, promise.'

I'm nearer half an hour by the time I sling my bag in amongst our gear to plump next to Jenny.

'Crap!' I say and jump up before Mr Goleniewski can shut the door. 'Stop! I left my purse in the flat.'

The glare from Mr Goleniewski would wither a sumo wrestler. I sprint back to the flat to retrieve the purse from my bedside. The smell of smoke from the fire still lingers. I thought the fresh coats of paint, new furniture and carpets would have killed that. The multiple air fresheners don't help. Their smell is no better. I lock the door and fly down the stairs. I am about to leap back in the van when I catch sight of Isobel. I freeze. She's standing in a close across the street, ducking back the instant I spy her.

'Get in!' says Mr Goleniewski.

'A minute,' I say.

'You've had all the minutes you need. Now get in!'

I stare at the close. I'm sure it was Isobel.

'Catherine, get in,' Mr Goleniewski growls. 'Now!'

I slide in, taking one last look for Isobel. As Mr Goleniewski bangs the door shut, I crawl over to my seat, wondering what the hell Isobel is doing here. I sit down and, with a deliberate stamp on the accelerator, the engine roars as Mr Goleniewski makes it clear that he's not happy with my tardiness. He throws the van into the first corner hard. Both Jenny and I slide from the chairs.

'Can't we fit bloody harnesses to these things to keep us in?' I ask.

'If you had been ready on time, Mr Goleniewski wouldn't be in a mood, and we wouldn't need harnesses.'

'Curly Sue ran late.'

With the van's interior light only working when the door is open, we'd be in darkness if it were not for another Umar fix; an electric camping light swinging from one of the van's cross beams. As the van moves the light sways, shadows dancing around us.

After a short while the van picks up more speed as we slip onto the motorway.

We both sit. My head thinking about Isobel. Jenny's deep in her own thoughts.

'Did Mr Goleniewski say when he was likely to make a pit stop?' I ask after about twenty minutes.

Jenny shakes her head. She's unusually quiet. Apart for admonishing me for being late, she's not said a word.

'Jenny, are you okay?'

She nods again. Her hand is lying on a large brown envelope, pinning it to the van deck.

'What's in the envelope, Jenny?'

She picks it up. Hesitancy in the action. She stares at it before waving it back and forward a little.

'What is it, Jenny?'

Now we are on the motorway, I need to lean in to speak because of the noise, but Jenny keeps her distance. She has her eyes fixed on the pile of equipment that lies in the middle of the van. It's neatly stacked and secured with rope. Umar was never that neat, but that's Mr Goleniewski for you. Jenny waves the envelope again.

'Jenny, what is in that?'

'Catherine, can I ask you a favour before I tell you?'

Our heads are inches apart, her breath sour on my nose, a wash of last night's excess floating over me.

'What?'

'Please don't get mad!'

'About what?'

We both brace our feet as the van shifts lanes.

'About this,' she says, holding up the envelope.

'What is it?'

She hands it over and says, 'Open it.'

I lift the envelope flap. There is a single sheet of paper in it. I extract it. The light isn't good enough to reveal any detail.

'Jenny, I can't read it.'

'Can't you?'

She takes the sheet from me. 'Sorry. I forgot how poor the light is in here.'

'What does it say?'

'I'd rather you read it.'

'I can't. Just tell me!'

She says nothing, playing with the sheet of paper rather than talking.

'Jenny, spit it out!'

'You can read it when we get to the service station.'

'Which could be hours, now just tell me!'

Again, she stops talking. I say, 'For crying out loud, Jenny, what is it?'

'I can't tell you.'

'Yes, you can. You've obviously read whatever it is. So, what's the problem with telling me?'

'I know, but...'

'Oh for f's sake!' I half-shout. 'Just tell me!'

'Okay, but promise not to get mad.'

'I promise, now talk!'

She leans right in. Closer than she needs to overcome the road noise. Almost as if she doesn't want anyone else to hear. As if there's someone nearby that could eavesdrop.

The van slides back into the inside lane and we both press our feet hard on the wooden bar to counter the movement.

'I was going to give you this earlier but the time never seemed right,' she says. 'Before the gig we were all so uptight and after, well... after the gig, the news with Geoffrey kind of made it awkward.'

'Will you just sodding tell me?'

'Okay, okay. I was at the library.'

'The library?'

'The Mitchell, up town.'

'You?'

'I like to go to the reading room. Catch up with the newspapers. I go most days, one way and another.'

'Really?'

'Things aren't brilliant with Mum. She's got this thing about wanting a grandchild. She'll bring it up at every turn. We argue a lot over it. I mean, it's my decision whether I want kids, but she makes it sound like I'm being the worst daughter in the world by denying her a grandson or granddaughter to dote over. When I was married she must have asked every week. Now she asks whenever I see her. She blames the band. Says it's no way to meet a decent guy.'

'I never knew.'

I never really think about Jenny's or Daisy's or Mr Goleniewski's problems. I suppose I've become a little too self-centred in the last few years. Not a good thing.

'Anyway,' she says. 'I like to sit for an hour or so in the library reading room, just flicking through the newspapers. I was never a paper person before, but it's kind of nice to see how screwed up other people are. Makes me feel a little better.'

The sadness in that statement is palpable.

'Are you feeling that bad, Jenny?'

'At times.'

'You should have said something.'

'I don't like to talk about it. Anyway, if this whole Geoffrey thing works out maybe that'll change.'

'We should talk.'

'Yes, we probably should.'

'And what did you find?'

'As I said, I was in the library on Friday morning flicking through the papers. I tend to start with the redtops and then move on to the broadsheets. Well, I was just thinking of calling it quits and was closing The Times when a name caught my attention.'

'Whose name?'

She pauses as the van negotiates more lane changes. The driving still feels aggressive. I suspect my lateness has not yet removed the lead from Mr Goleniewski's right foot. When we've settled back into the near lane, Jenny continues.

'I saw Mr Goleniewski's name.'

'He was in the papers?'

'No, not our Mr Goleniewski, another Mr Goleniewski. The name was unusual enough to catch my eye in the headline.'

'And who is this Mr Goleniewski?'

'It was an interesting article. All about a man called Michael Goleniewski. He was a Polish officer in something called the Ministry of Public Security back in the fifties. He was deputy head of the GZI WP.'

'The what?'

'Polish counterintelligence.'

'Oh.'

'He later headed up a technical division, but at some point, he became a spy for the Soviet Union. Then, later, he also became a spy for the CIA. A triple agent as they called him. Sometime in the late fifties, the Americans informed MI5 that Michael Goleniewski had told them that there was a mole in the Royal Navy passing secrets to the Russians. At first the Americans didn't tell MI5 that they had received the information from Michael Goleniewski. To hide his identity, they gave him the codename Sniper, but MI5 called him Lavinia.'

The names ring a bell. Were they some of the names in the papers in mum's lock box? They sound right.

'Go on!' I say.

'Well, after that it gets a bit confusing, but ultimately Goleniewski defected to the Americans in 1961. Somehow it all ties into a major scandal involving Russian spies in both Britain and America. In the case of the UK, it involved what became known the Cambridge Five and others. I didn't really understand it all.'

'And our Mr Goleniewski is tied to this?'

'I'm not sure if he is.'

'And why would I be mad about this?'

We have another hiatus as the van does a four-lane shuffle.

'It's what else was in the article, Catherine. The photograph. I wish you could see it.'

I take the sheet again and realise that it's a copy of a newspaper article but, I can only tell that because Jenny has put the thought in my head. There might be a picture at the bottom of the article, but no matter how I angle the paper, I can't make anything more out.

'What can't I see?'

'Who is in picture.'

'Who?'

She pauses.

'Who?' I repeat.

'Your mum.'

'What?'

I stand up, grabbing at the side of the van, making my way towards the swinging camp light. I let go of the van's side and grab the light with one hand to stop it moving, pushing the paper up against the lamp with the other hand to get a better look. I still can't make out the words but there's enough light to see the picture. The van swerves and I'm thrown off balance. I manage to catch my fall before crawling back to the seat.

'Did you see it?' Jenny asks?

I nod.

'Sorry, Catherine,' Jenny says. 'I wanted to tell you as soon as I found it, but as I said the timing seemed wrong.'

I hold the paper up to my face. I can no longer see the photo, but I know it's there. The same photo that hangs on the wall of Mr Goleniewski's bedroom. The same one that burned in my flat. Mum in the Marilyn Monroe dress. The man with some of Mr Goleniewski's features. Both of them standing in front of Manhattan.

'Did she ever mention Michael Goleniewski?' Jenny asks.

I shake my head. 'But I've seen this photo before.'

'You have?'

'Yes.'

'Where?'

'A blown-up version of it hangs above our Mr Goleniewski's bed.'

'You're kidding?'

'I wish I was.'

'Why has he got a photo of your mum over his bed?'

'He won't tell me.'

'God, that's creepy!'

'I also saw a copy of it in Mum's things just before the fire broke out in my flat. It was in with some old official looking documents.'

I pause, then, 'Did you say Sniper?'

'And Lavinia, those were Michael's code names. Why?'

'I'm sure those words were on the document with the photo.'

'What did they say?'

'A lot of nonsense, or so I thought. What else does the article say, Jenny?'

'Well, that's the odd thing.'

'What?'

'When Goleniewski made it to America he made a strange claim. He said he was the son of the last Tzar of Russia. The heir apparent as they call it.'

'That is odd.'

'Catherine, do you think our Mr Goleniewski is tied up with what I found?'

'Sounds like it. The man in the photo looks a little like him. What do you think it all means, Jenny?'

'Well, I don't know about the spy stuff or any of the Russian royalty nonsense, but I do have a thought.'

'Go on!'

'And I could be way out on this.'

'And?'

'This is the bit I need you to promise not to get mad.'

'I already said I wouldn't.'

'When were you born, Catherine?'

'You know when.'

'March eighteenth, nineteen sixty-five.'

'Correct.'

'And the article says that photo was of Michael Goleniewski and your mum—taken in the June of nineteen sixty-four.'

'So what?'

'Oh, come on, Catherine! Think on it! Your mum has never told you who your dad was, and you were born around nine months after that photo was taken. Put two and two together!'

The world around me seems to recede a little.

'My dad!' I splutter. 'Are you saying that this guy, Michael Goleniewski is my dad? The guy in the photo?'

'I don't know, but the timing would work. Maybe it's just coincidence but think on how our Mr Goleniewski has been looking after you all this time. Have you ever asked why he would do that?'

'Because he knows Mum.'

'Seems a bit much to me,' she waves her hand around. 'All this just because he knows your mum.'

'And?'

'I don't have an 'and', other than, if the guy in the photo and Mr Goleniewski are connected—maybe related—then there is something going on here. I'm sorry, Catherine, but I'd say that there's a good chance that the man in the photo might be your dad.'

22
THE CHAT THAT SHOULD HAVE
BEEN HAD LONG AGO

THE SERVICE STATION is somewhere between quietish and a little short of not quite busy. Given I've never been in a motorway service station in my life, this could also be its 'five thirty at Glasgow Central' or the 'wee small hours in Linn Crematorium' moment.

The four of us sit around a wood-effect plastic table attended by plastic-effect plastic chairs. The food in front of us is food-effect. The sandwiches are more rubber than a Good Year tyre, fillings older than the amalgam in my teeth. The sheet of paper that Jenny gave me lies between us.

In the cold fluorescent light, the faded grey of the photocopy gives it a vintage feel. As if the page has leapt straight from the sixties into our life.

THE LONGEST WAIT…

'Who is he?' I ask Mr Goleniewski.

He couldn't look more uncomfortable if I'd pulled down his trousers in a church aisle.

'Well?'

'It tells you,' he replies.

'I know it does. It says Michael Goleniewski. But who is he to you?'

'A relation.'

'What kind of relation.'

'A distant one.'

'How distant?'

'Not distant enough.'

Jenny slaps her hand on the table causing us all to jump a little. 'Mr Goleniewski, Catherine says you have the self-same picture on your bedroom wall. So, forgive me if I'm a little direct, but I think Catherine deserves some straight answers, not bullshit ones. Don't you?'

He pulls the slip of paper towards him, staring at the photo, rubbing his finger over it. For a moment his eyes glaze over, and he freezes, his thumb resting on Mum's dress.

'It's not my place to talk about this,' he says after a while. 'It never was and never will be. I made promises.'

I yank the paper from him, pointing at my mum. 'My mother,' I say. 'That is my mother! You know? The person that's been missing for fourteen years. And now I find that a relation of yours knew her. Maybe better than knew her, and you have the gall to tell me it's not your place. Then whose place is it, may I ask?'

'Not mine.'

'Is he my father?'

'I can't…'

I stand bolt upright. 'Enough, just bloody enough. Tell me, just bloody tell me what you know!'

'It's not…'

'Tell me or I'm out of here! I'm damned if I'm going to London with you.'

'But you have to! Look at the opportunity.'

'Screw that. Just tell me, or I walk!'

He looks at the photo again.

'I really mean it.' I add.

Jenny and Daisy look on in dismay.

'You can't do that to us, Catherine,' says Daisy.

'Then tell this man to talk!'

They both look at Mr Goleniewski. Daisy takes the lead, 'Don't you think it's time to talk, Mr Goleniewski? How can you say nothing with this in front of you?'

'And you have the picture on your bedroom wall,' Jenny adds.

'I'm not going to ask again,' I say. 'I'm sick and tired of this. I just want answers and I want them right here, right now.'

He studies each of us, his eyes flicking from person to person. There is a fight going on inside his head, but I don't care. I really have had enough. This boil should have been lanced years ago. And I feel like a fool for letting it go on so long. Fourteen years. Where have they gone? Why have I let it get to here?

'Okay,' he sighs. 'But I can only tell you much. And before you shout at me, it's because I only know so much.'

He takes the paper from me and re-reads the article.

I wait.

'What the article says is true,' he says, his voice a whisper. 'Michael Goleniewski was a spy. Quite a famous one, but I never knew him. He is related to me. He's a cousin of my father.'

'He looks a lot like you for a distant relative,' Jenny says.

'The Goleniewski forehead. Very recognisable. The men in my family are all blessed with it. If you ever meet my brother, Piotr, you will see what I mean. Also the shape of the beard.'

When I look at him, I can see what he means. His beard hides the bottom half of his face. I suspect if Mr Goleniewski shaved, the resemblance would be less pronounced.

'And his connection with my mother?' I ask.

'Catherine, do you know what your mother did before you were born?'

'A secretary with some shipping firm in Glasgow.'

'So she told you.'

'Are you saying she wasn't?'

'She was neither a secretary, nor did she work for a shipping agency, nor did she work in Glasgow. At least not back then.'

'What then?'

Daisy and Jenny are playing head tennis as each of us speak.

'Your mother worked for MI5, Catherine.'

'Mum? Mum worked for MI5?'

'Yes, for a number of years.'

'Don't be so stupid! Mum and British intelligence? That makes no sense at all.'

'It is true. She was not a spy,' he says. 'If that is what you are thinking. She was what was called a junior liaison officer based in London.'

'London? Mum was in London?'

'She started back in nineteen fifty-nine, I think.'

'And what is a junior liaison officer?'

'I'm not that au fait with the workings of MI5.'

'Tell me what you know!'

'From what I understand—and your mum never really told me too much about her time there—she was mostly involved in what she called processing work, with some low-level involvement with field operators.'

'And she met Michael Goleniewski?' I ask.

'He was called 'Sniper' by the Americans and 'Lavinia' by MI5. Those were his code names. They even gave your Mum one. 'Daylight' they called her.'

I remember that name from the documents. So it was Mum that was the go between – I say nothing.

'She met Michael in London. When he was defecting to the USA. MI5 intercepted him and she interviewed him a few times. Normally she wouldn't have got near such a valuable asset. But your mum had a way about her and Michael and she got on well. The British were desperate to know the ID of the Russian moles at the time. Michael had info, but he said nothing. It was the Americans he wanted to talk to. But your Mum had a thing for him.'

'And she told you this?'

'Yes.'.'

'Where?'

'I'll get to that.'

'Is that where Mum went?' I ask. 'To America, to be with him?'

'It's not that simple, Catherine.'

'Tell me how *not* simple it is!'

'Yes, your mum went to America, but that was back in 1964, well after Michael had defected to the USA—by then the Americans had lost interest in Michael.'

'How do you know all this?'

'I was in America at the time.'

'And Mum went there to meet Michael?'

'Kind of.'

'Either she did, or she didn't.'

'I told you it wasn't that simple.'

'Then make it simple!'

He picks up the paper. His eyes loose cohesion.

I take a punt, 'You!' I say. 'Was it you that she went to see? Is that where you met her?'

He says nothing and, in that silence, Daisy and Jenny do what I do. They draw an obvious conclusion. One that should have occurred to me the moment I saw the photo on his bedroom wall.

'You and mum? God, you and mum were a… thing?'

I stand up.

'Catherine, it's not that simple.'

'Stop saying that!'

'Sit down, Catherine!'

'Jenny thinks that man might be my dad? The dates work. Is he?'

'I don't know.'

Jenny's mouth drops open, and she points to Mr Goleniewski. 'Are *you* Catherine's dad?'

The question has the same impact as someone stabbing me. 'What?'

Mr Goleniewski drops his head.

'You?' I say. 'You can't be. You just can't be!'

'Please sit down!' he says.

I stay standing, hands on my hips. 'Oh my God! After all these years of wanting to know, and now I find out you are my dad.'

'Please, Catherine, sit down! This is not the way it should be. There are too many questions that I cannot answer. You are jumping to conclusions.'

'Just bloody tell me if you are my dad!'

Daisy pulls the photocopy towards her and looks at me. 'Or is Jenny right and this is Catherine's dad?'

I shout at Daisy and Jenny. 'This isn't some bloody quiz!'

Daisy drops the paper.

'Now!' I spit at Mr Golenweiski. 'Tell me now! Who is my dad?'

'I do not know,' he says.

'You don't know, or you won't say?'

'I am not sure who your dad is.'

He reaches out, touching my wrist, 'Please sit and I'll tell you what I can.'

I sit down, pushing my food to one side, all appetite well and truly gone.

'It is true that your mum came to America to see Michael,' he says. 'And yes, that is where I met her. I was a security officer with the Polish embassy. It is how I knew your mum had interviewed Michael when he was in the UK. The British wanted to know what he knew before handing him on to the Americans. When he defected, the Brits intercepted him in London. They didn't have much time with him. The Americans wanted Michael, and MI5 were getting nowhere—and under time pressure. They tried to use your mum to get him to talk, but as I said, he said little, and they had to hand him over to the Americans. When Michael landed in the USA, I was part of the team that was tasked with shadowing him, after all he was a Polish citizen. He was of massive interest to us at the time, but it was a fruitless task. The Americans kept him well and truly under wraps for a long, long time. By the time they let him go, he'd been wrung dry. We interviewed him, but there was nothing new he could tell us that we did not already know through other routes. We lost interest. But when we got wind that your mother was coming over, we wondered why. She did so of her own accord. We didn't know that at the time. We thought MI5 had some new information and your mum was being used as a go-between because she had clicked with Michael back in London. But that was wrong. MI5 never sanctioned her trip, and she knew she would lose her job if she came to see Michael. But we also knew Michael asked her to come.'

'And the photo?'

'Taken that summer by a journalist who was digging into Michael's claim.'

'Claim?' says Daisy.

'Michael claimed to be the heir apparent to the Russian throne,' Jenny says.

'Is that all?' Daisy laughs. 'Triple agent and royalty. What else was he?'

We all ignore her, and Mr Goleniewski continues.

'The journalist concluded that there might be something in Michael's claim, but most people didn't believe Michael. He said he was Tsarevich Alexei Nikolaevich, the only son of Emperor Nicholas II and Empress Alexandra Feodorovna and, to some, the rightful heir to the Russian throne. Alexei was not a well boy. He had haemophilia and was treated by Rasputin. Michael also had haemophilia.'

'Were the Romanovs not all killed?' asks Jenny.'

'Yes. After the Russian revolution the royal family were imprisoned before being shot on the orders of Yakov Yurovsky, the head of the Bolshevik secret police. They say that the family were asked to dress in the middle of the night, that they were being moved. Instead, they were shot. They also say that Alexia saw his mother and father shot first.'

'And Michael claimed to be Alexia and that he was not shot?' asks Jenny.

'He says that, far from shooting him and his family, Yakov Yurovsky saved them all by spiriting them away. It is a well-known theory, although discredited by many. Michael also said that he knew where a large sum of Tsarist money was but, again, this is disputed.'

'And then he asked Mum to come to America in sixty-four?' I ask. 'Why?'

'We checked with a contact in America who assured us that MI5 knew nothing about your mum's plan to visit. Michael was a busted flush to them and us, as they say, but your mum changed that when she turned up. After all, why had Michael invited her? It was my job to follow her. So to answer your earlier question, she came to see Michael but not for the reasons she believed. She met up with him at a hotel in Brooklyn but wasn't told that there would be a journalist there. She thought she was there because Michael had feelings for her. We talked to the journalist later. He said that Michael had told him that your mum was British intelligence, a special ops person code named Daylight and that she would back up his royal lineage claim. A few days later I found your mum wandering the streets. She was totally lost. I should have left well alone, but she was in such distress that I offered to help and, well, one thing, as they say, led to another.'

'And she never saw Michael again?' asks Daisy.

'I do not know.'

I take a breath before I ask the next question, thinking I've not got enough lung capacity for all the questions I have.

'So, you and my mum were an item? In America and what, back here as well?'

'Just America. I was with her for a wonderful week. She wouldn't talk about Michael much but I got the impression that she had thought there was something special between them. That she had flown over thinking he wanted to be with her. She was distraught when it didn't work out.'

'What happened?'

'I think they fell out. Maybe your Mum realised there was no relationship. Maybe Michael only needed her to add some credibility to his claim. Whatever happened, I found her wandering the streets.'

'You thought you had a connection with her?'

'So I believed, but when she returned to the UK, I had the devil's own time finding her and even when I did, she never answered my letters. When the chance to come to the UK arose six months later, I leapt at it, and moved over here with Polish security, not long before you were born. But your mum blanked me. I finally gave up chasing after her, and when I quit my job, a few years later, my mother died and left me some cash. That's how I started the club.'

'And Mum and I? All this time you've been keeping watch because I might be your daughter.'

'If you are, Catherine, I have a duty.'

I sit back, taking it all in. 'Mum said nothing to me about any of this.'

'What could she say?'

'The truth.'

'You'd have to ask her why she didn't tell you that.'

'Is that where the money Mum got now and again came from? You?'

'Every so often I would reach out, but your mother would have none of it. She refused any help from me.'

'So where did she get the money?'

'I do not know.'

'And why is she back in America?'

'That I do not know.'

'But she is in America?'

'I do not know. She was, but now? I do not know.'

'Oh come on!' says Daisy. 'You've talked to her? No?'

'Not for a long while.'

'And you never asked why she left Catherine alone?'

'I did, but she wouldn't answer.'

I rap my knuckle hard on the table. 'Just like you wouldn't answer me all these years!'

'She made me promise to say nothing. Made me swear.'

'Can you get hold of her?'

'Not since my father died.'

'Your father,' I say. 'What has he got to do with it?'

'When I moved to the USA, he came with me. He also knew your mum, met her a few times. She used him to get in touch with me over the years.'

'And your dad never told you where she was? What she was doing?'

'No. He was a stubborn man. But he knew that you might be my daughter, and it was him that insisted I help you. I would have helped anyway, but my dad was very old school, as they say. Your mum swore him to secrecy, and Dad was man of his word. He never told me anything. When he died, I lost touch with your mother. I have no idea where she is now.'

For a moment we all sit and watch the comings and goings of the service station. Tired people looking for some respite from travel. Truckers, delivery people, bus drivers, families on a long haul, businessmen stopping for caffeine. A herd of bikers wander in, leathered up, helmets under their arms, all heading for the toilets. The Café of Lost Souls they should call this place.

'And that's it?' I ask.

'I can say no more.'

'Mr Goleniewski, you can say a lot more. A lot, lot more.'

'I cannot. Now are you still wanting to go to London?'

'Why would I?'

'Because, it is a chance of a lifetime, Catherine.'

'I'm bloody furious at you.'

'Catherine,' says Daisy. 'You can't back out.'

'Please don't do that,' adds Jenny.

'I should. After all, I've been lied to this whole time.'

'Omission is not a lie,' says Mr Goleniewski.

'It is in my book.'

'So do you want to go home?'

'Yes.'

The girls look at me in horror.

'I will make you a deal, Catherine Day,' Mr Goleniewski says. 'If you come to London and you land a record deal, I will tell you everything else I know. I should not, but I will.'

'Well?' asks Daisy.

'No way. Tell me now!'

'I will not.'

'Don't throw this away!' says Daisy.

I glare at Mr Goleniewski, 'Who is my father?'

'I told you. I don't know.'

'Please,' says Jenny.

I sit down and boil. After a few moments I look up, 'And you will tell me everything only if we get a deal. That is not fair. Tell me now!'

'And break your mother's confidence. I won't do that now, but when you sign a deal, I will.'

'Why then?'

'My job is done. You will be successful.'

'And if we don't get a deal?'

'I will tell you anyway. But not until we know that there is no deal to be had.'

I look at him.

'God, Catherine!' pleads Jenny.

I'll be damned if I'm going to throw away the chance of a lifetime, but I just want to throttle the information out of him.

'No,' I say. 'Tell me, or I walk!'

'Then walk,' he says.

'Catherine,' says Daisy and Jenny at the same time. 'Please.'

'He knows more. Why not say it now?' I say to them.

'I have told you more than I should, and that is that,' he says.

I go to stand up again and Jenny reaches out. 'Catherine, we could have a deal in weeks and if we don't, he'll tell you anyway. How can a few weeks make that much difference?'

'It's my mother.'

'And would she want you to throw this away? Would she?'

I know the answer to that. I place a hand near Mr Goleniewski's. 'And you will tell me everything?' I ask.

'As much as I can.'

'Everything?'

'There are bigger things at play here.'

'So you think,' I say.

'So I know,' he replies.

A small light flashes in my head. 'Shit, I know where this is going!'

I push my chair back and sigh, 'You're not sure if I'm your daughter. You can't be sure. It could be Michael, or she could have met someone else. But that's not it. Is it? That's not your worry.'

He looks down as I speak.

'You're more worried that Michael *could* be my Dad.' I say pointing at the picture. 'Aren't you?'

'I do not know if he is.'

'But if he is? What then?'

'It would make things complicated.'

I laugh. 'Complicated! You've got that right. Very complicated.'

Daisy chips in, 'Why?'

'Daisy, that man in the photo believes he was the heir to the Russian throne.'

'And.'

'The one and only heir. Is that right, Mr Goleniewski?'

'In his eyes, yes.'

'So, I have three questions. And you need to answer them. If you do, I will go to London.'

'What are the questions?'

'Firstly, do you believe Michael was the heir to the Russian throne?'

'I do.'

'Okay, is he still alive?'

'He passed in 1993. And the third question?'

'If I am his daughter, and his claim was correct, then I'd now be the heir unless there are others. Would I be the rightful heir to the Russian throne?'

'If Michael's claim was correct, you could be the true and sole heir.'

'Even if that were true, there is no throne anymore. It's irrelevant,' says Jenny.

'Not everybody thinks that the Russian throne is irrelevant,' he says.

'And there, ladies and gentlemen,' I say 'is the rub. And I often wondered why I'd been called Catherine.'

'Sorry?' asks Daisy.

'Wasn't the last empress of Russia called Catherine?' I finish.

23
DEAL

THE THREE OF us stand on a postage stamp that purports to be a stage. The room is packed with bodies and, given the heat in here, a sauna would be more comfortable. We've watched four artists play before us. All have been brilliant. Each a touch better, in their own way, than the last. The silence in which we watched the act before us, Henry Mudd, a lone guitarist, gave testament to our nerves. He was damned good.

Geoffrey chatted to us for a few minutes when we arrived, appreciating the new army look, but saying it still didn't quite work. It would do for tonight. Then we were asked to sign our contracts. Mr Goleniewski was not happy, but Geoffrey made it clear we would not be getting on the stage unless we did. I'd seen two other acts sign earlier. Despite Mr Goleniewski's protestations, we all signed. I then asked Geoffrey who the crowd were. He said that it was just a few movers and shakers. Punters from the bar next door are excluded in favour of people clutching small yellow slips of plastic with the words: 'VIP – The Band Played On. Admit One.'

Daisy thinks she recognises a Radio 1 DJ, and Jenny is convinced there are at least two MTV presenters in the venue. If the crowd are truly VIPs, then they are the most dressed-down VIPs I've ever seen. I know pubs in Glasgow that would tell you to sling your hook if you turned up dressed like some in here.

'Ladies and Gentlemen,' says the announcer—a young woman called Rhonda, who is dressed in startling yellow jeans and a bright green crop top. Neon blue shoulder length hair waves as she talks. 'Next on stage, all the way from the wild north, we have, The Chug.'

We walk on to a smattering of applause—polite, reserved.

'Hi,' I say, as I reach the mic. 'My name is Catherine, and these are Daisy and Jenny. Together we are The Chug.'

Just before Jenny counts us in, I realise we haven't done our group chant. Is that bad luck?

Six songs later, dropping all the covers, we leave to another smattering of polite applause, maybe a touch louder than when we came on. To be fair, every act so far has had the same reception. We huddle into one corner to watch the final group, Slate Star—a grunge band with a lighter touch than most. They, too, are applauded on and off.

And that is it. No record Exec. beating a path to talk to us. No request for an interview from the supposed media types in the room. Just a few minutes of post-music chat with Rhonda and then the lights flick on. Twenty minutes later we are across the road in another bar, four of us squeezed around a table designed for two.

'Well?' Jenny says, sipping her expensive water.

We all shrug.

'That wasn't what I thought it was going to be,' Daisy says. 'It was hot and sweaty, but about as atmospheric as an office meeting.'

'How did we do, Mr Goleniewski?' I ask.

'You were really good,' he replies, sipping at his water. 'Dropping the covers worked well. I saw a lot of nodding heads.'

'It felt like we were playing some posh kid's tenth birthday party. I thought we might get a little more reaction. And where is our guru, Geoffrey?'

'I saw him working the room,' says Mr Goleniewski. 'He was flitting from person to person, never standing still for more than a minute.'

'So, what now?'

'I do not know, Catherine. We go back to the hotel and wait to be contacted I suppose.'

We give it another half an hour before we call it quits. Mr Goleniewski drives us back to our hotel and we head straight for bed.

The following morning, we had agreed to do a bit of sight-seeing. More for my benefit, as Jenny and Daisy have been in London once before. Mr Goleniewski was based here for years, and agrees to act as our tour guide. Breakfast is as muted as the pub last night and talk is thin. We all leave the hotel and wander through Hyde Park, cross to Green Park and make our way to Buckingham Palace. From there, we trip up the Mall to Trafalgar Square and down to Big Ben and the Houses of Parliament. We find a café on the south bank of the Thames for some lunch, and Mr Goleniewski calls the hotel. With no mobile phones between us, it's the only way he has of checking if Geoffrey has been in touch. His long face tells us all we need to know before he even gets a chance to sit back down.

After lunch, we backtrack through Trafalgar Square and up Shaftesbury Avenue, briefly stopping to look at Chinatown and Soho before we make our way out towards St Paul's Cathedral. The last sights we take in are the Tower of London and Tower Bridge. I should be enjoying this, taking in the wonders and marvels of one of most iconic cities on the planet. I'm not. I'm thinking back to last night, to where we went wrong. Why has

Geoffrey avoided us? Sure, I'd hit a few bum notes, as had Daisy. Jenny lost the rhythm once and my microphone seemed way too sensitive. I felt I was shouting at times. We blew it. Is that what's happened, and no one is telling us?

We find another café. This time for tea and a cake. Only, no one wants cake. Mr Goleniewski vanishes to call the hotel again.

'Well, what do you think,' I ask, as a I sip at the lukewarm tea.

Daisy answers, 'I think that our stay here will be a lot shorter than six months.'

'I agree,' says Jenny.

'Come on team, it's only out first gig down here. There's tons of time.'

Neither of them looks convinced at my optimism.

'Why is Mr Goleniewski taking so long? I want to get out of here,' says Daisy after ten minutes. 'This place is the pits. I'm of a mind to put on my glad rags and hit town this evening. Even if we screwed up, I don't want to go home to tell everyone that we spent our last night in a London hotel room.'

Neither of us bite.

'Okay,' she says with resignation. 'Maybe I'm not into that. A quiet night might not do us any harm.'

When, another ten minutes later, there's still no sign of Mr Goleniewski, I get up to look for him. With no phone in the café, I hunt down the nearest phone box and spot him, receiver in hand, talking. I give it a few minutes and return to the pub.

'He's still on the phone. I suspect he's talking to his club. He hasn't been in touch for a few days.'

We stare at the empty cups, Jenny drumming her fingers, Daisy scraping some dirt from underneath a fingernail, and me watching an elderly couple argue over the prices.

When Mr Goleniewski returns, we all stand up, ready to go.

'Sit down, girls!' he says. 'Please sit down.'

We sit back down.

'Okay,' he says, staying on his feet. 'Do you want the good news or the bad news?'

'Did you talk to Geoffrey?' I ask.

'Yes,'

'Well, give us the bad news first,' I say. 'Please just get it over with.'

'Okay, I did talk to Geoffrey, and he has been onto some of the Execs he met last night. He called them this morning to follow up.'

He pauses.

'And?' asks Daisy.

'He hasn't had a single offer.'

The air is sucked from the room and all our heads drop.

'What in the hell was all the rush to get us down here?' I ask.

'Does that mean we are dead meat? So quickly?' says Daisy.

'Hang on, I didn't tell you the good news!' he says.

'Which is?' I ask. 'We get our petrol money home, a discount on our hotel bill and a 'try harder next time' speech?'

'No. I said he didn't get a *single* offer and that's true.'

'There's no need to rub it in,' I say.

'We did not get a single offer.' He pauses again. 'We got four offers!'

The air rushes back in with the smack of a hurricane.

'What?' we all say at the same time.

'Four initial offers, details to follow, but four labels are looking to sign you.'

Jenny is the first to really react. She jumps up, pushing her chair over and shouts, 'You bloody dancer!'

Daisy joins her and punches the air.

'Four!' I shout. 'Four bloody offers! Tell me you're not kidding?'

'Details to follow and negotiations to take place,' he says. 'But Geoffrey said that he's confident of landing a good deal. We got more offers than anyone else last night.'

I reach out over the table and place my hand high in the air. Jenny, Daisy and Mr Goleniewski join me.

'After three,' I scream. 'One, two, three.'

We bang our hands together. Forming the pyramid. 'Chug, Chug, Chug,' we all shout. 'Let's Chug!'

24
BOYFRIEND?

AS WE CALM down, Mr Goleniewski suggests we go somewhere a little more suitable for a celebration. Talking twenty to the dozen, we weave our way up into the City of London and find a pub under the monument to the Great Fire. We are heading for five o'clock and the place is already busy with suits and power dresses. A group of six men, decked out in the finest cloth that city bonuses can buy, are sipping on quarter bottles of champagne through a straw. Four women, grouped around a high table are cocktailed up. The scene is repeated throughout the pub.

If ever I felt like a drink, it was now. I mean how much harm could one do? I've been sober a long time. I have this under control. Look what you've just achieved Catherine Day—a record deal—or as near as dammit. So, what harm one drink?

Mr Goleniewski approaches the bar.

'What will it be girls?'

'Champagne,' I say.

'Really?' says Daisy.

'Not for me. For Mr Goleniewski and Jenny. We'll celebrate with American champagne, Daisy.'

'American champagne?'

'Coke,' I say.

She laughs.

We settle into a corner and toast our success. Mr Goleniewski has a meeting planned with Geoffrey in the morning. We can't do anything until that meeting is over, other than wait. There are a few other gigs lined up, but Mr Goleniewski says these might change depending on what deal we get.

'So,' I say, once we've been round the houses a few times on what's next. 'Mum?'

Mr Goleniewski sighs. 'When the deal is signed and only then.'

I'd asked a dozen times after we left the service station, blagging the front seat from Daisy, and got exactly nowhere.

'And I mean signed,' he says. 'No earlier.'

I go to speak and Jenny places her hand over my mouth. 'Leave it for now. Let's not go there when things are so good.'

That rankles with me. 'You mean don't let my personal pain interfere with your good news.'

She shakes her head, '*Our* good news. For heaven's sake, Catherine, I'm not having a go. We've just had the best news in history. I just want to enjoy the moment.'

I sip at my Coke. She's right. I'm being an arse. For good reason, but still an arse.

'Sorry,' I say. 'To us and to many albums, a ton of tours and very healthy bank balances.'

The champagne lasts an hour, and we agree that a meal out tonight is a good idea. A wash and brush up first back at the hotel. Mr Goleniewski has an idea where to go for food.

'It is a little different,' he says. 'But then again familiar.'

Cryptic, but he'll say no more.

THE TAXI ARRIVES at the hotel at eight and we all pile in. There have been no further messages from Geoffrey, but Mr

Goleniewski's appointment with him is at nine thirty tomorrow morning. We've agreed that we'll find a café nearby and meet up with him after he's seen Geoffrey.

The restaurant for tonight's celebration is buried up near Farringdon in an area that looks a little down at heel. The taxi driver drops us outside a building painted light blue. There's no sign that this is a place to eat. A door, also light blue, has a small silver plaque on it. With a magnifying glass it reads.

Nieśwież-Szczecin Klub

'You have another club?' I ask Mr Goleniewski as he knocks. 'Not mine. My brothers.'

'It has the same name,' I say and then look again. 'At least I think it has the same name.'

'It is the same. There are four such clubs. One in Glasgow. One here. One in Nieśwież and one in Szczecin. We want one in New York, but that is proving difficult. No one can agree where it should be.'

The door opens, and a man with the Goleniewski forehead stands before us.

'This,' says Mr Goleniewski. 'Is my brother, Piotr.'

'Stanislaw, why have you stayed away from London for so long?' Piotr asks, ignoring us and embracing his brother.

In that moment I realise that I have never known or asked what Mr Goleniewski's first name was.

'Piotr,' he replies. 'Why have you stayed away from Glasgow for so long?'

Piotr smiles and turns to us, 'You are all welcome. We have a Polish band playing tonight, and you will be able to grab some food before they come on. But I would be quick. In here they do not so much eat food as... I forget the word. It means to absorb things through the skin.'

'Osmosis,' says Jenny.

'That is the word,' replies Piotr. 'It is a word that is written on many of our members stomachs.'

We enter and navigate down a set of dimly lit stairs. Piotr pushes open a door. We walk into an almost exact replica of the club in Glasgow.

'All four clubs are built to the same specification,' Mr Goleniewski says, spotting the look on my face. 'We have plans to franchise the business.'

There isn't a spare seat to be seen and, as in Glasgow, a large buffet table leads up to the bar at the rear. On the stage there are five young men setting up equipment.

'It as well that Stanislaw called,' says Piotr. 'We are sold out. The band is good. Come this way!'

He leads us across the floor to near the front. I was wrong about the place being full. There is one empty table with four chairs wrapped around it. A reserved sign sits in the centre.

'What are the band called?' I ask.

'The Nomadic Five,' Piotr answers. 'My son's friend is the lead singer. My son plays the drums. Have you heard of them?'

'No, I'm sorry.'

'Do not worry. You will soon. They are going to be big.'

As the crowd settles, we load up on food from the buffet, and I receive looks from some people while others look away. The memory of the fight in the Glasgow club floods back as Piotr announces that the band will be on in five minutes. We manage to order drinks, and get back to the table just as the lights go down.

If I was being truthful, I'd say that The Nomadic Five were just a touch too like Oasis for their own good. They even finish with a couple of Oasis numbers. Mind you, we only ditched the last of the covers for the gig last night, so what do I know?

Was it only last night?

The band finishes up, and Piotr brings the lead singer over. 'My son's friend, Jan. He wanted to say hi.'

We all say hello.

'May I join you?' Jan asks

Piotr finds a chair and squeezes it next to mine.

'I hear you are also in a band,' Jan says as he sits down.

'You are in the presence of the mighty Chug,' Jenny says.

'Piotr says you are about to sign a record deal?'

I look at Mr Goleniewski. He smiles, 'I told my brother about it.'

'We hope so,' I say. 'But I'll wait until I see the final contract before I believe it.'

'When do you play next? I'd like to see you.'

'I don't know. We had some gigs lined up, but that might change now.'

I find myself drawn a little to Jan. He's a good-looking man in his early twenties. He has an easy manner and a grin that's as cheeky as a comedian's.

'Can I get you a drink?' he asks me.

'I'm good,' I say.

'I need a beer, singing dries me out.'

He gets up and heads for the bar.

'You've clicked!' says Daisy.

'What?'

'Oh yes,' adds Jenny, smiling.

I blink hard. 'He's not said ten words to me.'

'He watched you all through the set. You must have noticed.'

It had struck me that he was looking our way a lot.

'So do you fancy a little Polish in you?' asks Jenny.

Mr Goleniewski scowls, 'What kind of thing is that to say?'

Daisy laughs, 'Mr Goleniewski, we are not children.'

'Sometimes I wonder,' he mutters.

I look at Jan standing in the queue, and wonder exactly how much Polish I could take.

25
THE LIE

TWO ALBUMS, an advance that removes my short-term money worries, a tour for early next year, a full makeover and a boyfriend called Jan. Five items that have been on my wish list forever, a day, and then some. The first four were a moonshot of a wish list. The magic four as Daisy calls them. All agreed that the morning after our night at the club, as we sat in a café. The fifth something that has just never happened. When Jan called the hotel the morning after we heard the details of the deal, he'd asked if I was free that afternoon to 'go for a walk'. I was still buzzing from hearing that Geoffrey had negotiated the magic four, and said yes. We'd met outside the hotel, and I'd half floated along the pavements and paths for the next two hours. When Jan asked if he could see me again, I'd agreed.

'Okay, I'd guess we need nine or ten new tracks, on top of what we have, to make an album,' I say.

The three of us are sitting in a three-bed flat just off the North End Road in Fulham; a stone's throw from the palaces and rollers of Chelsea, and a short hop from the pub we had first played. We have a three-month lease on the place. That's the timeline we have to write and record our first album.

'Is that how it works?' says Daisy.

That has become her favourite phrase as, like us, she has no idea how anything in this world works.

'Should we call Danny?' Jenny asks.

Geoffrey has left the scene to be replaced by Danny Wishart, a forty-three-year-old wannabe pop star that never made it. Danny is our day-to-day contact for all things music-wise. He liaises with the record company people, the tour people, the makeover people and any other people that touch The Chug. Geoffrey still keeps his hand in and materialises, unannounced, once in a while. I get the impression that he loves doing things unannounced.

'I don't think we need to ask Danny,' I say. 'I'd say we need a dozen tracks for the CD, and to get that we need some spares.'

'Most bands write much more than they record,' points out Jenny.

'Do they?' I ask.

'Actually, I've no idea,' she replies. 'But it would make sense.'

'So, we go for fifteen in total to start with?' I suggest.

'And how do we write them?' asks Daisy.

'Why don't we just stick to the way we wrote the last few songs. Everyone seems to like them,' I say.

'Sounds like a plan.'

We were a bit Elton and Bernie on those tracks. I'd scribble some lyrics and Jenny and Daisy would play around until they found a melody. Then we'd get together, wrestling the track into some shape. We are still highly influenced by early eighties electronica but with a far harder edge. Gary Numan's new album, *Exile*—a favourite of the band—is a good example of where we are going. Industrial is the word.

I reach into my backpack, pulling out a large plastic wallet.

'Here,' I say. 'Your starter for ten.'

Daisy takes the wallet and opens it. She drops a pile of A4 sheets on the kitchen table.

'Bloody hell, Catherine!' she says. 'When did you write this lot?'

'I never really stopped after we did the latest tracks. Let me know if any of them work.'

The two of them pour over my scrawls as I brew some more tea. Slowly three piles of paper appear. I sit back, watching the two of them work. A small smile slides over my lips. Jenny, my best friend at school, and Daisy, probably my best friend now, and me—a pop band. It's almost unbelievable. But it just feels so *right*. We watched *The Three Amigos* on telly last night, and agreed that we were the female version—only cooler. Or at least, we think we are cooler. The record deal will be formally signed tomorrow—we may or may not be doing some PR. In readiness, in case the world's media descend on us, Danny had escorted us all to a small but immaculately presented office in Fitzrovia for what turned out to be two days of torture. Otherwise known as media training. A media guru called Wendy showed just how bad we were in front of a camera, microphone or a recording machine. She showed us how easy it was to say the wrong thing. She interviewed us on film before playing it back. We cringed as she filleted us over everything from our view on drugs to bands that we hated. In every case, she twisted our words, and when she played back the result she took pleasure in scribbling up the sort of headlines that our answers could have generated on a whiteboard.

Wendy had asked, 'Catherine what is your view on drugs?'

I'd answered, 'I don't do drugs. They aren't good for you. But each to their own. It's their body.'

Headline: *'Catherine Day thinks drugs are harmful, but people should take them anyway.'*

Wendy had asked, 'Daisy what's the worst band you've ever seen live?'

She'd answered, 'The worst band ever were *The Rubettes*.'

Headline: *'Daisy Ali has a go at classic pop band.'*

Wendy had asked, 'Jenny did you drink when you were underage?'

She'd answered, 'Yes, I had a wee drink when I was at school. Who didn't? It was what you did to fit in.'

Headline: *Jenny Meadows believes underage drinking is cool.'*

By day two, we'd started to get the gig: if you didn't like the question, then you needed to reframe it. Reframe, be interesting, but don't bridge. That's the mantra. Who knew we'd know what that meant?

As I watch Daisy and Jenny at work, it takes another round of teas before all my lyrics have been read and sorted.

Daisy points to the piles, 'These ones work for us, these kind of work, and sorry to say these don't.'

I pick up the ones that work. I count twenty. I take all the others and bundle them back into the folder.

'What about the maybes?' asks Jenny.

'Twenty is plenty,' I say. 'Where do you want to start?'

'What? Start now?'

'The keyboard is in the living room, so is the acoustic guitar. Let's take one of the twenty and I'll watch you sweat.'

An hour later we have a working track. A Sony DAT Walkman, courtesy of Danny, lets us record a rough version of the song as Daisy makes notes. The combo will suffice to make sure we don't forget the tune.

'How Much I Know,' I suggest. 'Does that work for the title?'

Jenny rubs at her temples, 'Can I throw in an idea.'

'You have to ask?'

'I'm wondering if the naming thing for the tracks should be a bit of a signature for us.'

'In what way?'

'Well, all the titles could be one word or two words or all contain the same word or….' She pauses.

Daisy adds, 'I get you. Or they could all start with the word 'The'.'

'Or they all have someone's name in it,' I suggest.

'How many words do you think have 'ch' in them?' Jenny asks.

'Who knows?' I reply. 'Millions.'

'We could make sure that every song has a 'ch' word. After all we are The Chug and our last single was *Check That Back*.

'And do the same for the album title!' I say.

'I'm sure Danny and Geoffrey will have something to say, but 'How Much I Know' works as a song title for me.'

'And as the album title, maybe' I suggest.

'It does that,' replies Daisy.

'Agree,' says Jenny. 'So, the new album is called 'How Much I Know'?'

We all nod.

Over the next few weeks we work our way through my lyrics. Most nights I see Jan. This rubs Jenny and Daisy up the wrong way a little. Partly jealousy, and partly because I cut a few writing sessions early.

Jan is my first real boyfriend. I'm thirty-one years old and he's the only person that I've gone out with for more than two dates. I've met his family, but not read anything into that—Mr Goleniewski was there as a chaperone.

The actual signing of the record contract was more complicated than I thought it would be. Mr Goleniewski had insisted, after our keenness to sign Geoffrey's contract without advice, that we have our own lawyers present. In order to justify their fee they had argued over items on every page. This didn't please the record label, or Geoffrey, but when we did put pen to paper, I felt I knew what we are letting ourselves in for.

The announcement went out the next day. It was low-key, and will make the music press as a by-line. Once that was wrapped up and our songs are good to go, we hit the recording studio with an engineer that has worked on more famous albums than I've had hot cups of tea. He's called Dek, and is so cool that Daisy appeared wearing the same *Sex Pistols* T-shirt Dek had worn when we had first met him at the record label's place

Geoffrey pops in on day one for a pep talk. He's accompanied by our record label Exec, a woman that goes by three names, Chase Whitney Miles or CWM.

'Okay, The Chug,' Geoffrey says. 'This is your album and your album alone. Dek here is simply the wizard that will bring it to life. But we are on a fixed budget.' He looks at CWM when he says this, and she gives a small thumbs up. 'So, if you suddenly fancy the Philharmonic Orchestra as your backing group or think the acoustics would be better in the Amazonian rainforest, forget it. But, if you have a real desire to do something off the wall and can't shake it, you clear it with CWM here first.'

When they both leave, Dek surprises us by asking us all to follow him. He takes us to small room that has a piano in one corner, on top of which is an acoustic guitar. A single tom tom lies next to the guitar, a pair of drumsticks across it.

'Do me a favour,' he says. 'Play me the gig you did at The Band Played On.'

With this he settles into an armchair. Daisy checks that the guitar is in tune. I sit at the piano and Jenny picks up the drumsticks and settles the drum in front of her.

It is, by far and away, the worst gig we have ever played. We sound dreadful, the songs are pitiful, and we stop and start so often we lose track of what we have and haven't played. After an hour we grind to a halt.

'Okay,' says Dek, and stands up.

He takes us back to the studio.

'Play me the last two songs you did at The Band Plays On gig.'

Our equipment is already set up in the studio and we play Dek the songs. When we finish, he asks us all to join him in front of the nixing desk.

'Now tell me about your sound.'

He makes us talk about our favourite bands and where they fit into what we are doing. He yanks CDs from his bag and plays us tracks we've never heard from bands we don't know. When we hit something we like, he drops the CD to one side.

'Go back in and play that last track again.'

We do so and he makes us play it half a dozen times. Recording each take.

'Go grab some lunch!' he orders as we finish.

We do as we are told. The chat over sandwiches is all about how odd the morning has been.

We arrive back to find Dek munching on a banana.

'Sit down!' he says.

We line up in front of the mixing desk.

'Now, this will be rank shit,' he continues. 'Raw as a salt on a wound. You need to be honest with me.'

He doesn't say about what.

He hits a button and the track we played before lunch booms from the speakers. We are spellbound. It's fantastic. Our song, but so much more.

'God!' I say when it finishes. 'You did that over lunch?'

'Yeah, I know. It's crap, but is it going in any direction you like?'

We all nod as if our heads are on springs.

That day turns out to be a false dawn. The next day Dek asks us to play all the other songs we have written. We play him twelve of the fifteen. Again, we are truly dreadful. He makes us play the three others.

'Look girls,' he says, with us gathered at the mixing desk again. 'I kind of get where you are coming from, and you have six real killers in there, but the rest are for shit. Now we can play this one of two ways. I'll make the six great and the others I'll do my best with. Or you can try and give me four others while we are cutting the six.'

I suppose at some point in the future this conversation would take a different arc. Maybe we'd put our foot down about what we have written. Maybe we'd throw our toys out of the pram in a fit of artistic inspired rage. We do neither and agree that I'll play with lyrics and that Jenny and Daisy will play with the tunes while we record the six that Dek likes.

Six weeks later, new tracks have been written, and Dek wraps us up. 'How Much I Know' is born:

'How Much I Know' by The Chug
Track listing

1. *'How Much I Know'*
2. *'Check That Back'*
3. *'The Chairwomen.'*
4. *'I Never Had a Satchel.'*
5. *'Drink Is My Crutch.'*
6. *'Schism'*
7. *'Mother's Choice.'*
8. *'Check My Locker'*
9. *'My Couch Is on Fire.'*
10. *'American Bitch'*

The front cover is to be a picture of the three of us standing in a classroom with the title of the album written on the blackboard in chalk behind us. We're to be dressed in army fatigues but not Polish ones. A kind of hybrid designed by a fashion guru called Judy.

The launch date for the album is set. The record label is thinking that March 1998 will work. It gives us time to rehearse but, more importantly, it also means we can support Telegraph Code on the UK leg of their world tour. An industrial rock band in the style of Nine Inch Nails, they are the hottest thing out of the US at the moment, and musically a good match for us.

'So, what do we do now?' I ask Mr Goleniewski on the night we finish recording.

The two of us are sitting in the flat's kitchen. Daisy is out with Jenny doing some late-night shopping.

'Anything you want,' replies Mr Goleniewski.

'The record deal is signed.'

He says nothing, knowing exactly why I've brought that up.

'And you promised to tell me what else you know when it was done. And I've not mentioned it.'

'I think you overestimate how much more there is.'

'There has to be something else, otherwise why not tell me it all at the service station?'

'I made a promise and I'll stick to it. I'll tell you what I can.'

'What you know.'

'What I can.'

'Go on then!'

'What is it you want to know?'

'Everything.'

'Okay here's what I don't know. I don't know where your mum is, but she may be in America. If she is, I don't know *exactly* where she is. I don't know why she didn't come back at Christmas. I don't know how to get in touch with her.'

'Anything else you don't know?'

'Lots. I don't know how to do Algebra, cryptic crosswords or a decent Windsor knot.'

'And you expect me to leave it at this?'

He pushes back in his chair, the sound of scraping echoing off the kitchen's bare walls.

'Can I tell you a short story? I promise it's to do with your mum.'

'What?'

He pulls the chair back in.

'You met Piotr?'

'Your brother?'

'My brother.'

'What of him?'

'He was married.'

'I know, Jan says she's dead.'

'Did Jan tell you how she passed?'

'She went missing on a safari. It sounded awful.'

'It was. Piotr and Malina hadn't had a break since their son was born. Malina had a hard time conceiving, and their son was a bit of a miracle in their eyes. As such, Malina refused to go anywhere without him for years.'

'Jan said she was attentive.'

'I'd say clingy, but you couldn't blame her. Their son was sixteen when Piotr eventually convinced Malina that they all needed a real break. He was going to scout camp for a week. Piotr knew that Malina had always wanted to go on a safari to see big game. He didn't really have the money, but it had been so long since they had been away together that he called me, and I gave him what I could afford. Things went badly from the start. Even with my cash he was short. He booked through a London middleman who set him up with a bad hotel in Kenya and an even worse tour. On the third day, the tour truck broke down before it even left the hotel and Piotr demanded his money back. The tour guide convinced him that they would make up for it and promised a night on the reserve in a tent to see hippos at a waterhole. Piotr and Malina agreed, but the promised tent was nowhere near a waterhole and the next morning the truck didn't arrive to take them back to the hotel. They were on their own, too, as sometime during the night their guard had walked away. By lunchtime, Piotr, with no idea where he was, decided he would head back along the road they had come in on. He was convinced he'd seen a village at some point. He told Malina to stay put, as she'd twisted her ankle during the night when she needed the toilet. That was the last he ever saw of her. An hour after he left, he realised he was getting nowhere and turned back. When he reached the tent Malina was gone.'

'Jan said that they think she was kidnapped.'

'Maybe. The police were amazed that the couple were where they were. The tour guide had left them right in the middle of an area renowned for rebels. The police suspected that the tour guide had left Piotr and Malina to be captured by the rebels for ransom. It was a common tactic.'

'And she was never found?'

'Never. Piotr sold his stake in a bar he owned to fund a private investigation, and to hire some people to hunt for her. He pressured a government minister, but all to no avail.'

'And what has this to do with my mum?'

'Piotr has been waiting nine years for news of Malina; you have been waiting how long for your mum to come back?'

'Fourteen years.'

'And you think about her every day.'

'I do.'

'And you think what I know will help you?'

'I do.'

'I asked Piotr what I should tell you before we left Glasgow. Unlike you, he has little hope of finding his wife.'

'And what did he say?'

'Tell her everything, Stanislav! He said he would want to know everything.'

'And?'

'I have told you everything.'

'No, you haven't.'

'I have no more.'

'Then why did you say you had?'

I think back on the conversation in the service station and, before he can answer, I put up my hand. 'Please don't tell me what I think you are going to say. Please.'

'It was for your own good, Catherine. You needed to do this. Be here. As far as I know your mother is alive. Unlike Piotr you have much hope, and I couldn't let you throw away this chance. I had to promise I knew more to get you here to sign a deal if one came off.'

The sense of betrayal is overwhelming. 'You used my mother against me. Fourteen years, I've been desperate to know what happened, and you promised me something you don't have.'

'I really don't know anything more than what I have already told you but had I said that to you in the service station, you might have turned around and gone home. I couldn't let that happen. You would be throwing away your life for nor reason.'

'And did Piotr suggest this deception.'

'No, but I know he would do just about anything for a sliver of proof of what happened to Malina. I guessed you would do the same. I am sorry, but it was the best way I could think to make you come to London. I really thought you were going to turn back. I knew I had to tell you I had something more. I shouldn't have, but I did. I had no choice. It was for the best.'

'Best?' my voice is hard. 'Best for who?'

'You now know what I know. You do not know any less because of what I did, but what you do have now is a bright future. If you had not come here, you would not have that. Your mother would have wanted this.'

I clatter my hand down onto the table, 'How the hell would you know what my mother would want for me? How?'

'Because I have been there when you and your mother needed me. She would not let me get close to her. For that I am sorry, but I would not force myself on her. When she left you, I did the best I could, but she made me promise to say nothing about where she was. What would you have had me do?'

'Tell me everything!'

'I did that in the service station.'

'Before then.'

'I could not.'

'Yet you have now?'

'You forced me. I needed you to come here. I have betrayed your mother's wishes.'

'You lied to me.'

'A small lie in the scheme of things.'

I stand up. 'Why should I put up with this? Put up with you?'

He copies me and slams his hand on the table, so hard something cracks underneath. 'Okay! Enough, enough,' he says, his voice loud in the small space. 'I'll tell you why you should put up with this. So, your mum left you. Join the club, Catherine! My mother too left me when I was young. Fourteen to be exact. As have millions of mothers and fathers since time began. Let me be frank. Shit happens, Catherine. Do you get that? Okay, so it was tough. Okay, so it wasn't fair. But life isn't fair. Yet here you are. A dream in your right pocket and a nightmare in your left. Most people don't have anything in their right pocket. Most people have to suck up the vanishing of a loved one and just get on with it. Many fail. Yet what do you have? You have all you bloody want and a mother that is still out there. She isn't gone. Just not here. What would you rather I had done in the service station, let you run back to Glasgow? Then where would you be. Better off? No, you'd be back on the bottle in no time. I have tried all I can to help. Every inch of the way over the years, but you feel so hard done by, that you throw it back in my face.'

He stands up.

'I could have walked away long ago, Catherine. When your mother turned me down, I could have just tried to forget her. Stayed in America. And don't think I'm doing this because you might be my daughter. If you are or aren't, it makes no difference to what I have done. To what I will do. I loved your mum, and I did what I thought was right. I obeyed her wishes, I looked after you and I did what I thought was needed. Do you get that?'

He walks to the window.

'And what was right was to get you and the rest of your band here now. Do you know how hard it was to get you into T in the Park, or to get Geoffrey to even watch your set? What about funding the other gigs, the van, the petrol?. You got a grand for appearing at my club, and I paid that out of my own pocket. The lawyers at your signing. Did they come free? For the last two years I've pulled every string I know to get you to this point.'

'We got here on our own talent!' I shout.

'You have talent, yes. So do many others, but you did not get here on talent alone. And you know that. Without me there would be no band. You would probably be in your grave or, at best, on the street begging for coppers. I knew nothing about managing a band. I knew nothing about treating an alcoholic. I do know something about being abandoned as a child, and at no point did I ever threaten to call it quits and fuck off. And I was damned if I was going to let you do that.'

'What do you want from me - thanks?'

'Damn you, Catherine Day! Yes, thanks would be nice, but what would be nicer is to see you fly. See the band rise. See you set up for life. Then I can do no more. I don't ask for anything else. You do not care about me. That I know. You did not even know my first name until we got to London.'

'A martyr, is that it? You're a martyr?'

He slaps his hand off the wall. 'You make it so hard. I have so often wanted to take you by the jacket and shake some sense into you. I have tried to do what I thought right with one hand tied behind my back. All I ask is that you grab this opportunity and take it as far as you can. Come the album launch, if you want, I will leave. You have my word. You will never see me again. I cannot bring your mother out of hiding. I cannot play the instruments for you. I cannot make you successful, and don't think I'm doing all this for the money! In case you hadn't noticed—which I know you didn't—I am not in the contract. I waved my right to any fee to make sure you three got as much as possible. I have done as much as I can. And if you want me to leave right now, then I will go.'

He storms from the room.

I've never seen him that mad or even close.

'Whoa!' says Daisy walking into the kitchen. 'What did you say to Mr Goleniewski?'

'It's nothing to do with you.'

Jenny strides in behind. 'Did you and Mr Goleniewski have a super argument. He just swore at me. I mean, how often does Mr Goleniewski swear?'

'He was being a dick.'

'Mr Goleniewski?' they both say.

'No way,' says Jenny. 'He's the least dickish person I know. A bit awkward, but not a dick.'

'What went on?' asks Daisy, throwing her shopping bag on the table.

'I'm not talking about it.'

'Oh,' says Jenny. 'I get it.'

'Get what?' I spit.

'Your mum, right? It was about your mum. Time for him to tell all and you didn't like what he had to say.'

'It's none of your business.'

Daisy sits down and pulls a Coke from the shopping bag, pops it and leans back.

'It is,' she says.

'What is?' I ask.

'It is our business, Catherine. In case you haven't noticed we are all on the same train, in the same carriage and sitting next to each other in pre-booked seats that are not transferable. The three of us are joined at the hip, and what cooks your goose fries in everyone's fat.'

'What are you talking about?'

'Just deal with it, Catherine!' she says. 'Deal with your mother issues as best you can but don't let it screw *us* up. Sorry to be so brutal, but all I'm wanting to do is to get this album off the ground and, if that means parking all our personal issues, then so be it. I want us to focus on the group. We've recorded the music. Soon we'll have to hit the road and PR the hell out of it. We need all the help we can get. Pissing off Mr Goleniewski helps none of us. Now, before you lose your rag, I'm only saying what needs saying. Jenny?'

Jenny chips in, 'I'm with Daisy. Band first for the next wee while. It's all we are asking.'

'Have you been talking about this?' I ask.

'Of course,' Daisy replies.

'Yip,' says Jenny.

'And where do I figure in that conversation?'

'Anywhere you want. Do you disagree with what we are saying?' says Jenny.

'I've been lied to by Mr Goleniewski.'

'We know.'

'You do? Were you both in on it?'

'Yip,' says Jenny.

My hand slips from the worksurface it was resting on.

'You were?' I'm stunned.

'Of course, we were,' admits Daisy.

I can't take in what they are saying, nor the casualness that goes with it.

'You needed to know about your mum at some point,' says Jenny.

'Mr Goleniewski gave me that article,' she continues. 'No library was involved. I lied to you. I've not been near the Mitchell since I was a kid. He knew that once you saw the photo on his wall you weren't going to let it lie. He asked me to show you the article on the way down to London. But not until we were well on the way. He thought if you were locked up with me in the van we could talk it out. Break it to you gently. But he always thought that enough would never be enough for you. So we had plan B. If you still wanted more, then he'd promise you more to get you to play ball. Stop you bailing out on us all.'

'You...'

'And before you say it, we both knew that you'd hate us for the whole thing and we still did it.'

'I don't even know where to start.'

Daisy slugs some more Coke, 'Let's be straight here! It wasn't like we planned it months in advance, or that we've been holding out on you. Mr Goleniewski gave us the article half an hour before we got in the van. Okay, we could have told you there and then, and we'd never have left Glasgow. Jenny told you less than an hour after we knew. We weren't trying to stop you finding out about your mum. We were actually trying to help. We just agreed with Mr Goleniewski's take on how to do that. And as far as we can see, it was the best way.'

'Best?'

'Catherine, we can't do anything more about your mum. As far as we're concerned, you know everything there is to know. If we'd known anything else, we'd have told you.'

'When?'

'Well, before now.'

'You both lied to me.'

'We did,' says Jenny. 'And I'd do it again. Being here, doing this, it's the best outcome possible. Not being here, not doing this wouldn't have helped you one little bit.'

'You mean it wouldn't have helped you.'

'Or you.'

'That's not the point.'

Daisy stands up and makes for the door, 'Actually, Catherine, it is.'

'You are both selfish?'

'We're selfish?' says Jenny. 'Really? Tell me this! Are you better off or worse off right at this moment than you would have been back in Glasgow?'

'Who knows?'

'Not true. We know, you know, the bloody postman knows. We are all better off.'

'And you just expect me to accept the way I've been treated?'

'We both knew this moment was coming and if we've blown it with you, well, at least we got the album done. So, you decide how you want to pay us back. Jenny and I are going out for the evening.'

'Your call, Catherine,' Jenny says, as she joins Daisy. 'We'll be at the pub on the corner when you've decided what you are doing.'

With that they leave.

I am stunned.

Simply stunned.

26
LIVE AND DANGEROUS

Six Weeks Later

'LADIES AND GENTLEMEN, welcome to stage the hottest band to come out of Glasgow since Simple Minds. Catherine, Daisy and Jenny—otherwise known as... The Chug!'

How I got through that single song is beyond me. I've watched the video recording of the TV show a hundred times since, and I can see the total panic in my eyes. The sheer fear. My life in danger of being ripped away by one stupid action on one stupid day long ago.

The interview after we finish the song is less than two minutes long; the host, cheery and non-aggressive, asking how we met, why the odd band name and what makes Glasgow such a great place for music. My total contribution to the answers is a grim smile and a muffled thank you at the end. Daisy and Jenny did all the talking.

One hour before we appeared on live TV to sing that song, we had been sitting in the cramped BBC dressing room, nervous like we've never been nervous in our lives.

The call from Geoffrey telling us that he had secured us a slot on the late-night chat show had only come the night before. Telegraph Code, the band we were due to start supporting in a week's time, had been booked to appear. A fault on their plane put their departure from Los Angeles back a day and they could no longer play the slot. Re-booked for the following week, it was

Telegraph Code's lead singer, Ding Radical, that suggested we fill in.

The runner for the TV programme is sitting in front of us. 'Okay, your gear is good to go. When I give the signal then just walk out and take up your positions. The interviews on the stage will still be going on. Just watch and when you're introduced, it's over to you. And remember Catherine, keep your eye on the main camera, just pretend it's a member of your fan club that's asked for you to sing to them. When you've finished, Terry will walk over and interview you. When the interview finishes, stay where you are until the floor manager signals the programme is finished. Got it?'

I don't really want to get it. What I really want to do is slip away into a corner and throw up. We all nod.

'I'll be back in thirty minutes.'

As she leaves we can hear chanting in the distance. One of the guests on the chat show is a local MP turned author. In his autobiography he admits to meeting with an African leader in secret twenty years back. His encounter gave the leader some much needed credibility with key individuals just at a time when he was teetering on the edge of being dumped as the head of his party. The MP's visit shored the leader up and helped him become president at the next election. The country in question is now a basket case, the leader a despot and the people outside Television Centre are taking the opportunity to protest against the MP and the regime he supported.

We had to be escorted through the crowd, which by the admission of our runner, was much larger than had been anticipated. 'We thought maybe a dozen or so protestors,' she had said. There were a hell of a lot more than that when we arrived.

I look at myself in the dressing room mirror. My make-up looks way to heavy, but I've been assured that it is perfect for telly. We are all wearing cut down boiler suits in green khaki - our makeover artists suggestion for a new look. Danny and Geoffrey had 'loved' it. I'm not so sure that we don't look like environmental Ghostbusters whose outfits shrank in the wash. My hair has been shorn short and dyed blonde. Daisy's short and red. Jenny's short and black. I have a fringe that falls over my left eye. I constantly flick at it and, once this is over, I'll gel it out of the way. Daisy's hair is slicked back, Jenny has a pudding bowl cut across the front. We had all been asked to wear killer heels but we all declined. We stuck out for Doc Martins, thinking it more in keeping with the boiler suit look, but now I look down at my feet, I'm of the opinion that, as style gurus go, we won't be setting any trends this century.

'I could kill for a cup of tea,' I say. 'Do you think it's okay to go and hunt one down?'

'The runner will be back soon,' suggests Daisy.

'I need one now. Any later and I'll sweat like a dog when we get on stage.'

I open the dressing room door and look out. The corridor is quiet, no sign of our runner. I remember passing a tea and coffee machine on our way through the maze that led us here. I check my watch. Plenty of time.

I wander down the corridor. A few people squeeze past me in the opposite direction. There seems to be an air of calm that I hadn't expected. To be fair, the BBC have been doing what they do for a long time, and though live TV might sound scary to me, it's bread and butter to the people in this building.

The protestors chanting gets louder, which reassures me. At least I'm heading in the right direction. A few turns and a few doors later, I stumble on the machine, pinned against one wall.

There's a small queue. I tag on at the end, wondering if I should get Daisy and Jenny a cup—I forgot to ask. A few minutes later, and I'm the only one in the corridor, waiting on the machine to spit me out my drink. I've heard so many on-screen jokes about the quality of BBC tea that I'm thinking I'll dine out on the fact that I've had a cup of the stuff.

THE REVENGE WAIT II…

'Fancy meeting you here!'

I spin to the sound of the voice.

'Isobel?' I exclaim.

If anything, she's thinner and more distressed looking than when I last saw her. And I wouldn't have thought that possible. Her crew cut is now shaved to bald. Her jacket is more a parachute on her than a loose fit. Behind her is Billy. He's Hardy to her Laurel. A gut the size of a beer barrel pushing out through an ancient 'Frankie Says Relax' T-shirt. His hair is down to his shoulders, as greasy as a Healy's scotch pie.

'What are you doing here?' I ask. 'How did you get in?'

'We're here to see you,' she replies. 'And getting in was easy. There's so much nonsense going on outside, it was a doddle to slip in through the back way. You've just saved us the job of tracking you down. We were clueless where you might be.'

She smiles, revealing a set of nicotine-stained teeth, a few missing, giving the smile all the warmth of cold pound of tripe.

'I'm calling security,' I say.

'Good luck with that,' Billy says. 'They are all out front. Be our guest, but aren't you on telly shortly?'

'What in the hell do you want?'

A man, holding a clipboard, breezes by, giving us all a sideways glance.

'Let's use that room there,' says Isobel, pushing open a door.

Beyond is another dressing room, larger than ours, but no less tired.

'In!' she orders.

'No way!' I reply.

For a fat bloke, Billy moves quickly, shoving me hard in the back, catapulting me through the door. They both slip in behind me and shut the door. Billy takes up station as a guard, hands folded, standing in front of me. Isobel switches on the light. She points at the dressing table.

'Take a seat Catherine!'

'I'm due on telly.'

'This won't take long.'

'What do you want? Money?'

She scratches at the palm of her hand. 'Funny you should mention money. Isn't an itchy palm a sign you are about to come into some?'

'Just tell me what you want?'

'Want, Catherine, want? Well, what *do* we want, Billy?'

Billy smiles, his teeth, if anything, an even better ad for not skipping out on your annual dentist visits than Isobel's. 'You tell her, sis!'

'Well, Catherine, what I really want to do is fuck you over. Good and proper. Royally stick it to you. Does that make sense?'

'No. I don't understand.'

'Let me put it another way. When we first met you, which, by the way, was no accident—the queue in the Bru was our go to for mules back in the day. You could always spot the desperate ones. And you were so desperate-looking we thought you'd be good for at least a few years of transporting shit. Anyway, we gave you your wee job and, like a good little slave, off you toddled and made the delivery.'

The way she's talking, I get the impression that this is a speech that she's been practicing in her head for a long time.'

'But that was also your last day. Wasn't it? We got lifted before you could shift anything else for us.'

God, someone saw me at the back green! They know I was responsible. My legs fold and I slump back on the dressing table, barely staying upright.

'And that's the issue here,' she says. 'We meet you and like some magic trick we're banged up in no time. Like you're some bad luck omen or something. We've recruited loads of others and never a hitch. We recruit you and things go south in a big way.'

'I had nothing to do with that.'

'That's not what we heard. A wee birdy says you were in the vicinity. Was it you that called in the polis?'

'No.'

'No matter. I'm treating it as if you did. It makes what comes next both satisfying and easy. You mentioned money, and although I haven't read it anywhere, I'm assuming that your little band got an advance. Isn't that what they call it? A bit of cash in hand?'

'I'm not giving you any money.'

'So you think,' says Billy.

'I'm not.'

'I think, Catherine, that you will,' Isobel points out. 'It might be the only way to save your fledgling music career from imploding before it can get off the ground.'

I brave up, 'I want out of here.'

Billy moves closer. He places his hand on my shoulder, 'Just take a wee rest there, darling!'

'Now,' says Isobel. 'We don't want you to miss your big break on telly, do we? So I'll make this swift. You see, me and Billy here are right short on readies. We had to blag our way down on the train. Nae bugger checks your tickets if you hide in the bog. We haven't any accommodation lined up for tonight and we need to find some. So, I'm going to make this quick.'

She joins Billy, close to me, hand on my other shoulder. I think about kneeing Billy in the ball sack. It would be easy, but he senses something and backs away a little.

'So, I think you need to start paying towards our pension, Catherine,' says Isobel. 'A wee contribution on a weekly basis to keep us in ciggies and booze. Let's say a hundred quid a week.'

'What?'

'Make that two hundred. I'm sure you can afford it. Just pop it in an envelope. I'll give you an address to send it too.'

'You're mad,' I say. 'I'm sending you nothing.'

'I thought you'd say that, so I have a wee mind sharpener to counter that thought. Now, you and I know that you delivered a package to BarL for us. And you know that it wasn't a birthday cake with a file in it. And you're thinking, after all this time, what does that matter? Well, here's how I see it. We're not dumb, Catherine, and we knew, back then, that our mules were our weak link. Some of the mules thought they could get one over on us. Indulge in a little blackmail. Threaten to out us to the polis. So, we needed to make sure we had our arses covered on that one.'

She presses down harder on my shoulder, and I wince.

'To do that, we bought a few handheld videocams. Amazing how good the picture quality is. We have a wonderful tracking shot of you at the Mount Florida station picking up the package and taking it to the park. Just wonderful! And we have a few shots of you on the bus to BarL, walking up to the prison, your little detour up to the golf club. We even managed to get some cracking CCTV footage of you in the prison reception sticking the package in the locker.'

'None of that means squat. That package could be anything.'

'We also thought of that. We even have the wrapper of the package. Go figure, for all these years, it's been sitting in my flat. And I'd wager that your fingerprints are still there. And if all of that is for shit, so what? All I have to do is release the video anyway, and your record label will dump you like a cold bowl of sick—whether our story stacks up or not.'

'That is all nonsense'

'No, Catherine, it's not. It really isn't. You know it and I know it. No smoke without fire. Deny it all you want, but I still think your record deal will die.'

'Bollocks!'

'Okay, if all that doesn't convince you, what about this? Do you want to know what the money you smuggled in was used for?'

'I don't care. It'll be drugs or drink.'

'Drugs and booze? That's not even worth talking about. The place is so awash with both, who would care? But if you do want to know what the money was for, do yourself a favour, and read up on an inmate called Cam Reid, also known as Heavy Cam.'

I don't need to. He's famous. He was accused of burning down a flat with an entire family in it. Mother, father, three kids, granny and a grandson. He'd nailed the front door shut. Being on the fourth floor it was the only way out, then he'd poured a gallon of four star through the letter box and lit the lot with a firework. He then broke into the neighbouring house before throwing a three-piece suite, and a sideboard down the tenement stairs to block it, slowing down the fire brigade. His dumb attempt at abseiling from the other flat by a clothes line, left him dangling two floors up. He was rescued, but by the time the fire brigade got to the fire, the entire family were dead.

The story doesn't finish there, because Cam escaped. And, as far as I know, he has never been caught.

'You see, Heavy slipped out of BarL on the back of a couple of hefty bribes that led to a fortuitous lack of diligence on the part of a few guards. And your money made that possible. So, forgive me if the headline 'Rock Star Smuggled Family Slayer's Escape Money Into Prison' doesn't make your record label feel warm and cuddly.'

I've nothing to say.

'Anyway, you are due on telly and the more famous you are, the more money you'll have. And that's in Billy's and my interest. So off you go and sing for your supper!'

'Why now?' I ask.

'Because you are just about to hit the big time. And that means money. Why bother before?'

She moves to one side, and Billy stands clear of the door. I glance at my watch. Five minutes to show time. I leave, and more by luck than design, navigate my way back to the dressing room.

Daisy, Jenny and the runner are none too happy at my last-minute return.

I'm none too happy at life.

27

EXPOSURE

THREE WEEKS ON from that night and I'm still sweating on what to do. With no address to send any money to and no sign of one, I'm of the opinion that Isobel and Billy are playing with me, planning to pull the plug at the most opportune moment. Namely the day we launch our album. Until then, hang out the threat of revelation and sit back and enjoy watching me fall apart. For that is what I'm doing, one panicky hour after another. It doesn't matter that their claim of videos could be horse shit. Or that opening up this old wound could incriminate them. Or that the idea of my fingerprints having survived for all these years sounds far-fetched. Or, or, or…

Daisy and Jenny all but stopped talking to me last week. My erratic behaviour since the BBC show has blindsided them at every turn. Moody silences, unjustified accusations, throwing stellar tantrums over trivial transgressions, no-shows at rehearsal, diva-esque demands over food, drink, dress—the list is extensive. I'm more than aware of my deeds, but I fight back.

'You've no idea what I'm going through.'

'If I want to do X, I'll bloody do X. And Y and Z, and any bloody thing I want to!'

'I'm not a robot.'

'I need time to myself.'

'Go take a f….'

The tour with Telegraph Code kicks off tonight, and I'm sitting on the edge of my bed in the down at heel guest house that is our accommodation. Telegraph Code are slumming it at the five-star Hilton along the road. Daisy and Jenny are out on a retail therapy trip. We've a sound check in an hour. This should be one of those moments in life. The gig is a sell-out. They all are. Even for us as support, the venue will be easily a quarter full, maybe more, when we take to the stage. With a capacity of two thousand, that will make our share of that the biggest audience we've ever played to. To add grist to what should be a sweet, sweet mill, Radio 1's Steve Lamacq is bigging up our single, *How Much I Know*, and we've been approached by Dave 'Storm' Raider to do a dance remix. Storm has three number one dance hits under his belt in the last year. We got five stars on the NME review of the album and nothing less than four on most of the rest of the music press. Although still a year away, there is already talk of a BRIT nomination.

I rock back and forth on the edge of the bed, working through the range of options that I've ground to death, including grinding Isobel and Billy to death.

There's a knock on the door. I open it and Mr Goleniewski is standing there.

'Can I come in?' he asks.

I step back and let him enter. I drop back to the bed. He hands me a quarter pound of mint humbugs—my favourites.

'Thanks,' I say.

'I need to talk to you, Catherine.'

'What's stopping you?'

He grimaces.

'I need you to be honest with me, Catherine.'

'Okay, I'll be honest. Can you leave me alone right now? We have a big gig tonight and I don't need any lectures.'

The room isn't large enough for a chair and I've spread my arms out across the bed, preventing him sitting down. So he stands.

'I'll go,' he says. 'But first I need to say something.'

'If you've come to tell me I'm acting like an idiot, don't bother. I know, and I don't care.'

'Do you have a self-destruct button, Catherine?'

'Yeah, under my left armpit. I forget it's there, and every so often set it off by mistake when showering. Do you want to see it?'

'Stop this. Do you know how well things are going?'

'Not so much for me.'

'Daisy and Jenny are angry with you.'

'Thick as thieves those two. They're supposed to be my friends, but act like a married couple. I'm the unwanted elderly aunt that smells of cats and piss.'

'You push them away at every turn. And me. And to be frank, everyone. Ever since the night of the chat show.'

'So?'

'Geoffrey came to see me.'

'Nice for you.'

'He's seen a lot of acts come and go in this business, Catherine. A *lot*. The Chug are just another pebble in his pond. And once your ripples stop, he'll let you sink to the bottom in a heartbeat. But he thinks you have real potential. He also thinks, to put it in his words, that you, Catherine Day, are doing your best to throw it all away.'

'Really?'

'Really!'

'Look, I'm tired.'

'Do you know that Daisy and Jenny have talked to me about replacing you?'

'What? They can't do that. I'm the lead singer, the song writer and I'm on the contract we have. They can't.'

'Yes, they can. Jenny can sing, you don't write the tunes, and the contract has a clause specifically for this type of thing. If you think that you're irreplaceable, then think again.'

'Why? Because I've been a bit moody.'

'There is no 'bit' in this conversation. Since the TV appearance, you've gone out of your way to hack everyone off at every turn. Walking on eggshells, I think they call it. Well, we've been walking on a desert of eggshells and it's taking its toll. Daisy and Jenny should be having the time of their life but they feel like they are trapped in some sort of Catherine-generated hell. And I'm not exaggerating here, Catherine. No one wants to be in the same room as you at the moment. The rehearsals have suffered. Ding from Telegraph Code sneaked into watch you yesterday, after which he asked his management if they could change their support act.'

'Do you mean drop us?'

'That's exactly what I mean. Geoffrey had to step in late last night to stave that off. He wanted to come to see you, but I convinced him to let me talk to you instead.'

The rehearsal had been horrible. I'd sang like an idiot, cracked up at the slightest thing and knew fine well I was screwing it up.

'Daisy and Jenny were left crying after your histrionics,' he says. 'First, they asked if they could replace you, and then they asked if they could walk out. Do you realise how close this all is to imploding? Do you?'

'And it's all down to me? Is that it. Catherine the Bad!'

'What is going on, Catherine?' he asks, staring into my eyes. 'And don't tell me it's your mother. You don't get to play that card today.'

'It's nothing. Now can you leave?'

'Are you going to be there tonight?'

'Yes.'

'Don't let yourself down. But, more importantly, don't let Jenny and Daisy down!'

There's another rap on the door. I roll over and lie down, 'If that's Daisy and Jenny tell them I'll make my own way to the soundcheck.'

He opens the door.

'Yes,' he says.

'We're here to see Catherine.'

Isobel's voice comes from behind Mr Goleniewski.

'And you are?' he asks.

'None of your business.'

'Catherine is getting ready for a gig.'

'I don't care if she's getting ready for an OBE, just get out of the way!'

Mr Goleniewski turns around, 'Do you want to see anyone?'

I shake my head.

'She doesn't want to see anyone.'

'Catherine,' Isobel says. 'Do we want to discuss prison visits from out here.'

I push myself upright, 'Let her in!'

Mr Goleniewski stands to one side and Isobel pushes past.

'Can you tell this old fart to bugger off?' she says.

Billy squeezes in.

'Catherine are you okay with these people,' Mr Goleniewski says.

The word 'these' is squeezed between his teeth as if it's a bad taste.

'I'll be fine Mr Goleniewski.'

'Are you sure?'

'Yes,' I say. 'I'm fine.'

'Okay, see you at the soundcheck.'

He leaves, reluctantly. Once the door is shut I say, 'What do you want?'

'You're behind on payments,' Isobel says. She's wearing exactly the same clothes she had on back in the BBC's building.

'In case you haven't noticed, you never gave me an address.'

'A clever girl like you could have found that out.'

'How? I don't know where you live.'

'Let's call it two grand and we'll be on our way.'

'I don't have that kind of money on me.'

'You got an advance.'

'Of which I haven't seen a penny yet. It could be weeks. That's the way it works.'

'I'm sure that if you ask nicely, you can unlock that particular bank account.'

'I can't. I have eighty quid in my purse and could probably get a hundred more from the hole in the wall. Once the advance is in I can pay more.'

Billy laughs, 'A ton eighty? Is that it? Do you know how hard it is down here to find food and shelter?'

'You've been down here the whole time?' I ask.

'An old friend of mine has a squat,' Isobel says. 'Real comfy and the old dear that owned the place had stashed some cash. We've had a fine time, but the money has run out and we are on the hook for some favours from a few friends.'

I grunt, 'You mean dealers.'

'Friends.'

'So, I'm your get out of jail free card. You owe some bad types and it's time for me to pay up.'

'You're so on the ball, Catherine,' she says. 'So, call who you have to, and rustle up the cash!'

'I told you. I can't. If I ask for anything like that amount, they are going to ask what it is for.'

'Your problem. I've got a ten pence piece in my pocket and the number for a journalist that interviewed me not long back. He's promised me a little folding for any good stories I might have. Not much money - but if you are going to stiff us, better than nothing.'

'I just can't get it.

'We'll give you until tomorrow morning or I make that call. Come on Billy, let's see if the squat has anything new to attract us!'

When they've both gone, I sit and stare at the floor. I look at my watch. I need to go. With legs of lead, I stand up. The last thing I want to do is a sound check, but I can't afford to get the bullet from the band. Maybe I can blag some cash from Mr Goleniewski. Two grand is a stretch, but if I can get a few hundred I might hold off Isobel and Billy until I can figure out what to do.'

As I walk down the stairs, the owner of the guest house appears. A small, grey-haired woman of late vintage who seems to spend most of her time in the back room with the telly on full volume.

'That man Jan phoned again,' she says.

'Thanks.'

'He asked to talk to you, but I told him what you told me to. That you were out.'

'Thanks.'

Since the evening at the BBC with Isobel, I've put Jan on hold. Blanking him at every turn. He's been persistent, even turning up here twice. He's on the guest list tonight, so I'll have to see him.

The walk to the venue takes me past a thousand people with a thousand lives, and a thousand people that I'd swap with right now. When I reach the stage door, I stop and lean on the wall, wondering if it would be better to walk away. Do a Mum. Vanish.

Maybe make for the States, New York. Track down Michael Goleniewski's contacts, PI Catherine Day back in action. A gumshoe on the streets of the Big Apple. It has a romantic ring to it. Slapping leather on the sidewalk, sipping coffee from Dunkin' Donuts, the ring of drain covers echoing amongst concrete canyons as yellow cabs zip over them. Maybe a bagel in Bryant Park, a trip on the Staten Island ferry at midnight, a stroll across Brooklyn Bridge. Chewing pizza on Brooklyn Heights while looking down on Governors Island, staring out to Ellis Island, the Statue of Liberty, to New Jersey and beyond. Bruce Springsteen on the Walkman, telling me where he was born.

I mean how hard could it be? Wouldn't I be closer to what I really want?

I turn my back on the venue and take a step. The first step? The beginning steps? No Isobel. No Billy. No return to the dank flat in Glasgow scraping a few coppers for some cheap wine when they have grassed me up. Cornton Vale avoided, a stretch in prison a sure way to hammer home that life-ending nail.

Just keep walking!

'Catherine?'

I realise that I've wandered more than a block away from the stage door. Daisy is in front of me.

'Where are you going?'

A good question.

'Eh, just getting some air.'

'The venue is the other way.'

'Is it? Oops.'

'You *are* going to turn up tonight. Aren't you?'

'Like you care? Wouldn't you be better as a duo? Seems to me, that the two of you can't get enough of each other.'

'What are you talking about?'

'Mr Goleniewski told me all about your plan to throw me out.'

'Don't be stupid!'

'Are you saying he's lying?'

'No, but we were angry after yesterday. It needs to be said— you were crap, and you were crap in front of Ding. Bloody *Ding*. Shit, he's got more influence than Bill Clinton at the moment, and you chose to sing like a turkey with its throat cut. And then you stormed out in another one of your hissy fits. Did Mr Goleniewski tell you that Geoffrey had to save us from getting booted off the tour before it's even started. And why? Because you're a moody, angry cow that doesn't seem to understand what damage she's doing. What is really going on here?'

'Nothing.'

'This is our fucking future, Catherine Day. Yours, mine, Jenny, even Mr Goleniewski's. It's our fucking futures!'

She's belting out the words, turning the few heads that are walking this back water.

'We have the bloody chance of a lifetime, Catherine Day. The album won't sell itself. We need this tour, and we need it now. Twelve dates and we could be made, and you're acting like a fucking spoilt teenager. That's why we asked last night if we could dump you. We don't want to lose you, but we *really* don't want to lose this—and you're making us choose. What in the hell is wrong?'

At that moment, Isobel appears, Billy by her side, standing at the next corner, her crooked smile wide and on full view. She lifts her hand and rubs forefinger and thumb together, mouthing the word 'money' at the same time.

'Well, screw this,' I say and Daisy jumps. 'Let's get this done!'

I storm along the road, Daisy in tow, trying to breeze past Isobel and Billy. Isobel grabs me by the arm and whispers; 'Change of plan. Money before the gig tonight. We can't wait until the morning.'

She lets me go and Daisy throws me a look.

'It's okay,' I say and carry on

Ten minutes later, we're on stage. I've no idea what I can do next. There is no way I can get the cash Isobel wants, but I owe the girls and Mr Goleniewski.

'I'll see you tonight,' I say, as we finish the check.

'Promise,' says Jenny.

'I promise.'

For the next few hours, I wander through the heart of London, finding myself up by Vauxhall Bridge. I stop and watch the dirt brown water as it slides beneath me, the roar of traffic a constant behind. In the distance, I can see Battersea Power station, the four iconic chimneys poking into the London evening sky. I walk back to the guest house with not a single thought on how I'll get any money. I think about confessing all to Mr Goleniewski, Jenny and Daisy. And dismiss that. Isobel will still make the phone call when she finds out I've blabbed, and I'll still be screwed. I've never felt less like doing something than this gig.

I dress, and when there's a knock at the door, Daisy is there, standing ready.

'Mr Goleniewski has the van downstairs.'

I fall in behind her and we descend to the ground floor in silence. I take the front seat without asking, and Daisy and Jenny take the cinema seats. We rumble through London, me saying nothing.

At the venue we get to work with our set up. We've been allocated the front of curtain space, with Telegraph Code already set up behind. We'll perform here, and when we're finished we'll clear our stuff and the curtains open. That will be the same set up for all the gigs, with or without curtains. In every case, we have a six feet strip of stage to play with.

Once we are good to go, we walk back to our dressing room—a cramped space that has less room than a phone-box. It smells the same.

More silence.

I'm waiting on Isobel to appear. I'm not sure how she'll get back here but she managed to slip security at the BBC. Jan appears half an hour before we are due to go on. He wishes us all good luck and gives me a peck on the cheek. Seeing him doubles the hurt. I'm going to lose all this. Jan, the band, the lot. It hurts so bad that I start crying. Jenny shuffles over.

'Jesus, Catherine, what in the heck is wrong? Please just tell us!'

The tears want to flow hard but I sniff back.

'Anyone got any gin?' I say.

'No way, Catherine,' says Daisy. 'You can't drink. You've been off it for too long. Not tonight.'

'If I want a drink, I'll have a drink.'

'Please, Catherine, please don't!' pleads Jenny.

'I've had enough.'

I'm about to stand up when there's a bang on the door. It flies opens. Isobel dives in and bounces into Daisy. Billy follows.

I'm so screwed.

And then there's Mr Goleniewski standing behind them with another man next to him—a stranger, but a stranger built like a granite lavvy.

'Tell her what she needs to hear!' says Mr Goleniewski to Isobel.

Isobel looks back over her shoulder.

'Now!' shouts Mr Goleniewski.

Daisy pushes Isobel away, 'Who the hell are you?'

'Now,' Mr Goleniewski repeats. 'Talk. Right now!'

'Okay, okay,' Isobel says. 'Look Catherine, I think you might have got me a little wrong. I've been having a wee think about our chats…'

'Just tell her!' shouts Mr Goleniewski.

'Okay, okay. There's no video tape, Catherine, at least not anymore, and there's no package. Billy and I are going home.' She turns back to Mr Goleniewski. 'Will that do?'

'No,' says Mr Goleniewski. 'The rest.'

'For fuck's sake.' She spins back to look at me. 'Okay, we can't tell anyone about what went down. Your man here has made sure of that. You'll not hear from us again.'

She turns to Mr Goleniewski. 'Am I done?'

'Yes. Now get the fuck out of here and remember what we talked about! One wrong word and you'll be inside so quick that your nose will bleed. And that goes for your brother. Now, fuck off!'

Mr Goleniewski moves to one side to let her go. When they have left, he steps into the room, standing right in front of me.

'Right, Catherine Day. Is that things sorted?'

My head is a mill race.

'Tell me, Catherine,' he says. 'Is that it all sorted? Is there anything else, or is that it?'

'How?' I stammer.

'We can chat tomorrow, but whatever you think those idiots had on you is gone—for ever. So, tell me, is that things straight?'

I nod.

'And are you going to knock it clean out of the park tonight?'

He raises his hand into the air. Daisy and Jenny are looking so confused it almost makes me smile. I raise my hand and touch Mr Goleniewski's. Jenny stands up and, slowly, raises hers. Daisy does likewise.

'Chug, Chug, Chug,' we all shout, but before the others can finish, I shout 'Let's Chug!' They join in, and Mr Goleniewski leaves.

'What in the hell?' says Daisy.

'Catherine?' says Jenny.

'Later, team.' I say. 'Let's get this done.'

The call goes out for us to hit the stage.

I float along the dark corridor, the sound of the anticipatory crowd growing in my ears. We walk out to cheers, and I glide to the microphone. I look out on the crowd. I feel like a hundred tons has been lifted from my chest. I breathe deep. 'London. I am Catherine and these are Daisy and Jenny. Together we are… The Chug!'

That night we don't just knock it out of the park. We slug the bloody thing clean out of the sodding city.

28
ACROSS THE POND

THE FOLLOWING MORNING dawns as if the sun has never risen before. I'm up by five o'clock, in another half hour I am downing a coffee from an early morning riverside van. I'm not sure it's possible to feel any better than this. I have no clue what Mr Goleniewski said or did to Isobel and Billy, but they both looked down-and-dirty scared.

After the gig, Ding apologised to me for asking to dump us.

'You've got something,' he'd said. 'You were awesome tonight. Really got something.'

We sold out of CD's and T-shirts after the show, and a beaming Geoffrey appeared to tell us that he'd rarely seen such a good first support gig. When he left, Daisy, Jenny and I bounced around the room for an age. No one asked me about the incident in the dressing room earlier. I've no doubt they will, and I'll need to work out what I'll say. The truth is probably the best bet. I owe them that at least.

I stroll along the riverbank, drinking coffee. I'm so buzzing, I could break into a run and keep going all the way back to Glasgow. Except we have a gig down in Brighton tonight, and Mr Goleniewski is picking us up at ten o'clock. I wander back to the guest house. Mr Goleniewski is sitting in the small park opposite. He waves to me, and I cross the road.

'Couldn't sleep, Catherine?'

'No. You?'

'I always get up early. It's an age thing. My bladder hasn't got the capacity to make it through the night anymore. Three hours max between pees, even if I don't drink a thing for a month.'

I need to know, 'What happened with Isobel and Billy?'

'You should have told me all about it and what they were planning on doing.'

'I couldn't.'

'You could have. When did they first approach you about money?'

'I saw Isobel in Glasgow not long before we left for here, but she didn't ask for cash until the night we did the BBC show.'

'They were at the BBC?'

'Sneaked in under cover of that protest.'

'Which is why you were so bad that night?'

'Isobel told me what she would do if I didn't find money, just five minutes before I went on.'

'And what did you do that she was blackmailing you about?'

'She didn't tell you?'

'She did, but I want to hear from you.'

And so I offload, and not just about the trip to BarL. I talk and talk, until I can talk no more. When I finish, he suggests we go for a short walk. We find a greasy spoon café, and both of us load up on a hot breakfast.

'So, tell me, what did you say to Isobel and Billy?' I ask, once my first roll and sausage is gone.

'I heard you talking to her in the guest house room after I left. I just listened at the door. She should have checked I'd really gone. She's either not very bright or she's over-confident.'

'I think the latter.'

'Either way, when I heard what you talked about, I knew I had to do something.'

'You could have asked me about it all once they left.'

'And what would you have told me?'

'Probably nothing.'

'So, I got to work,' he says. 'I still have some contacts in the security world. I called them, told them I needed info on Isobel and Billy, double quick.'

'How could they do that? Where would they even start? And with such speed?'

'Do you really want to know that I have had someone spying on you for a while? That I had them follow Isobel back to her flat in Glasgow after she first appeared? Just in case?'

'No.'

'I thought not. Anyway, I also followed the two of them after they left your guest house, and then called in Borys. He's like me. Old school. Let's say he can be persuasive, got the info we needed, and we'll leave that bit of the story alone.'

'Did they have a video of me?'

'Yes. It was found in their place in Glasgow.'

'Who found it?'

'Someone.'

'And they got the video?'

'Yes.'

'Isobel could have a copy.'

'I doubt it, but even if she does, she'll not want a visit from Borys again. We also lifted the package with your finger prints that she talked about—although it was just a crumpled-up piece of paper next to the video in an old shoe box.'

'And that's that?'

'Well, we did suggest that should they come near you again, not only would Borys visit them but that the drug squad were always interested in tip offs. They got the idea'

'But what I did was wrong. Back then at Barlinnie. It was wrong. A killer is on the loose because of me.'

'The one that used your money to escape?'

'You know about that?'

'Isobel made that up. We checked. He broke out months after you were there but not from BarL. He escaped while on a visit to hospital. Your money had nothing to do with that.'

'But what I did was still wrong. I smuggled that money in.'

'Given what you've just told me, I'm not sure that I might not have done the same.'

'And if the story gets out anyway?'

'What proof is there?'

I think on that before asking, 'And what about Daisy and Jenny?'

'They need to know. And from you.'

'God, they will hate me!'

'You might find that they are better friends than that.'

I munch on the next roll, and I see Mr Goleniewski in a whole new light, 'I don't know how to thank you.'

'Just don't keep stuff to yourself in the future.'

'I have one more question?'

'Not about your mum?'

'Kind of, but it is a personal question.'

'Go on.'

'How will I know if you are my dad?'

'DNA would tell us.'

'You'd do that?'

'If you want me to.'

'And if you are my father?'

'We'll deal with that when it happens.'

'And what if my dad is Michael?'

He takes a small drink of his tea and a bite of his roll before he replies, 'Well, if his claim of being the rightful heir to the throne of Russia is true, you may be in a different world. But that is a long shot.'

'What him being my dad?'

'No. Him being the heir to the Russian throne.'

'But you believe him?'

'There is a difference between believing and proving.'

'You once said people are interested in me.'

'More than you can imagine. Michael's claim may be a long shot, but there are groups out there who still think Russia needs an Emperor or, in your case, an Empress, and they believe in Michael's claim.'

'What groups? Where are these groups?'

'Who do you think the members of the Nieśwież-Szczecin Klubs are?'

'Really?'

'That night in Glasgow. When there was a fight. That was because some of our newer members lied to us. They were non-believers. We've got lax and some of the people that disagree with us got into the club. Only believers are allowed in now.'

'How can you tell if someone is a believer?'

'You can't, that is why we will have to be on our guard. There are others out there that want to make sure no royalty ever returns.'

'Bloody hell! Am I in danger?'

'To be honest. Maybe. But I am here, as are others.'

'But why are the Polish so interested? Why not Russians?'

'Do you know why the club is called the *Nieśwież-Szczecin Klub?*'

'Lena told me it was named after two towns.'

'That's correct. Nieśwież or Nesvizh as it is now, had been, at one time, in Poland, then in Russia, then Lithuania, and now it is in Belarus. More importantly, it's the city where Michael Goleniewski was born.'

'And you were also born there?'

'Correct, I was.'

'And Lena said that Szczecin was the birthplace of Catherine the Great.'

'Yes, it was. The last empress of Russia, Catherine the Great. It was in Prussia back then, but is in Poland now and some of us Poles use that to lay a small claim to Russian royalty.'

'And if I'm royalty, I am seen as Catherine the What?'

'Catherine the Pop Star, if you are my daughter, and Catherine the Second if Michaels' claim is true.' Then he adds, 'I have one more question, Catherine.'

'What?'

'I said I'd leave if you didn't want me to stay around. I will stand by that offer.'

I stand up and take his hand, pulling him up. I lean forward and kiss him on the cheek and say, 'Don't be so bloody stupid.'

WE WALK BACK to the guest house to meet up again at ten. I force Mr Goleniewski into a cinema seat, and convince Daisy to drive, with Jenny making it three up front. I use the journey to Brighton to confess all. And Mr Goleniewski is right; they are far better friends than I deserve.

We arrive in Brighton, see the sights, check out the venue, do the sound check, set up, and later that night we are ready to knock 'em dead when Ding walks into our dressing room.

'Hi girls,' he says. His hair follows ten minutes later along with the most gorgeous scent of expensive cologne. He's such a rock star. 'I loved last night. So much so, I've got a proposal for you.'

We all sit like giggling teenagers.

'After we finish the tour in Glasgow,' he says. 'We have a week's break and then we're touring the States. We have twenty-three gigs lined up on the east coast.'

He smiles. A row of pearly whites that probably cost more than my flat.

'And' he says. 'How would you like to open for us in the States?'

All three of our mouths drop open at the same time.

'I've cleared it with your management. They think it's early to go to the USA, but I don't. We are on the same label, and they are up for releasing the new album in the States. After that, you are free to come back here and do your own tour. You'd be back in month. I think they have some dates here for you already.'

Our jaws drop even further.

We say nothing, and he shrugs. 'Anyway, let me know what you think!'

Jenny jumps up. 'What do you mean think? Yes! Yes! Yes!'

Daisy screams an even louder yes.

The USA.

Mum.

Mum is in the USA.

The answer to why she left me is in the USA.

And, right now, my future and past are in the USA.

I also holler my own 'yes!', throwing my hand in the air. Jenny and Daisy leap, hands up with me and we shout, louder than we have ever shouted.

'Chug, Chug, Chug.'

'Let's Chug!'

ACKNOWLEDGMENTS

This was a book written during lockdown (I forget which one). I rose at five to five thirty each morning and took a mental trip back to the eighties and nineties.

For those who are interested, Michael Goleniewski was a real triple agent during the cold war and he did, indeed, claim to be Alexei, the son of the Nicholas II and Alexandra. He even married under the name Alexei Romanoff in 1964 and had a child (although in reality she was called Tatiana – not Catherine). As to whether he had a cousin who ran Polish clubs, I doubt it. And he never met Catherine's mum, or was interviewed by MI5, save for in my imagination.

As to any factual errors with the world of 1984 to 1997, you can blame my memory for that.

Can I thank my beta readers, Irene Sutherland, Tracy Hall and Lucy Sampson. And a big thanks to Gwen Jones-Edwards for all her editing skills. Can I also thank Sean Coleman, my publisher and editor, for giving so much time to my book. To Kirsty Nicholson for the idea behind the cover. Can I also thank Sharon Bairden for all her help, and my agent, Kevin Pocklington.

And to Lesley, my wife, for putting up with me waking her every morning as I tried, unsuccessfully, to slip from bed to write without waking her.

ABOUT THE AUTHOR

Gordon J. Brown was born in Glasgow, and lived in London, Toronto and a small village called Tutbury before returning home. His day job, for many years, was as a marketing strategy specialist, and he helped found Scotland's international crime writing festival, Bloody Scotland.

Any Day Now is his tenth novel. He's a DJ on local radio, has delivered pizzas in Toronto, sold non-alcoholic beer in the Middle East, floated a high-tech company on the London Stock Exchange, compared the main stage at a two-day music festival, and was once booed by 49,000 people while on the pitch at a major football cup final.